THE OPEN MIKE

To John
thankyou for all the great music
and loving care.

Rod MacDonald

8.1.15

THE OPEN MIKE

Rod MacDonald

Archway Publishing books may be ordered through booksellers or by contacting:

Archway Publishing
1663 Liberty Drive
Bloomington, IN 47403
www.archwaypublishing.com
1-(888)-242-5904

ISBN: 978-1-4808-0901-7 (sc)
ISBN: 978-1-4808-0902-4 (e)

Library of Congress Control Number: 2014914865

Printed in the United States of America.

Archway Publishing rev. date: 12/5/2014

Contents

The Book Of Reo

1–The Last Audient 1
2–The Birth Of Radio Free America 8
3–Reo Learns The Kama Sutra. 14
4–Dylan Reed 19
5–Raven. 25
6–Number 90 31
7–The Derailment 35
8–Ships Passing In The Night. 40
9–Times Square 42
10–The Pilotfish 49

The Open Mike

1–The Open Mike. 55
2–Graduation Day 60
3–Making A Living 64
4–The Road To Ruin 69
5–Disappearing Act. 77
6–The Weary Traveler 82
7–Number 30C 86
8–New York Nights 90
9–Battery Park 94
10–Lost Days. 100
11–Slow Dissolve 106
12–A Free Meal. 110

13–Chance Encounter 117
14–Back To Basics 122
15–The Threat 130
16–Number 13c 135
17–Hanging Out 140
18–Tools Of The Trade 147
19–You Gotta Have The Girl 152
20–See You Around 156
21–Dog Days 163
22–Chicago By Storm 169
23–Music Business People 178
24–Duke La Monte 185
25–Recording Session # 1 189
26–On The Road In New York Town 194
27–On The Job 201
28–O Please Don't Follow Me Home 205
29–It's Not About You 212
30–Folk Music 217
31–Now We're Getting Somewhere 224
32–To See The Great Man 229
33–The Gig 235
34–Lightning Strikes 239
35–The Search 244
36–Recording Session #2 249
37–A Place To Call Home 255
38–Here 261

Afterword, by Robert S. Koppelman 268
Selected Bibliography 279
Selected Recordings 280
Acknowledgements 281

The Book Of Reo

1–The Last Audient

Finally, there was no one left in the room but himself, the bartender, the waitress, and the blond-haired girl at the corner table. One by one they had all left; the harder and more passionately he had sung, the more of them had tuned him out, paid their checks, and split.

She was the last one left, and he didn't even know her.

He finished his last song, put down his guitar, and walked off the stage, threading his way through the tables until he had reached the bar.

"Tough night," the shag-haircut barman droned, wiping a glass squeaky clean.

"You said it." Then he felt the tap on his shoulder and turned around.

"Excuse me." He looked at her and was immediately knocked out. Close up, she had clear blue eyes and a wide-awake face: a rare photograph, yet comfortable in its beauty.

"Excuse me," she repeated. "What's your name?"

"Reo," he said.

She giggled. "Just that? Reo? Nothing else?"

"Reo MacGregor. What's yours?"

"Ilsa. Ilsa Breitmuller." He noticed for the first time she had an accent, a soft retaining of her native speech.

"Are you European? Scandinavian?"

"No, I am German."

"Would you like a drink?"

"Yes. Very much, thank you."

Two beers later, they were seated at the corner table, and he was lost in her blue eyes.

"Is this what you do? I mean singing? Yes?"

"You mean for a living?"

"Yes?"

"Well, I ...that is, I do this sometimes. I...wash dishes most of the time."

"But this is what makes you happy?"

"You could say that. Wish it made other people happy too."

"Oh, now don't be bitter. Perhaps these others don't understand you. But you sing very well."

"Oh. Thank you." He felt embarrassed and instinctively wanted to turn the conversation around. "What do you do?"

"I am a graduate student. In psychology."

"You came from Germany to study psychology?"

"You make it sound like something terrible."

"No. I mean it's a long way, oh, I don't know. I just..." He let his eyes drift around the room until they came, and then rested, on the now-empty stage, still glimmering under the bright spotlights that had not been turned off. For a moment, he forgot she was even there, as she silently ran her thumbnail along the stem of the glass.

"Does it bother you when the people leave during your set?" she asked, her soft tone taking the biting edge out of the words.

"Yes," he said, "I guess it does." He craned his neck forward and looked down at the floor momentarily. "Maybe they couldn't hear it," he murmured.

"You mean it wasn't loud enough? Oh, no," she said with a laugh. "It was loud enough. Have you been doing this very long?"

"Since ten o'clock," he said. Then he smiled. "That's a joke." He felt very pleased with himself.

She frowned at him. "You don't have to assume that I don't have a sense of humor just because I have an accent..."

He put his beer glass back on the table, sliding it around in the tiny puddle of water that condensed there.

"I've been singing for a couple of years, maybe a few. It's not that easy to get gigs. You know gigs?"

"Of course I know gigs." She pronounced it with a long ee sound, almost like *geegs.* "But you wash dishes usually?"

"Well, it's a job. What do you do for money?"

"I'm here on a fellowship. And I teach a class."

"Oh, yeah? In what?"

"A basic introductory course for undergraduates. In psychology." She smiled at him.

Beautiful, he thought, *don't stare.*

"You seem a little defensive about washing dishes. Does it bother you to do that?"

He exhaled hard. Someone came in and went past them on the way to the bathroom.

"I think I should go soon," she said.

He stared at his beer glass, still half full. "May I walk you home?"

"Yes, that would be very nice, thank you."

He shut off the stage lights, hitting the switch the manager had shown him before leaving for the night. He put his guitar in the closet and locked it and then gave the key to the bartender. The bartender turned around and leaned over the cash register, as if waggling the insignia from his designer jeans, too cool to speak. He knew a dead night when he saw one.

The barman shook his head, tossing his hair around a bit, and then handed Reo his $25 without speaking. He was not even going to say, "good night."

Fuck him, thought Reo, and left. Ilsa was standing on the sidewalk, the street still crowded on the hot autumn night, still full of the smell of roasting meat, pizza, beer, and sweat, as the last couple hundred of nightly revelers danced and belched their way along the Village sidewalks.

"Where to?" he asked her, and she took his arm and started walking. They reached the corner and turned right.

"May I ask you something?" she began, her voice still cool and bubbly, her hand in his jacket pocket with his.

"Sure."

"Why do you sing?"

"Do you mean what got me started?"

She smiled, as if to herself. "If you wish."

"I was sitting on a wall in San Francisco a few years ago with a friend. I was about to head back east. He asked me what I was going to do. I said I didn't know. He said I should sing. I was already playing the guitar and making up songs, and I always liked doing it. So I said, 'Okay, sure.' Well, here I am, I guess."

"What were you doing before that?"

"Oh, I was in school, and I worked as a reporter for a while."

"Yes? Was that fun?" Her voice rose up to its soprano.

"Sometimes. I didn't like the fact that you don't have direct access to the public. You can't really say a lot, because the publications edit it all the time. At least that's what I used to think. Now I think it was probably just an excuse I made to justify wanting to do this instead."

"But you do have direct access, as you call it. No one edits you?"

"Nope." Then he shrugged. "They can leave, though."

"Do you think that's because of what you're saying?"

"I hope not. I mean, I sing anti-war songs and stuff, but I don't think people are that narrow-minded."

"What, then?"

He scratched his head, right behind the ear where it itched.

"I don't know. Maybe I don't sing very well."

"I think you sing very beautifully," she said.

That stopped him, and as they approached a massive gray church with its iron-fenced greenery out front, she turned toward him. He stepped back.

"You know, you can't take yourself too seriously," she said, smiling all the while. And for the first time, he realized that he needed a lot more from this woman than to walk her home.

"Want to have some tea or coffee somewhere? I know a place near here," he asked, putting his hands in his pockets.

"Yes. That would be very nice." She smiled back.

Minutes later, they were sipping tea in an all-night restaurant, a place where nothing would interrupt them but the occasional clanking of dinner plates.

"Have you ever been to Europe?" she asked.

"No. I'd like to; haven't made it yet. Have you seen much of America?"

"Some places. I have been to Boston."

"Oh, yeah? Boston. What do you think?"

"I think in America, people are much more defensive about their way of life. In Europe, the bourgeoisie—you know that?"

He nodded, resisting the temptation to insist she shouldn't think he was dumb just because he hadn't been to Europe.

"They are more cynical about why they are that way. In America, the middle-class treats being middle-class as a religion, all this capitalism and democracy. In Europe, I think the people who are well off are more cynical about the system that makes them that way."

"Do you think they're both materialists, though, mainly?"

"Of course. But the Americans think it's this glorious state of something, while in Europe, people realize being bourgeois is just a way to survive." She looked straight into his eyes and smiled.

Their faces were mere inches apart, silently regarding each other.

"Can I ask you something?" he said, very quietly.

"What?" she whispered back.

"May I kiss you?"

She was still smiling, silently. He reached out slowly, gently, toward her face with his hands, but she drew away.

"Oh, no. I can't do that, please, I…go with someone. He wouldn't like it at all."

He put his elbow on the table and sank his forehead into the curvature of his thumb and forefinger, staring blankly at the green tea.

"I'd better go home now. Do you still want to walk me?"

He stood up and put his jacket on without saying anything; then he paid the check and went out to the street with her. Again she looped her hand through his arm.

"I am sorry if I hurt your feelings. You make me sad we have met, when before I was very happy." Now she would not look at him.

"I…don't know what to say. A minute ago, I was feeling so amazed to meet someone as nice as you, and then this. I feel stupid."

"Is it so terrible, then? We're not friends? You see, in Europe, we would not be that way. One has a lover, one has friends; having one does not exclude the other."

"I'd like that," he said. "I'd like to be friends with you." But he already had a sinking feeling.

They reached the door of her building. She turned toward him, put her arms around his waist, and drew herself close to him. He didn't know whether to hold her close or just let his arms hang. Slowly he returned her embrace and felt the gnawing ache of her body on his; then, smoothly, she slithered away, slipping from his arms like smoke leaving through an open window.

She tried to smile but couldn't find it.

"Good-bye," she whispered huskily. "It was nice meeting you."

And then it was that strange time in New York, when everything is cast in streetlight yellow-orange and distant taxicab horns talk to each other from avenue to avenue. He started walking up the street, but only made it past three doorways before he had to sit down and think it over.

He got up and went back to her building. He opened the door and went into the foyer, and looked at the names on the buzzers. There was no Breitmuller on it. None at all. There was a Miller. He pressed it and heard it ring faintly on a middle floor.

Seconds went by. There was no answer. He tried again.

More time. More silence. And slowly it dawned on him that he'd probably never see her again, unless he did something about it.

He went back outside and sat down on the steps.

Okay, he thought, I can wait until morning or even afternoon. It's already getting light over there anyway.

But he could not sleep on the cold stone steps, and minutes later the chill got him. He stood up and started walking. And he thought of his empty apartment and how there would be no sunlight there, wedged into the basement under the store, and he did not want to go there. In a few blocks he reached a park; the birds were chirping their morning notes as they woke up, and the sound of it was peaceful and very soothing.

He followed his nose to a pile of leaves, their drying into brown filling the air with the smell people know as Fall: leaves on the grass, piled up as if asking to be torched. Burning leaves, one of the favorite smells he had ever known.

He sat down, then lay down, in the leaves; then he reached around behind his head with his hands, watching the sparrows flitter around in the branches above him, all lining up for their chance to sing. Did they meet beautiful sparrows when they sang, he wondered? Do sparrows practice monogamy, or even love?

Okay, Reo, he said under his breath. "Forget it. She's not for you," he mumbled out loud. "Why not? She's got someone. Oh, that. Wouldn't you want others to respect your relationships? I suppose. Anyway, if she really liked you she would make that decision herself.

"Yeah, that's the bottom line. It's up to her." But in fact, Ilse Breitmuller was already on the phone with her love, and Reo would, in fact, never see her again. In the tree above, a sparrow was tooting merrily away, ringing up the notes like a runaway flute.

"Hey, bird," he said, breathing through the words. "I'm all out of songs, myself. Sing one for me." And he sank into the leaves and closed his eyes as the sparrow twittered over him, twitching its head from side to side. Soon it would fly off to join the other sparrows, to fill the park with their songs.

But for now, the bird was singing for him. An audient of one.

2–The Birth Of Radio Free America

"Women," he said. "They're like Chinese handcuffs. The further in you go, the harder it is to get out."

I squirmed in my small chair. The café had seats that were precise little things, steel frames shaped like flowers with a thick cushion. They were designed, no doubt, to keep the weekend tourists from nursing their coffee too long.

"Now you take Castillo," he continued. "I can't even figure out what you found so fascinating there. But you got more stuck on her every time you saw her. Only thing is, she's not stuck on you."

"You don't think so, huh?"

"Well, maybe she thinks you're interesting. You know what I read today? The Soviets are bombarding us with radiation from high-intensity transmitters in Cuba. I tell you, it won't be long before we start shooting at each other."

Zeke stared out the window. The rain was streaking the glass as two women police persons strolled by.

"Look at that. Some of these new ones are pretty nice." He stretched out the word "pretty," spitting through the "t's."

"These people," he went on. "They don't even see what's coming. They think it's gonna be like this forever: get up, go to work, eat burgers, plug the wife, watch the tube, die, lie there staring while the worms eat your flesh. Boom Boom. All gone. What are you gonna do then with your gold records and your pretty cunts? Huh?"

The waitress came to our table, her eyes painted black all around to match her miniskirt.

"Ready to orda?" she asked through her gum.

"Coffee?" he looked at me.

"Coffee," he said authoritatively to the girl. "Two coffees."

The waitress shifted her weight and rolled her eyes.

"Isn't that enough?"

"Two coffees. Coming right up."

She twirled on her foot and bounced away.

"Look at that. Whatsa matter, you disappointed we didn't order the surf and turf? So anyway, the Russians are actually doing that, directing radiation at us. They must mean it. They want to bury us."

"Sounds pretty stupid to me."

"Oh yeah?"

"Doesn't radiation stay in the air? It'll get around to them."

"Yeah, huh. Well, it all gets around, right? Wow, here's an idea. Buy a huge radio transmitter and put it inside a truck so you can't see it. Then drive around the city broadcasting. The government could never catch you, you'd always be moving just when they got a fix."

"Why would you want to do that?"

Zeke took out a pen.

"You could tell people the truth. Think of it! The truth! What an outrageous concept!"

Our coffee came, and I poured some honey into the cup. It was strong coffee, almost gritty.

"The truth, the truth," Zeke rattled on. "How do you like that."

It sounded so matter of fact.

"I don't know. Do you know what the truth is so infallibly? You think every word you'd say would be so valuable?"

"Well, don't you? What do you think your songs are for? Do you think about it at all?"

"I write as honestly as I can," I bristled.

"Don't get defensive. It's the same thing. Your songs, my transmitter. Listen, I'm building a recording studio. I want to record you. Okay?"

I sat up and looked at my coffee. Slowly I started twisting the spoon.

"Why?"

"I want millions of people to hear what you've got to say. But you've got to do it my way. I know what I want to hear."

"What's that?"

"I want to hear your voice and your songs coming through with nothing fake in it, no show biz or rock and roll, no bitterness. Sometimes you hit something that's very beautiful. That's what I want."

I thought about the last time a friend had asked me to his studio. He had two decent quality tape decks and a couple of mikes, and I sang "Marcie Jane" from midnight until seven in the morning. But we had to stop every time I got excited and tapped my foot, for it popped onto the tape. Finally, at seven a.m. we had a take we both liked.

"Let's make a copy before something happens to it," my friend had said. He slapped a second reel on the other machine, hit a bank of buttons under his desk, and discovered thirty seconds later we had erased the good take.

On the other hand, no one else had asked to record me for two years. And I was sick of washing dishes.

"What kind of studio are you building?"

"A good one. We'll make good records there, as good or better than the big companies. We'll do even better, because we know what's really going on and they're just trying to peddle shit to children."

"Come on. It's not that bad."

"What are you defending them for? They don't give a shit about you. If they did they'd have your records out. But I'm going to do that."

"You mean it?"

"Damn right. Why don't you come over and look at my studio?"

We finished our coffees and headed through the streets. It was only a few blocks away, in a neighborhood being transformed from old industrial warehouses to loft apartments: big, spacious empty rooms. We walked in the door and Zeke flipped on his phone machine.

"Hi Zeke, this is Gabriella. I just wanted to see you tonight. I'll call you tomorrow. Bye."

"Ooh, that Gabriella," he cooed, rolling his eyes. "She's a horny one. Loves to get on top. I like that in a woman, it shows she appreciates you. Let's go inside."

The room was just being sanded and marked off. It was empty.

"Here it is," he said proudly.

"There's nothing here."

"There will be soon enough. You'll see. I think I'll put the drum booth over in that corner. I'll have to cover the windows. We'll put the floor on a six-inch cushion and build a lower ceiling. Air tight. No sound leakage. I want to be able to record at three a.m."

"I'll believe it when I see it."

"Oh, you'll see it. Just be ready to sing."

I found myself staring vacantly out the window. In the background I could hear Zeke playing Gabriella's voice again, humming in anticipation of the next time she would appreciate him.

Six months later there was snow falling and a cold wind when I threaded the streets to Zeke's. I walked in and couldn't believe my eyes. There was a perfect plasterboard box of a room, about twenty feet square, built into the loft, complete with a waxed hardwood floor and a huge, black grand piano. There were drums in the far corner and three shiny microphones on stands. A double window of glass separated it from a control booth where two enormous tape machines were flanking a large flat gray slab covered with rows and rows of knobs.

"Zeke, you did it!" I exclaimed.

"That's not all, look at this," he offered, holding up a small metal box. "This little critter is gonna smooth out the sound, make it all sound wonderful."

His face was shining and he seemed to overflow with energy.

"We'll show them," he smiled. "I told you, right?"

"Yeah, you did."

"Come on, let's get something to eat."

"Don't you want to check it out?" I was excited now.

"Oh, I've been playing here all day. I need a break. Come on. I'll treat."

We went to an eastside diner, a place full of fluttery neon fluorescent lights.

"How's the music going?" Zeke asked me.

"Oh, okay. I have a couple of concerts at high schools next week."

"Oh, good," he said, but it seemed to travel up through his nose, as if it really wasn't so good.

"When do you want to start?"

"Start what?"

"Recording. You said you wanted to record me."

He shifted on his seat and scanned the near-empty restaurant.

"Well, that might take a while. I want to upgrade my equipment first, get a newer board. I want to do this right."

"So we're not going to do this right away?"

"Let me tell you a story. Once there was a man who had a large fortune, land, all that. Then one day he was wiped out by a hurricane. So he went to his friend, the king, and asked for some help. The king gave him seventy-five sheep and said, 'here, take care of these.' But wolves came and ate the sheep. He went to the king again, and again the king gave him seventy-five sheep. This time the sheep ran over a cliff and were killed. He went to the king again, and again the king gave him seventy-five sheep. This time a year went by and he had a hundred sheep. The king gave him a hundred more, and two years later they had doubled. The king called him to his court and said, 'You've done so well I want you to take care of all my sheep,' and gave him thousands of acres of land.

"The man asked, 'Why didn't you do this before?'

"'Well,' said the king, 'If I had done that, I'd have lost them all.'"

He broke some crackers in his soup.

"Is there a moral to this?" I asked.

"Only that you have to do things in their proper time," he answered, running his hand through his thin brown hair.

"Are you saying this isn't my proper time?" I asked.

"Well," he laughed, "I don't want to lose all my sheep. We'll do it, don't worry. But don't rush me. Have you seen Castillo lately?"

"I've run into her once or twice. I think she has a new boyfriend."

"Of course. Well, at least you got her out of your system."

"I suppose," I replied, wondering if I had. "Are you still seeing Gabriella?"

"Oh, her? No. I had to end that. I need to meet some women with simpler names, like Mary or Linda. Enough of these fancy names. These women with fancy names think their asses are something fancy, too. Who needs it? I don't need it. I can have any girl I want. Any girl. Poof. You just have to know how. But I don't want just anyone."

"Oh, no?"

"Nope. You'll see. Good things are coming. Do you dream?"

"Sure."

"I've been writing down my dreams. It's great, you should try it. Last night I had a beautiful one. A beautiful girl in a long white dress gave me a flower."

"Someone you know?"

The check arrived. We fumbled for cash and left it on the table.

"No, but I'm going to meet her soon."

We stood up and went outside. The sky was just turning light in the east, and the soup felt good in my stomach as we faced the icy air. I watched him pull the wool cap over his balding head. He slapped his gloved hands together twice and started running in place. It struck me that we had almost identical builds: five foot ten, slender, in shape but not very athletic.

"How can you be so sure you're right all the time?" I asked him.

"Oh, well, that's easy. If I'm wrong I'll figure out something else anyway. And if I'm right I'll see it coming so I can grab it when the chance comes. It doesn't matter. But you might as well go ahead as if you're right. Just cover the exits."

I wondered why I always felt so much like I should take notes. We walked back toward his door. It would be light by the time I got to sleep, another night turned upside down; I was going home a little later each night, or should I say each day.

"You don't like sleeping alone, do you?" he asked.

"No. but I don't have a girlfriend right now either."

"Yeah, it's tough. Well, I won't see you for a while."

"No? Going somewhere?"

"I'm going to go fall in love." He stepped inside and winked at me. The wind caught the door and slapped it shut behind him.

"Good luck," I said, but he was already up the stairs.

3–Reo Learns The Kama Sutra

He did not remember how they met, for it seemed to him that they had always known each other; each conversation seemed less like the fluid, feeling interchange of two lovers getting acquainted than like the climbing into each other's mental space and pushing out the walls, like ice exploding a bottle. She was Castillo: the lithe, fair ice queen who called him to read her poetry to him:

> I see the edges of cards
> rather than the faces on them
> I cry
> For the ripped, the marked aces
> who yield to prying eyes

and since they had walked a whole night on the Manhattan streets, crisscrossing Broadway from Canal Street to the Battery, he had felt his life come alive, even as he felt himself seeing things in terms of the playing-card metaphor she affected.

"That man," she would say, "the king of diamonds," and he knew she meant the dark-haired business-suited commuter across the way, "has a wife he doesn't understand. But he'll knock himself out to buy her stuff. At least until he drops. Maybe after. Who knows?"

Now it was Sunday night, and all weekend he had hoped to see her, to run into her, for she had said she was breaking up with her boyfriend. Should I call her? He wondered. Bad idea, he told himself. But will she call me? He was wandering around in his apartment when he first saw the book: *The Kama Sutra of Vatsyayana*, it said. He opened it, and it broke naturally where his friend Zeke had left it: Chapter 2, "On making acquaintance with the woman," and on efforts to gain her over. But it was the next chapter that grabbed him:

> Examination of the state of a woman's mind:
>
> When a woman reproaches a man, but at the same time acts affectionately toward him, she should be made love to in every way.
>
> When a woman gives a man an opportunity, and makes her own love manifest to him, he should proceed to enjoy her.
>
> And the signs of a woman manifesting her love are these:
>
> She speaks to him tremblingly and inarticulately;
>
> She calls out to a man without being addressed by him in the first instance;
>
> She shows herself to him in secret places;

There was the buzz at his door. He got up and pushed the intercom button, then, still enmeshed in the book, picked it up:

> She places one of her hands quite motionless on his body, and even though the man should press it between two members of his body, does not remove it for a long time;

And suddenly he heard her voice.

"Reo? Reo?" he heard faintly through the door. He opened it and she stepped in, dripping wet from the rain and looking drained.

"Castillo. Hey. How are you?" He started to kid her, then realized she was shaking and weak. She collapsed against him, reaching with her hand for his neck and leaning all her exhausted weight into his ready arms. They stood there quietly. He felt her shiver.

"Are you all right?"

"I....took some pills. I shouldn't have," she mumbled, putting her lips against his shirt. "Lie down. Got to lie down."

He led her over to the slim mattress and helped her lie down, but she was still too wet. He sat her up and forced her arms back as he peeled off her raincoat. Her clothes had soaked through, the stripes beginning to blur in the cotton. He got up and went to his closet and pulled out a flannel shirt.

"Here, put this on," he told her.

"No," she mumbled, tossing her head, shivering.

"You're soaked. You can't lay there in those clothes."

"You go ahead, then," she said. He sat there, undecided. Then he reached out and unclasped the buttons from the top down. She was wearing no brassiere, sitting there, eyes closed, teeth chattering, her breasts very full and beautiful, more than he had expected under the loose clothing. He was pulling the blanket over her when she snaked her arm around him and drew him toward her.

"I'm cold," she whispered. He lay down beside her and put his arms around her. She turned her face to his, and then they were kissing, their mouths open, their bodies pressing against each other, their hands unfastening belts, undressing jeans and slacks; and in one easy movement, they sank onto the mattress and fell into a sweet embrace.

Abruptly, she stopped moving and cocked her head, looking in his eyes.

"No, please, wait," she whispered, drawing back, slipping away, leaving her tears on his face; and she lay with her head on his chest, holding on as if afraid of rolling off the side.

Stunned, Reo lay motionless, his arms barely holding her, listening to his heartbeat; he was thinking she had passed out when, without a word, she moved firmly downward and put her lips on him, giving him what she thought he wanted.

He woke in the morning while she was still asleep, got up and made some coffee. After a while he heard her feet hit the floor.

"Hey, I've got to call my job. What time is it, anyway?"

She got up and walked across the small flat to his phone.

"Can I use this?"

"Sure." She dialed it.

"Hi, Leslie? This is Cassie. Can you cover for me? I'll be there in half an hour. Oh, thanks. I owe you one, ok?"

She hung up and walked over to her clothes.

"Good morning," he smiled. "Want some coffee?"

"Oh, hi. No, thanks, I've got to go. I guess I was in pretty bad shape last night, huh?

"Any time," he replied.

She stopped and, for a moment, stared at the jeans she was holding in her hand.

"Did you undress me?"

"Well, yes, I guess so," he answered slowly. "Don't you remember?"

"Oh, I remember finding your buzzer. It's pretty dim after that. Was I a real problem?"

He thought for a moment.

"Well, no, not really."

She pulled on her blouse and slacks, then studied him.

"What do you mean?" she asked quietly.

"Well, um.....don't you remember anything?"

"Remember what? Did you fuck me? YOU BASTARD!"

She threw her shoe at his head, knocking his coffee onto the floor. He stared at the cup on the floor, the puddle of coffee, and didn't get up.

"No," he said quietly, "I undressed you because you were soaking wet and asked me to."

Her eyes were furious; she wasn't kidding.

"You were kissing me too, you know."

"I was? I was too fucked up to know anything!" She threw her other shoe against the wall and slumped into the chair, crying. He went over to her and put his hand against her face.

"Hey, look at me." She blinked under her bangs.

"I wanted something to happen. Didn't you?"

She fought with herself and won, looking up.

"What did happen?"

He glanced away, thought about it, then came back to her grey, unblinking eyes, and broke it to her in a gentle, quiet voice.

"We got naked and made out a while. Then you passed out."

She looked at the floor for a moment, then stood up.

"I've got to go to work," she said. "It's all too fast. I didn't want to...I don't want to rush into anything."

He wanted to put his arms around her but stood there motionless.

"Look, I've got to go," she repeated. "You had your fun."

"Hey, it's not like that," he recoiled, straightening up. "I thought you wanted to be here."

She watched as he stepped back, crossed the small kitchen to the door, turned the knob, opened the door to the hallway and moved out of her way, still returning her steady gaze.

"Sorry to find out otherwise," he said sadly, turning away, addressing the coffee stain on the floor.

She paused at that, realizing she had hurt him.

"Oh, Reo," she sighed. "Please don't fall for me."

Now it was his turn to stand there, feeling her reproach, watching his hopes dissolve right before his eyes.

"I've got to go," she breathed, and started for the door, her coat on her arm. At the last second she turned and kissed him on the cheek, so faintly he felt it only as a breeze, her eyes cool as a winter sky.

"Maybe...maybe I wanted this too," she mused. "But it's too soon. I've got some hurting to do before I can feel anything again. I'm sorry."

And now she waited.

"I'm...sorry, too," he answered. "I want to see you again."

"I know."

"Can I?"

"I don't know."

"What should I do?"

"I don't know. Nothing. Whatever you want. I...I'll come to you sometime. Maybe. Please don't ask anymore."

He answered her the only way left to him, saying nothing. With a faint smile she was out the door, out of his morning. He had the day off, a whole empty day in front of him, and some ideas that might become a song. But that would be later. For now, he wanted to be very still.

4–Dylan Reed

For a while I roomed with a guy named Dylan Reed. He was a quiet, moody sort of guy sometimes, but then he'd burst into some amazing, hilarious monologue that would somehow connect a whole slew of unconnectable ideas, and he'd get you laughing like crazy.

"Hey, Reo," he'd say. "Did you ever wonder where our thoughts come from? Past lives? Some guy down the street who puts them out every other night, like the garbage? Or maybe inside ourselves, bubbling up from some interminable vat of slightly undigested life, like fart gas festering on a load of beans you didn't chew well enough? But try, just try to shut them off. You can't do it, really, not for more than a few minutes of dead air. What a load. To me, I admire somebody who can walk around in simplicity, keep his head uncluttered. But I can't, I have to do this or I go nuts."

He'd be sitting at a typewriter about then, drilling away in his two-fingered style on the keys. What people didn't realize was that he was a fucking genius. I say "a fucking genius" because the truth is, though he didn't make a point of walking around and spouting off, in private he could simply open up his mind and make sense of things better than anyone I ever heard.

Mostly, though, the local crowd thought he was just another aspiring songwriter/singer type. He hung out, played the open mikes, got the occasional gig and had a few fans, though I doubt anyone really knew the extent of his ability. But I read some things he had typed, at least one novel, dozens of stories, poems, lyrics he hardly ever sang, and they were brilliant. Just brilliant.

He wouldn't say what he real name was, though. I once asked him if Dylan Reed was his real name.

"Not the name I was born with, no," he said. "But it's real now." So I asked if it came from Dylan Thomas or Bob Dylan.

"Well, really," he said, "I was given the name in a dream. By a dream character other than myself. Where he got it I don't know." He'd run his fingers through his shaggy blond hair and keep on talking.

"It probably shows some latent impulse I have toward self-aggrandizement or something, I don't know. But my friend, it's just a name anyhow."

As a songwriter he was pretty good, sometimes great; "Analog Nightmare" was my favorite, though I could easily name six or seven that I took the trouble to learn. His love songs were often poignant and sarcastic at the same time, as if he couldn't decide if the whole thing that made him so turned on was worth anything deep down. And sometimes he wrote political stuff, songs that made the way society does things look pretty silly, like one song (whose title escapes me) about the politician who gets elected President and turns out to be a computer-generated robot (and gets impeached because he's not 35 years old). I loved that song, actually, not because of the premise (anyone could've thought it up, they said) but because the robot says the same mindless stuff every politician says to get elected, and then after winning starts to think for himself! In fact, if the robot hadn't started to think they never would have found him out.

We used to hang out a lot together in those days, late nights at the Bucket of Blood, one of the favorite local venues. Mostly it was a male scene, the singers drinking beer and talking about it all. Women came and went at their own pace, sometimes settling in for a few months, then landing some uptown guy with business connections and moving on in their careers, or going on the road. But the guys hung out, year after year, hanging on to the same old ways.

Reed—the name he preferred being called—was a bit different. He didn't spend long hours talking about himself, like Denny, or make a shtick out of putting anybody down. He was a quieter type, which really infuriated Jonas, who considered himself to be the "voice" of the scene.

"Who the hell does he think he is, anyway?" he bellowed one night at the Bucket. "Taking a name like that for himself."

"Ah, shut up, Jonas," groused Denny. "You're just pissed that he didn't ask your permission."

But Jonas couldn't leave it alone, so he went over and butted into a conversation Reed was having with some very lovely young lady who'd recently been seen around.

"Just where the hell do you get off taking a name like that for yourself?" swirled Jonas, wrapping his cape around himself and sucking his pipe: a long, low-slung pipe he seldom lit.

The sweet brunette and Reed exchanged glances; the bar got quiet.

"Well, I usually get off at West Fourth Street," he answered.

The place went nuts. Everybody knew Jonas loved nothing better than to get the screws on somebody; he was forever talking about the need for "truth" in folk music. So he got a little nastier.

"Then the least you could do is pick a name you're worthy of," he rasped.

Reed just sat and stared at him for a minute. I always admired that; Jonas was a very intimidating type, a good writer and a real bastard, but Reed never let himself be overwhelmed by him.

"Well, you know," he went on, "I used to be Go Fuck Yourself, but they wouldn't print it on my checks, so I had to change it."

There was too much laughter for Jonas to win this one. I stepped in and handed him a beer.

"Can't you see the guy's busy? Come on and sit down," I said.

"I want to know."

"Yeah, well you're not likely to find out tonight." He sat down and started in on me. This always happened when he couldn't get the best of somebody, he'd go after me instead. And, since he never really got the best of Reed, I absorbed a lot of it.

"The trouble with you, Reo, is you're too easily satisfied with things that you've no right to accept. Don't you want to know what his real name is? Maybe he's a complete phony, or trying to use the poet's name for selfish purposes."

"Sure, I want to know," I said. "We'll find out sometime." In fact, I didn't care that much; but it did interest me that he preferred to be called "Reed."

Once I asked Reed about Jonas. It came up because we all went to Chinatown one night for dinner and ran into some old friend of Denny's who'd gone to graduate school with him.

"Graduate school?" Jonas had practically screamed out. "We didn't know about that, did we? And all this time we thought you were just a humble servant of the muse." Denny was pretty embarrassed, and later I overheard Reed trying to cheer him up.

"Hey, a little education never hurt anybody," he said. "Jonas'd be the same if he found out you'd once had halitosis. Just so he's got something on you, that's all he wants, Denny Boy. Forget it."

"Oh, he's not so bad," I put in. "He's just a stickler for the truth."

Reed wheeled on me; it was probably one of the few times I saw him angry.

"The truth! Hey, you want the truth? It's what it is, the truth, which may or may not have anything to do with Jonas, or you or me, for that matter. You want to know the truth you better start to figure it out for yourself and stop letting people cram it down your throat."

Reed and I roomed together for about a year, and I never did find out his real name. I don't think it makes much difference to me, he was a good friend and that's what counts in the end. Hell, you can take any name you want, it's how you are that makes the difference. But I used to come home and find him pecking away at that typewriter, and once in a while he'd let me read something. He was good. I hope sometime the winds change and they publish his stuff. It would do people good to read it.

My favorite time with Reed, though, was when we started the "Radio Free America" sessions. We spent a few nights putting down tracks for a tune—"You Speak My Name" it was—and the song was meant to have this big vocal note at the end. I brought home a cassette and was playing it when he walked in and sat down, listening without saying anything. When it ended I decided to risk asking his opinion.

"You do that at Zeke's?"

"Uh huh."

"I like the song."

"What's that mean?"

"Well, I think you could sing it better."

"It's just a rough track. I haven't done my vocal yet."

"Oh, that's different. What's it like working with Zeke?"

"It's...uh...kind of hit or miss. Sometimes he's real easy to work with, things go smoothly. Sometimes he's in a bad mood and we'll do half a take and he'll stop the machine and give me a long lecture and then say he's too tired to record anymore."

"Hmmm," he mused. "Hard to psyche yourself up when you don't know if you're gonna be left hanging out there to dry, huh?"

I sat up. He'd hit the nail on the head, the problem I was having.

"You know, Reo, you're much better than you know," he told me. "You deserve to be working with pros, people who don't push their own neuroses into the situation. But until somebody hears you, Zeke's worth your time, I suppose, right?"

"I suppose."

During the next couple of days I thought a lot about "You Speak My Name," what would help me get a finished version of the song. And I asked Reed to come to the studio with me.

"What for?" he wanted to know.

"Just help me sing the vocal. I'll stake you to dinner. It'll give me someone to sing for, someone who's listening with open ears. I mean, Zeke listens sometimes, but I can never relax because he's so volatile, if he's fixated that day on the end of the world or something he won't hear anything. He'll just start a monologue whatever I do."

"He'll do that anyway, whether I'm there or not."

"Maybe not. Maybe he'll just settle down a bit if someone's there. He thinks I'm hard to work with."

"Okay, okay," he gave in. "But if Zeke starts some Gestalt on me I'm going to remember a previous engagement."

The funny thing is, he was much more of a bastard than Zeke. He made me sing the whole song about eight times and then we spent more than an hour on the last note, the long one I had to hold while the band played the crescendo. Finally they stopped the machine and stared at me through the glass.

"God damn it, Reo," Reed's voice came on in my headphones . "You have this beautiful lyric, expressing this beautiful love for someone, how she speaks your name and you want more than anything in the whole world to give her your love. So sing it like you mean it! I want to hear you bleed, I want to close my eyes and feel your bond with this woman written on your soul. I don't want any fucking nice notes. A song like this, it has 'Don't Waste My Time' written all over it unless you're going to make me believe it."

I got a bit mad at that. Hey, I'm a good singer, I don't need this shit,

I was thinking. But I finally sang one note that really hit it. Reed got out of his chair and ran into the recording room.

"That was great! All right!" he cheered at me. Zeke said he didn't think it was good, but he was tired and wanted to stop.

"Let's mix one copy of it right now," Reed said.

"Can't do it," Zeke said.

"Sure we can. After what he's been through Reo deserves to take a copy home with him tonight. You afraid it might be good or something?"

Zeke sniffed. I think Reed had touched a nerve there; I'd often thought Zeke wanted to keep everything in a permanent state of incompletion, never being good enough; and now Reed wanted to listen to it again.

"Oh, all right, if you have to. But it's a mistake," Zeke said.

So we mixed it. Later I played the cassette for a lawyer and he helped me sign one of my first contracts, long after Reed had disappeared to who knows where. I never got the chance to thank him, though I did treat him right at that Greek sandwich place down the block.

5–Raven

One day Reo was standing in a bar, dreamily staring at the backside of a skin-tight leather skirt, when the contents of that skirt turned around and spotted his entranced eyes across the room. By the time he looked up, straight into her twin green lenses, she had him. By the next night she was all moved in, living in his dust-infested apartment behind a late-night bar where bad bands massacred "skiffle" music, that golden-era shuffle-and-wink craze from England having left its mark on the young American guitarists who were trying too seriously to revive it in the States. A pretty sight she was, too, from her slim legs on up to her long, straight black hair; and she called herself Raven, proudly arching her neck ever so slightly.

"Ohh, she's great," he told Zeke the next night. "I feel very lucky."

"What do you mean?"

"I can't believe this is happening, man. She's so beautiful, and when she kisses me, man, that's it. Right there."

"That's all?"

"Huh?"

"That's all? Kiss?"

"Well, you know, man."

"Know what? Have you had her or not? Don't you at least get to lick the little red spots, get her all squishy, you know?"

"Hey, man, that's enough."

"You brought it up. I mean, don't you at least get to slide the ole cigarillo into the smokehouse, put some flavor in that bacon?"

Reo led out a long exhale.

"That, you know, is none of your business," he said, smiling just enough. But it went on.

"The only thing bugs me about her is she makes up some bullshit phony name for herself. Raven. Big deal, she's got black hair. She's got great legs, too, why not Giraffe? Stork. What's her real name, anyway?"

Reo smiled.

"I don't know, she won't tell me. What the hell, she can call herself anything she wants to, I don't care."

But a few days later, when Zeke put on his best sport jacket and went to their apartment for an "intimate dinner for 7," he asked her the same question in front of everybody, right over the steamed vegetables.

"My name is Raven" she said, quite nicely.

"That's what your parents called you?" he persisted.

"It's my name," she reiterated. She had the class to stay nice, but he wasn't going to be denied.

"I don't know, I doubt it. I mean, really. I just don't believe parents would name somebody that, all bald and just born."

She sat back and looked across the table at him. Everyone was quiet.

"Does it matter?" she said. There was an edge in her voice.

"I like to know exactly who I'm dealing with."

"Is that so?"

"Suppose I found out, oh, say Reo here wasn't Reo at all but Schverzenheimer or Wang Chug or Lester Van Clydesdale the Third. Don't you think you'd say, aren't you trying to fool people? Maybe even fool yourself a little? I don't know, just wondering."

For a while no one said anything; the guests pushed their food around with the chopsticks. But Reo and Raven exchanged a glare that needed no words to understand.

"Uh, Zeke," Reo started carefully, "why don't you lay off?"

"Hey, no problem Mister Alzheimer."

"You know," Raven said softly, "my parents wanted to call me Rebecca. But as for you knowing people, I could tell you my name, rank and serial number and every detail of the life I'll ever have lived and you would never, ever know me."

Zeke sat chewing, silent.

"And since you and Reo are such great friends, maybe you should pursue this with him," she continued.

A long silence passed before Reo spoke up.

"You know, my parents called me Ruarachan. For years I went as Rory. But I shortened it myself after I read this poem."

Zeke looked around at the other diners, who all stared adamantly at their plates as Reo continued.

"It was written by a friend of mine. He and I roomed together for awhile."

"What happened to him?" came the soothing womanly voice of Raven's friend—what was her name? he couldn't remember.

"Last I heard, he was traveling somewhere out west. He was an interesting guy, taught me a lot. He used to say 'Don't ever give in. Never. Make them respect you, every inch of the way.' He didn't mean violence, though, he was a pacifist. He meant, don't let them convince you to be like them, no matter what."

"'Them?' Be like who?" Zeke broke in. But the quiet, professional-sounding woman carried the field.

"When did you change your name? When for you, I mean?"

Reo laughed.

"When I first moved to New York he sent me a letter. Want to see it?"

Suddenly the other three diners, all quiet til now, murmured "sure" and "yeah, let's see it" and "out with it," and Reo went and dug through a pile of old papers behind a desk.

"Here." Hands grabbed for it.

"Wait," said Raven. "Read it out loud."

Reo picked up the paper. He smiled, almost sadly, as if he had meant to keep his secret always. But it was too late for that now.

Telegram from Reo Starkey

Come the revolution I'm going to resign my post
As a senior worthless individual
Among many such types
(I say, have you seen the hot air balloon
No
Yes
Yes? It landed today. A sight.
A sight? Yes. Darkest I've seen.

The skies?
No, no, her eyes)
Who spend their spare time thinking
When they could be
Supporting the new order
By harvesting wheat
Or smelting steel
Or digging graves
For just enough to eat
And a warm place to
Sit down. And words?
Could I leave behind
This war of words
For the glory of one great Workerhood? Well,
To poetry, I say Adieu!
Shazam!
Get lost!
Poeticize THIS piece of
Expandable skin-covered
Cartilage-like protuberance
Possessing the propensity
To propel its perpetuation
Whenever penetration is performed!
So much for poetry.
As for revolution,
Why does it keep coming around
Just when you thought it was safe
To hate the government?
(Words only, she said, and
I would leave them both
for the real thing, your love and freedom;
see how high I fly?
Her voice like sweet summer breezes
On the bay where I have sailed.
You have sailed?
The world over.
Always wanted to sail.)

But at least poetry beats working;
Come the revolution
Please publish
Stop

It took a few seconds to sink in that it was over.

"That's very interesting," gushed one of the non-participants in the earlier talk, rolling up the sleeves on his checkered sport coat.

"And you, Rave," said another, a middle-aged woman whose date had eaten all of the carob-coated raisins earlier, "why did you choose the name Raven?"

The black-haired beauty smiled, as if making a private joke.

"I want to fly like they do. I think they're very beautiful."

"And you, Zeke," came the smooth womanly voice. "Why do you call yourself Zeke?"

He crossed his legs and spoke with an air of indifference.

"It's my name," he answered.

"What a pity," the woman returned. "You've not used your imagination at all."

"Well, this is all very fascinating, but really I must be going," said the checkered sport coat, patting the side of his hair. He and his date, the smooth-voiced woman with the strawberry purse, stood up as one and thanked Raven for the lovely dinner. The other, older couple did the same. Of the six people Reo had invited, only Zeke had come.

"Good night, Mr. Zeke," teased the now-standing woman who had questioned them all so calmly. "Here is my card if you'd like to come by for a talk sometime." And she extended him the strip of cardboard.

"Counseling," he read aloud with distaste. "No, thank you, I was counseled in my last life."

"Yes, goodnight, Zeke, thank you for coming," said Raven, extending her hand with utmost politeness. Zeke looked across the small party at his friend, but Reo couldn't help him and said nothing.

"Yeah, well," he said, standing up, putting on his coat and walking to the door in one even swirl of motion.

"Thank you for the food."

Raven turned to Reo and then stopped herself from speaking.

"Let him go," Reo said, a little sadly. "Forget it."

"Goodnight, dear, thank you for the nice party," the older woman said, and in a moment they were all gone.

For a few minutes they avoided looking at each other, busily cleaning up the dishes and pans. At last she broke the silence, loudly flinging the spoon into the dish-filled sink.

"This is the kind of polite little gatherings my parents used to fake their way through all the time. I don't think I can take much more of it."

He didn't answer until he had sat down.

"You know, Raven, I don't care what you want to call yourself. And I'm sorry I expected you to sleep with me last night. You go ahead and sleep on the couch if you want to. Make yourself at home. Do whatever feels right. I'm going to bed."

And he went into his back room, where he had built the platform sleeping loft to give himself more floor space, and climbed the wooden stairs without pausing to undress or shut off the lights.

For a few minutes she didn't believe it. Then, for a few minutes more, she listened to one of her tapes on her headphones; but she had heard that one, at least a dozen times. And it was much later, almost light outside, when she peeled off her shirt and jeans, down to the thin cotton t-shirt that clung to her curves, down to her bare legs and lime-green panties, and climbed the stairs to his loft.

6–Number 90

Just before we met, I'd counted up on a piece of paper the initials of every woman I could remember sleeping with. There were a couple where we didn't actually have intercourse (no birth-control handy, that sort of thing), but I counted them anyway because we'd enjoyed each other so thoroughly. The total came to 89, and I stared at the number for a few minutes, wondering if I'd forgotten anyone—a sure admission of meaningless physical gratification for itself, I figured—or if I wasn't truly a fickle person who'd known only sex and never love.

But I stopped counting when I'd made love to Raven a few times, for we had something I'd never felt before: a natural chemistry that left us feeling close and satisfied, as if we'd gone somewhere great together and then come back to lie still for a few moments, wondering at the magic we'd made.

After a few weeks, I asked her about this.

"You know," I started. "I've never really asked you about other men, have I?"

"No. And I appreciate it."

"There is something I'd like to tell you, though."

"What?"

"It's that....well, I've had sex with a few women, but with you there's some amazing electricity or something. It always feels right, and I've never had a relationship like that before."

She smiled at me with real pleasure.

"Well, I haven't either," she said. We were lying next to each other in the loft, and it was late or early, for the vague daylight was sneaking down the airshaft between the buildings and lightening up the room.

We had gone to bed late, slept awhile, and now could see each other in the faint morning.

Raven had her kimono on: a silk, peach-colored wraparound that opened in the front. I slid my hand under it, and found the smooth, soft skin of her upper thighs; she edged closer to me and opened her legs slightly.

"Reo," she whispered hoarsely. "Come here."

We rolled over and she rode me, arching her body while I held her waist and smooth, slim legs. As she bore down on me, I started to pull out of her; it was our birth control.

"No, stay," she said. "It's all right." I stayed inside her; and then, like a bolt of lightning or electrical current, my mind's eye saw a streak of light pass through me and into her. She began gyrating wildly around, somehow staying on me as she bounced all around the bed so violently I thought she might throw us off the loft; but I held her, and slowly she calmed down. As I relaxed, the wave came back to me like a white light, my body completely out of control.

It was late the next day when it occurred to ask her if she might get pregnant.

"I don't think so," she answered. "I had my diaphragm in."

"Oh," I smiled. "Good thinking." But we had been out drinking with some friends, and had climbed straight into bed when we got home.

"When did you do that?" I asked, curious. She looked away. "Oh, I don't know, sometime."

Now I was really curious.

"No, really. When?"

"If you have to know, it was yesterday afternoon. What difference does it make?" And she turned and looked at me, straight in the eye.

"Hey, no big deal," I backed off. "Listen, I have to go to work tonight." And off I went, singing my songs for a few beer drinkers on the lower east side; so I was glad when my shift was over. Newly paid, I stopped by The Folk Life for a few minutes of music.

"Who's this?" I asked Susila, the barmaid.

"Raphael Marcout," she said. "I think he's from Spain." The fellow had a nice sound on his guitar and an agreeable voice, though I couldn't understand the words. Sometime around the fifth song I was staring at my beer when a woman began singing along, and when I looked up Raven was on stage, singing along with him perfectly, her eyes watching the lips move under his long, dark bangs.

After the set had ended Raven came walking up to the bar. At first she seemed a little surprised to see me, then recovered as Marcout came walking up.

"This is Reo MacGregor, Raphael, remember I told you about the man I live with?"

"Oh, yes, it is so nice to meet you, " the Spaniard smiled, extending his hand graciously. "Raven is such a beautiful singer, I am honored to share the stage with her."

Raven and Marcout insisted I join them for dinner at the big Mexican place next door. We sat down and he handed her a small bottle of something, with which she went off to the bathroom.

"So, you like the music?" he asked me.

"It was pleasing. I don't know your language."

"Should it matter? If the music speaks to you, it needs no words, no translation."

"I suppose. What are the songs about?"

"Most of them are old, old stories, very sad, actually. Everyone dies. But here in America the people who miss the Spanish love to hear them again, and the ones who don't need not concern themselves with their sadness."

"Are they popular songs in Spain?" I asked.

"Oh, no, not any more. I understand you write songs. Raven says you are very good though hardly anyone knows it. I hope I may hear from you some time. And I want you to know, I will respect your relationship with Raven." He reached across the table and put his hand on mine for emphasis.

Raven returned and handed him the bottle. He excused himself.

"What is this? Are you doing coke?"

"Shhhh," she giggled. "Do you want some?" But I didn't, and the dinner turned sour for me, two hours of being a part-time member of a bilingual conversation, usually punctuated by their laughter at something they would try to explain to me in English, then give up on. I'd had more than enough when we paid the check and went out to the sidewalk.

Raven reached out and took his face in her hands, then planted a warm kiss on his cheek.

“Goodnight, Raphael, and thank you,” she said with a big smile.

“Goodnight, Raven,” he answered. Then, in what seemed slow motion, they turned and walked separately away, down the street in different directions.

Raven looped her arm inside mine and scooped me down the sidewalk.

“Let’s go home,” she said. “I’m really bushed.”

7–The Derailment

The next few days were predictable.

"Reo, we have to talk."

The guitar was on the couch he had built of plywood and two-by-fours. He picked it up and let his thumb drift across the strings.

"Raphael says I can do a tour with him, in two weeks."

He strummed a chord, a low A, and added some fingering: the low string didn't sound right. He twisted the tuning peg and the string popped.

"This will really be a great opportunity for me. I've been studying his music for years. Well, when I was in Madrid in college I first found his albums—and now he wants me to tour with him as a singer. Imagine! I've got to get busy. Get some clothes, get my guitar fixed, plane tickets. If you don't mind I'm going to bed now. I have to get up early and do all this. But feel free to stay up as long as you want to." And she went to the stairs that led to the loft, changed into a woolen nightgown to her ankles, and climbed up the stairs.

The next day he caught the noon train for Boston. He took the Red Line out to Harvard Square and walked two blocks to The Collective, a basement coffeehouse where he was booked for one of his better-paying jobs, arriving early enough to watch the crowd file in. He went back into the concrete dressing room, a modified bunker that had outlasted all attempts to clean it. He was working out a melodic progression on a G chord when the owner came in.

"Someone here to see you."

A young woman walked in behind the voice. She stood about five-feet-five and had a white blouse and blue jeans on her slender frame. She had a round, soft face with a mass of curly reddish hair on top, and he ended up staring into her eyes for thirty seconds before either spoke.

"Um, I was at your concert in Providence."

"You mean the gym at RISO?"

"Risdee?" she giggled. "Well it was fun. Could you sing 'When I get Younger' tonight?"

"Huh? Oh. Okay. Sure."

"Thank you," and she vanished out the door.

When he got on the stage she was right in front of him. He sang all the songs he had planned, and for once the owner wasn't waving at him from across the room to cut his set short. And he remembered her request.

"Here's one," he told the audience, "that's a bit of autobiography, going backwards and forwards at the same time."

He began the rolling, fingerpicking guitar piece, droning the A string with his thumb. The room stopped shifting its weight on the squeaky chairs and grew quiet.

When I get younger I'll find me a girl
We'll go out on some typical night.
Go to a restaurant, take in a show
Drive around, maybe look at the lights.

The audience sat perfectly still, leaning forward on their chairs.

When I get younger we'll sit by a fountain
And say 'why don't we make it right here?'
When I get younger, she'll show me her window
And say 'why don't you wait for me there?'

The attentive, quiet crowd seemed to crackle with energy. He almost missed a chord change but got there in time. He stole a glance at the woman just below him to his right; she was looking straight into his eyes, though she made no overt expression. By the last verse, he was drifting away on a memory, both singing the song and wondering when, or how, he had written it; unlike most of his songs, he couldn't recall specifically.

When I get younger, I'll think of the future
As a ribbon of musical thread
When I get younger I'll not be a soldier
I'll go as a weaver instead

He mumbled "Thank you" into the mike, then threaded his way through the crowd back to his concrete dressing room. The crowd of 35 clapped and clapped. But the lights came on and the owner began taking down the mikes. There were a few boos, but sullenly the audience gave up, stopped clapping, and began to leave.

In the dressing room, Reo put away his guitar and sat by himself.

"Not a bad show, Reo," declared the owner, Bill Hanson, in his clear Boston accent, handing him 50 dollars. "I'd have let you do an encore if you hadn't already gone overtime."

Reo hit the street, by himself and hungry. He found a hot taco at a nearby bar, had two beers and a salad, then caught the Red Line back to South Station. He got there at 1:15 for a 3 a.m. train, and was just settling into a plastic chair when he spied her across the waiting room. And the seat next to her was empty.

"Excuse me," He said, sitting down. "Did you like 'When I Get Younger'?"

She turned and recognized him.

"Oh, yes. It was very beautiful. I wish you could have sung all night. I don't know, I guess they were in a hurry to go home there. But I wanted to hear a lot more. So I walked around for an hour."

He looked down the hall of the train terminal: an old baggage cart, a wooden platform on steel wheels, sat empty in the corridor. When he returned to her wide, blue eyes he spoke low and conspiratorially.

"Really? You wanted to hear more?"

"Oh, yes," she whispered.

He took her by the hand and led her to the baggage cart. He slid his case onto the cart, jumped up and bent down to help her climb up too. They sat down, and he took out his guitar and tuned it, and began stroking the quiet strings with his fingertips. He had sung a few songs, and she had listened to them all, when the voice on the loudspeaker announced the 3 a.m. train to New York. He packed up the guitar. They stood up, but neither moved toward the train.

"Thank you," she said. "Oh. Really, I don't know what to say."

He looked at her sweet face, the tousled hair hanging into the sleepy eyes.

"May I kiss you?" he whispered.

"Um hum," she whispered back. And he set down the guitar and kissed her softly on the lips. But she wrapped her arms around him and pressed her body into him, soft and yielding; ignoring the bustle of late-night train riders, they kissed for two minutes, and when he felt her move against his pelvis, he let her.

They ran for the train but just missed the gate closing. Before they knew it they were alone in the terminal. And according to the signboard, the next train was at 5:30 a.m.

"Come on," he said, and led her out to the street. In the frosty January night everything was crisp-smelling like a New England winter night gets. He got them into a cab.

"Harvard Square, please."

How much money did he have left? Maybe twenty dollars, he figured. In the back seat she stretched out on him as they kissed; he had unbuttoned her blouse and opened her jeans when they reached Harvard Square.

"Right or left side?" the cabbie inquired, hiding whatever he was thinking very well.

"By the newsstand." Reo got out and bought the early morning edition of *The Globe.*

"Just checking the reviews," he told the cabbie. "How about Kenmore Square?" And they drove off again, as he kissed her smooth, lovely breasts, as she opened his shirt and ran her hands over his chest.

"Where in Kenmore Square?" The cabbie sighed heavily.

"You hungry?" He asked her.

"I could use a juice," she answered.

"How about a store or diner?" he told the cabbie, and when the cab stopped he buttoned his shirt and went inside, down the long, chrome counter beneath the fluorescent lights, and bought an orange juice from the curly-haired waiter.

"South Station," he told the driver, knowing they would be there too soon. And they were, using 18 of his twenty dollars in what had seemed like seconds. They sat together in the terminal until at last it was time for the train.

"Cissie," he asked, "Do you have a boyfriend?"

"Yes," she said. "And you?"

"I don't have a boyfriend."

They laughed. But he didn't really tell her any more, and when the train left Boston they were alone in the car. They went together into the restroom, undressed in the smelly, metallic toilet, and stood looking at each other, shivering in the cold, and stopped.

"Cissie, it can't be like this, the first time. I want it to be somewhere better than this."

She smiled and nodded quietly and reached for her jeans, then leaned forward and kissed him.

"Are you in love with someone?" she asked him.

He buttoned his shirt and looked out the window. It was going to be morning; the gunmetal grey waters of South Boston Harbor would start twinkling any minute, and the gulls were zooming thru their warm-ups along the waterfront.

"Yes."

"I'm sorry."

"Why?"

"Does she love you?"

"She says she does."

"But?"

The train arced away from the coast, darting alongside a highway not yet choked with commuters.

"I don't know, really," he said, half to himself.

8–Ships Passing In The Night

He had told Raven he would be home at 9 a.m., so he expected to have to explain. But she was sitting at the table in her jacket, her travel bag on the floor, when he walked in at 11:30.

"Oh. Hi. I was writing you a note. I'm going away for a couple of days."

"Oh, yeah? Anywhere interesting?"

She pushed her hair off her face and crossed the blue-jeaned legs.

"On tour. Philadelphia and Washington."

"Oh. With Raphael again?"

She looked at him and tried to act natural.

"Yes. Are you worried about it?"

"Should I be?"

She smiled.

"No."

He helped himself to some freshly brewed coffee, nearly stepping on her bag. She got up and started pacing.

"Taking much stuff?"

"Just some clothes and a small flute."

"Excited?"

"Well, you know." She beamed. He took a sip of coffee.

"Did you pack your diaphragm?" he asked politely.

"What did you say?"

"Did you pack your diaphragm?" he repeated.

She sat down and looked at her feet. Her face was bright red. "Yes," she whispered.

"Sleeping with Raphael, too, huh?" he murmured. She looked up at him, her eyes perfectly tearful.

"I was going to tell you if you'd just given me time. Now I feel I've hurt you."

He sipped his coffee, watching her.

"Are you taking all your stuff?"

Her eyes widened.

"No. Why?"

"Aren't you leaving?"

"Reo, I'm not leaving you. I love you. This is just a tour."

"What kind of tour is it when you have to fuck him to go? Are you trying to tell me this is just a musical experience?"

"I don't have to. He likes my singing; In fact he says he's honored to share the stage with me. I could go anyway."

"You mean you fuck him because you want to."

She got up and started pacing.

"God, everything's so black and white with you. Look, this is just something I've got to explore."

The buzzer honked twice. She picked up her bag, reached over and kissed him on the lips.

"I'll be back Wednesday. I love you, Reo. Please don't be angry." And she hustled down the hallway as fast as she could go. He picked up the coffee cup and threw it into the sink. It shattered, spraying dark brown coffee on the yellow kitchen walls. But he didn't bother to clean it up. He simply went into the bedroom and climbed into the loft with all his clothes on.

9–Times Square

He had a slow Tuesday, drank a lot of coffee, read the *Daily News*. His horoscope (Leo) told him:

> "You may be feeling edgy about living up to your commitments; the urge to cut your losses and get out will be strong until the moon leaves Scorpio on Wednesday."

He made a can of soup and ate it, drank some more coffee and got very edgy. He ransacked his desk drawer for a pen, finding a pencil instead, as well as a small gray object. He turned it over in his hand. It was like a piece of bark, something rustic. He bit into it. It tasted woody but familiar. Then he remembered: magic mushroom. Reed had left this.

He popped it in his mouth and chewed it up. In the meantime the faucet caught his ear, and he tuned it tighter, interrupting the beat. He spied the guitar on the couch, left sitting on the green mattress cover. He sat down and hit a single note on the sixth string; absent-mindedly he walked his fingers down a scale, down to the fifth and then the fourth string, alternating the finger-strokes with a droned thumb note. They clashed, and as he went back up the scale he found different notes, switching from the major to a minor chord.

Like a cat he sprang up and found a pen and paper. Playing the guitar line, he hummed the melody and wrote a line:

> I remember the night, the band was playing
> She came down the stairs with a glass of red wine

He played another line, and wrote to match:

Gave me a smile and sweet conversation
I was out looking for love at the time

It needed a chord change; he moved to a dominant one by barring the first fret and adding two fingers to the lower strings, and wrote again:

I've spent time like so many others
Watching the girls, their skins young and fine
This one was different, more of a woman
I was out looking for love at the time

As if in a fever he scrawled the words, sometimes stopping to play the melodic line, twice twirling to his feet and bouncing into the kitchen, only to return to put the words on paper. Near the end he had a great surge of emotion, and, fighting through the tears he often had when the writing became more instinctive than conscious, he finished the lyric.

Was that one two three four women so tender
Sometimes I forget these ex-true loves of mine
I love 'em all but of course I remember
I was out looking for love at the time

He sang it one more time, softly and mournfully, as if it said everything he had at that moment in time.

Oh oh, love at the time

Humming a long "ohh," letting it trail off over the descending guitar line that had started the song, he rejoined the small world of his apartment; the dirty sink, the squalid table and chair, the scrawled words on the white paper that were his only redemption in the solitude of his morning, all came back into view, then blurred away as water filled his eyes. Drained and exhausted, he sank into the couch and rested the guitar across his legs.

The door buzzer went off. Stiffly, he rose and pressed the button to open the front door of the building, without asking who it was. He began to wash his face, but Zeke walked in before he could get himself together.

"Hey, what's wrong? You okay?"

"Yeah." He sniffed.

"Raven not around tonight?"

"No." Reo looked at the paper back on the couch.

"I was just working on a song, that's all."

"Oh, a good one too, I'll bet." Zeke laughed quietly. "Can you play it?"

Reo picked up the guitar and started playing the downward melodic line. He slid into the voice and sang it quietly, listening to the words, until he had sung all of them. He stopped playing, abruptly, and sat there, crying his bitter tears, his stomach convulsing, unable to control himself or his shame in front of his friend.

Zeke walked over, knelt down, and put his arm around Reo, holding his head against his shoulder. He let a few seconds go by without speaking.

"It's tough, loving a woman," Zeke said softly. "They don't play fair."

Reo pulled himself together and sat up; he noticed Zeke's eyes were full of tears, too.

"That's a great song, Reo. What it must have taken to write it, I don't want to know."

Reo washed his face again and blew his nose in some paper towel.

"Want to get some wine?" Zeke asked.

"Sure, why not?" Reo answered, and they went across the street, into one of the nineteen restaurants on Reo's block of MacDougal Street. It was already well into the evening, and the place was crowded. They sat in a booth where the punk-rock waitress, her hair some shade of laminated wood, handed them menus, then took them back when Zeke ordered red wine.

"You know, Reo," Zeke began, "that's a beautiful song. But I think you take women too seriously. You think love is this great exhilarating thing. It isn't. Real love is something else. You can really love someone and never sleep with them. And you can sleep with someone for years and never truly love them."

The wine, a bottle of cheap Bordeaux, arrived with two glasses. The waitress offered Zeke a sip.

"Terrible. Just what I wanted. Leave it."

"So what's the point?" Reo interjected.

"The point is, you'd be better off to think of women as furniture.

Like a chair. A chair will hold any ass that buys it or sits comfortably on it. And why not? What's it matter as long as the ass is comfortable and the chair doesn't fall apart? And that's how it is. Do you always sit on the same chair? No, of course not. Well, women are like that, they'll give a seat to whatever asshole sits on them. If you want one, sit on her. They're furniture. They don't really care that much for love, I mean, they say they do, but that's just to fool some guy into thinking they're his chair so he won't throw them out for junk. But love? No, I think most women are simply looking for the proper living room in which to sit. The guy who pays the freight probably makes a lot less difference than he thinks, as long as he has good taste in couches, coffee tables, and lamps."

Reo sat back.

"Are you through?" he asked.

"Sure. Drink up. Drink the wine and here's a toast: A nice, tight little cushion in every garage, two chickens in every bush."

And like good soldiers, they drank deep and poured heartily.

The next thing Reo would remember was waking to the telephone with a throbbing headache.

"Reo? Hi. I won't be back today after all. I'm going to stay on the tour. It's working out! So I have to stay at Raphael's manager's house to rehearse. I guess I'll be gone another week."

"Why don't you just stay there for good?" he grumbled.

"Do you mean that?"

"What do you bother asking me for? Would you really give a shit what I think?"

"Oh, Reo, can't we talk when I get home? This isn't the time. I'll see you next week. I'll call." And she hung up. He was almost asleep when it rang again.

"Um, hi, this is Cissie. I got your number out of the book. Um, actually, I'm at....Penn Station. I took the train here. Is it ok to call?"

He sat up.

"Yeah. It's okay."

"Do you want to meet me?"

"All right."

Thirty minutes later he found her in the waiting room, sitting beneath the mass of red hair in a floor-length white cotton dress. They walked out to the street and started uptown, going nowhere in particular.

"Um, I broke up with my boyfriend."

"Really?"

She laughed.

"The morning we said goodbye the six o'clock news was doing a show on commuters. Someone taped us kissing in the doorway. A friend of my boyfriend who works there saw me and told him. He was pretty mad."

"We were on TV?"

"No, it was just some random stuff that his friend saw in the production room and told him about."

Reo laughed. It sounded so fantastic, so coincidental. As if anyone could catch you doing anything, anywhere.

"So he broke up with you?"

"He yelled at me. So I told him to go away. I think it's good. Actually, I was kind of unhappy. I like to think we've already had the best of each other, so why go on any longer?"

"Don't you love him?" Reo asked her.

"Not any more. I mean, I hope he's okay. But I don't think I'm good for him anymore anyway. How's your love thing working out?"

He laughed.

"My love thing? Let's not talk about that. I wish I didn't even have to think about it. What do you want to do?"

They were a few blocks north of Penn Station, just entering Times Square. Above them was a marquee that said, "She Can' t Get Enuff: $3 matinee."

"Want to see a movie?" he asked her.

"How much would a hotel cost?" she replied, but he shook his head.

"You know, I've heard of this movie. It's not porn, it's a comedy. Why don't we see it?"

"Okay."

They threaded their way down a hallway into the basement theater, where a sparse crowd of 25 or so was laughing loudly at the heroine's attempt to convince her two suitors they should get used to her sleeping with both of them. The actors, all African-American, were talking with exaggerated inflection, the small audience roaring in waves.

"Honey, I'm a good lovin' woman. Takes a lot to keep me feelin' alive," she was telling them both. Reo and Cissie slid into the back row, unnoticed. No one was within several rows.

"Look, I don't min' either o' you banging on the side," the heroine continued. But the phone interrupted her. "Hello? Tonight?" She looked at her two suitors and said to the phone, "Okay."

But Reo and Cissie weren't watching the movie; as soon as they had their coats off they were kissing, groping, unbuttoning each other. He reached down along her leg and drew up her white skirt, his hand landing on thin leggings underneath.

"I can take my tights off," she whispered.

"Bitch, you got a lot of nerve," one of the on-screen males yelled as a door slammed on the soundtrack. Cissie peeled off her tights and Reo drew her up on top, cramming her knees behind him in the tight theater seat. She kissed him all over his face while he tried to see if anyone was watching them.

"I don't care if they see us. Look what they're watching anyhow," she said.

Up on the screen the remaining suitor was demonstrating his virility by humping the woman, bent forward and rolling her eyes with mock emotion, from behind. Cissie unzipped his jeans and pushed herself onto him, moaning softly; but nobody was listening while the buck on the screen huffed and puffed, rocking the bored heroine, slapping her on the ass. Cissie dug down on him and moaned again; the woman on the screen took it all in stride. Reo grabbed her head, digging his fingers into a handful of hair; burying her face in his shirt, he closed his eyes as they made love in relative silence, quietly holding each other on the single seat. At last she raised her head and kissed him lightly on the lips, and he looked out into the theater again.

People were standing up. The lights had come on and the audience all filed out; no one even noticed them as they rearranged their clothes, got up, and left. They walked two blocks before speaking.

"What do you want to do now?" he asked her.

"I guess I should go back to Providence," she said. "I have to study for a test tomorrow."

"You mean you came all the way here to make it with me in a movie theater?"

She grinned at him, her face round and pink in the winter cold.

"I guess so. Fun, wasn't it?" she said. He walked her back to Penn Station, hardly saying anything.

"You really love her, don't you?" Cissie asked.

"I don't know anymore. I thought I did."

"You know, I dreamed about you. Or us, I should say. We were sailors together, drinking, hanging out with tavern girls in some old port. It was fun. I think we've been together in other lives. I think of being soldiers with you, and also doing magic, and being kids, and living in the woods, and travelling and singing. There's a lot there. And we always had things in fours. Like four ships, four songs to sing. I hope....do you understand?"

He stopped walking and looked at her. She seemed much more a woman to his eyes then, as if the connection she described affected him more than the sex.

"Yes, I....could see it. When we were sailors, we had four songs to sing?"

"Um, huh, and throughout each thing. Will you write me a song?"

He put his hands in his pockets and looked at her.

"All right."

"Then I'd better go. Think the news is watching?"

He shuddered and drew his coat closed. The evening's commuters hurried by.

"You never know. Do you?" he answered. And he kissed her goodbye and watched her walk down the stairs to the train that would take her back home.

10–The Pilotfish

For a while it seemed I knew every drug dealer in Greenwich Village. Nearly all of them were dilettantes, artists, actors, musicians and free-lance bohemians who found it easier to deal with the secrecy of drugs than the regiment of a straight job. On some occasions I'd find myself with three or four of them in a café or watching television in somebody's apartment, and it amazed me that there was no competition between them; each one had his or her sources and outlets, was well aware of the operations the others had, and was very private about that side of making money. It was a very genteel scene.

Probably every neighborhood in town had a scene just like it, in which the participants were more or less vicious toward each other. But there was always a third element, and that was the police.

"They broke down our door at three in the morning," Emilia was saying, "and took Eddie away. They found two thousand dollars we had stashed in a vase. He could get three to five. Three to five? For selling people acid and marijuana?" Emilia was crying. We had all heard about the bust: it had been particularly messy, spilling over into the hallway and ending in the street with more than twenty uniformed cops on the sidewalk. At three a.m. the streets were still alive, and the word traveled fast. I felt sorry for Emilia, she seemed so slight and unable to cope with losing her boyfriend for three to five years. What do you do when your lover is locked away? Pine? Wait? Leave town and start a new life?

The fact that drugs are illegal is a major philosophical axis of the black market. On one hand, if they were legal the black market would be very hard pressed to compete against the drug and cigarette companies, which could buy whole blocks of acreage and mass market the stuff.

Whenever the topic of legalizing marijuana comes up in this crowd, the line goes as follows:

"Sure, Reo, great idea. Just think of the good chemicals they could put in it to make it burn longer, smell more enticing, and rot holes in your lungs. All for the greater corporate profit."

On the other, "You know, Reo, selling drugs is about the last area left where a man can make some money. You can't get anywhere holding a job anymore, the faster you make money the quicker they make it worthless. I can make a thousand bucks a week selling people something to get high. Sure there's a risk, that's why it pays. Look at the Kennedys. They started their fortune with prohibition booze. That's what it's like now. Legalize and all that opportunity goes to the upper floors of those buildings over there." That said, my friend swept his hand up at the New York skyscrapers.

Emilia disappeared a few days later, gone, someone said, to the west coast. Eddie was rumored to get a suspended sentence. Jane, Alec and I went upstairs to watch television, one of those PBS nature specials with gorgeous photography and stern, heartfelt narration.

"The shark's method of locating prey is still mysterious to many researchers," the voice said. "It is believed they have a sense of smell that can detect blood from miles away, but have only a weak visual perception that does not extend much beyond shadows against light. If you are in the water, and not bleeding, the safest thing to do is to make as little motion as possible, for sharks react most strongly to the turbulence of sound waves and quickly-changing light patterns that are produced by fear."

A huge mako shark swept onto the screen, quickly followed by others. At its nose was a small, quick-darting fish that seemed attached to the shark's front end by some uncanny sense. I jumped out of my chair, first thinking the shark was about to swallow this lithe little fish, then realizing the tiny fellow was leading the shark forward by the nose.

"What's that?" I yelled.

"That? Oh, that's a pilotfish," answered Alec, who goes ocean fishing in the summers."It's like a companion to the shark, like flies on a cow."

"Why doesn't the shark eat it?"

"Too small. Too fast. I dunno, really."

"Maybe it has something the shark needs," volunteered Jane. We sat quietly. The pilotfish led the sharks to a swimming tuna, which had been gliding along peacefully and most assuredly was not giving off either blood or wild, turbulent action to attract the predator. We saw it all together.

"Eyes," I said it first. "The pilotfish has the eyes."

Three months later Eddie turned up again at his old hangouts. For two weeks he was completely clean, he had a little leftover money and said he had a job uptown, so he hung out at night in his usual places, saying he missed Emilia and didn't know when she'd be back. Then one night Brian walked by, dressed (as always) in style: a long wool coat with fur collar, and underneath a three-piece suit with a gold watch chain. His was a class act. Eddie ducked out on the sidewalk and had a conversation with Brian for a few minutes, then came back. I stayed an hour and went home. The phone rang.

"What do you know lately of Eddie?" Brian's voice asked.

"Nothing much," I answered. "He was saying tonight that his people were asking him for supplies but he was having trouble deciding if he should go back to it."

"I'll bet he is," Brian said. "Next time it's five to seven."

"Are you going to help him?"

"I suppose. I'm a soft touch. He says I owe him for working three years for me."

"In your business, can you afford to owe anybody?"

"Good question. Want to come over?" Twenty minutes later I was at Brian's house when Eddie showed up. He stood on the carpet looking nervous.

"I need five," he said.

"Do you realize the risk you're taking on?" Brian said solemnly.

"I think so. I want to fight it, you know, not let this fear thing take hold. I'm like the guy that fell off his horse. I got to get back on."

"What about your apartment?"

"I'm still living there. But I'm stashing the stuff somewhere else now. It's ok, really." Brian took a deep and long breath. He looked at Eddie, and at his shoes. He looked at me. I didn't move.

"All right," said Brian. Eddie got his load and left. Five minutes later the doorbell rang again.

"It's Eddie. I left my book." True enough, it was sitting on the counter. Brian opened the door and four other men walked in, three in uniform, guns drawn.

"We're going downtown," said the trench coat. He looked at me and added, "I don't know who you are or why you're here, but beat it."

I put on my coat and went out the door. Across the street I stopped to watch. They all came out together and got in the car, Brian in handcuffs. At the last second Eddie did not get in; he would move uptown for a few weeks and work a different neighborhood, and the cops would protect him from Brian, if they could. The waters were getting dangerous.

"Eddie," Brian shouted out the car window. "I feel sorry for you, my man."

The Open Mike

1–The Open Mike

Reo MacGregor took the downtown train to Greenwich Village, a train that squealed to a grinding halt as signs flickered past the windows, ending with a final shrug that bounced his guitar case away from the chrome pole it was leaning against. Narrowly missing a seated passenger, he swung the case by its handle and started toward the door.

"Sorry," he called back, but the rumpled man slumped on the bench never even looked up.

Reo exited the subway onto West 3rd Street into the cool, damp, late spring evening, hauling the heavy fiberglass case just above the pavement, its nose pointed forward. He spotted the large, pink vertical neon sign— Folk Life—about fifty yards ahead, just as a short, toothless woman dressed in very dirty clothing stepped in front of him.

"Money for food?," she pleaded, her extended hand bobbing in front of him as if she were steering him towards her. He stopped, set down the case on its heavy end, and jammed a hand in his front jeans pocket. It took him a few moments, but he sorted out a quarter and held it out it to her.

"Wish me luck," he said.

The woman blinked and continued holding out her hand.

"Money for food?" she repeated.

"Here," he said, placing the silver coin in her palm. The woman drew it toward her face, and the quarter slid off, clinking on the ground and rolling a few feet away. Reo started after it just as a large truck honked its horn, almost hitting him as it raced to make the light. Waiting until it passed, he found the coin, placed it in the woman's hand again, and rolled her fingers into a fist.

"There you go," he said.

"Money for food?" the woman implored unstoppably. He squeezed her fist and walked away.

He crossed the street and reached the club in a few steps. There was a small window to the left, as he turned through the open door into a narrow passageway that made a second turn through two swinging doors. It was a clumsy entrance for a guitar case, and he whacked one door loudly as he passed through; the murmur of conversation inside suddenly ceased. A roomful of strangers looked toward him, mostly young men standing over a field of black, brown, baby blue, white, and even red guitar cases, so that walking forward required stepping over their characteristic shapes—round at one end, narrow at the other—propped against the wall or flat on the floor, handles facing out and ready.

He picked his way, step by step, across the floor to the bar, where a blond, mustached man in wire-rimmed glasses sat watching him, a clipboard balanced on his knee.

"Let me guess, you want to play the open mike," he greeted Reo.

"Yes, if it's not too late."

"It is too late. Signup ended at 7:30," he returned. He looked at his watch. "It's 7:31 exactly. Tony's rules."

A voice sounded from behind the bar; an older man, wearing a white shirt and glasses, stood there cleaning a glass with a cloth towel.

"That's a right," the man echoed. "7:30 we stop a with the names."

Reo stood there, nodding slowly, then exhaled.

"I'm sorry, I came on the subway."

"Oh, another subway prophet," the blond man nodded knowingly. He looked at Tony, who looked back at him and continued rubbing the glass with the towel.

"Okay, but that's a the last," Tony smiled, then turned his back and walked away.

The blond man stood up.

"Lucky us. What's your name?"

"Reo MacGregor," he pronounced it carefully.

"Spell it, please."

"R-E-O, M-A-C-G-R-E-G-O-R," he intoned.

"Number 30C." The man smiled, almost sadistically, Reo thought; then, twirling the end of his handlebar, he went into the back room beyond the far end of the bar. Working his way through the wooden chairs and little tables arranged in two large semi-circles facing a stage along the right wall, he came to a desk with a small light bulb glowing over it. Reo watched as he sat behind a metal console, flipped a switch, and began talking though the club's sound system.

"Okay, music lovers, welcome to the Open Mike. This is your friendly host, Sonoma Sal, and I'm the guy who puts you on, so don't piss me off. In case you don't know the drill, you get two songs or eight minutes, that's it. Talking during someone's performance is rude, so don't do it. Tune up out in the bar, and please, *be in tune* when your name is called. We start with 1A, then 1B, then 1C, all the way to 30C, which, no doubt, will be very, very late. Any questions?"

"You want a beer?" Reo heard someone ask behind him; it was Tony, who stood smiling behind the bar.

"You gotta long a wait." In the background he heard someone's name being called, followed by a smattering of applause.

"Sure," Reo answered, setting down his case. "How long do you think it'll be?"

Tony smiled, drawing a beer from an ancient metal tap with a black plastic handle.

"Oh, two three, maybe a five hours,' he shrugged. "Who knows? You in a hurry? I see you before somewhere?"

"I was here one night last week."

"Oh. Who you see?"

"Giant Mountain."

"Oh, yeah, those a boys bring a good crowd," Tony said, setting down the beer. "That's a dolla. Since a you play. Usually two."

"Thanks," he said, opening his wallet, sliding a bill across the bar.

Tony went down the bar and Reo studied the scene: the back room and the bar were full of people, mostly young guys in blue jeans and denim jackets. There were only a handful of women in the bar, all either standing with their hand on a man's arm or in the center of a small circle of men. None of the women, interestingly enough, were talking with each other. One of the women, a willowy blonde with shoulder-length hair, stood surrounded by at least six men, who were all laughing at something she said; but when she finished, five of them deferred to the man next to her, a man in his mid-twenties, Reo guessed, which seemed five or six years older than the young woman. Running his hand over a head of sandy-colored hair, he made a comment that made all the men laugh, just as she looked across the room straight into Reo's eyes. He started to look away, but she smiled, somehow conveying a hello without any of her companions noticing, before returning to their conversation.

He counted the guitar cases; in the bar there were twenty-seven, and in the back room, where the crowd was at least paying attention, he could see fifteen. There were seven blue cases with the word *Martin* embossed in the side, advertising that its owner was a serious guitarist, or at least owned a serious guitar. Most cases were black and nondescript, except for the gleaming white one leaning on the wall behind the crowd surrounding the blond woman. Forty-two cases, he added up, and he was last with number 30C, the ninetieth performer on the list. At two songs or eight minutes, there was the theoretical possibility he could wait twelve hours to play.

The first performer finished; Reo had barely heard him. What if no one listened when he played? He grabbed his case and went into the back room, moving behind the main body of seats until he found an open spot on the vinyl bench at the back wall. He rested the guitar against the seat and sat down, banging his head against a framed photograph behind him.

"Ah, the past rears its ugly head," a round voice spoke from the next seat. "Don't worry, that photo has probably been there twenty years, if you broke it you'd be doing everyone a favor."

"Sorry," Reo replied.

"For what?" The speaker reached across and tilted the frame so he could look at it.

"Oh, the Children of Paradise," he grimaced. "I think they played here once in 1969."

Reo looked around the room; the walls were dotted with similar framed photographs.

"Is that what all these photos are? People who played here?"

"This is the folk museum," the man smiled, holding out a hand. "Ted. Imbonanti."

"Imbonanti?"

"That's my name. Ted Imbonanti." This time he emphasized the third syllable.

"Reo. Reo MacGregor," he answered, shaking the hand. Ted released it, then reached down and picked up a pack of cigarettes.

"Smoke?"

"No, thanks," Reo shook his head.

"You're new, aren't you?"

"First time."

"Oh, great. I remember mine. Two months ago. What do you think?"

"Well, I just got here."

"No, I mean, what do you think of this place? Pretty incredible, like a throwback to another era. All these famous people played here and Tony has kept it going all this time. Now he's got the best, hell, it's the only good open mike around."

"Are you playing?"

"Number 10B. You?"

"30C. I guess I'm gonna be here awhile."

"Hey that's cool, it's your first time. Not everyone gets such a lucky number their first time. You'll get to see it all. Most people leave for a couple hours, then come back later. You gonna stay?"

"I came to play."

"Great," Ted nodded through a cloud of smoke. "What do you play?"

"Some songs I wrote."

"Oh, we all do that. No, I mean what kind of guitar?"

"Gibson. Its an old LG1. Mahogany, it's small but I like it."

"Great. I have a Martin D-35. It's big and heavy but I like it too." He laughed, a quick, easy laugh that made Reo relax.

Someone in the row ahead of them turned around and shushed them.

"Oops," Ted whispered, his eyes wide in mock regret. And then they both laughed, as if they had arrived together at some secret location.

2–Graduation Day

Somewhere there is a picture of it.

The moment when he was free, not of any prison, nor of any physical restraint, but as surely as anyone can be freed from jail or any box in which one's life is constrained, was as clear and well-documented as any of those, at least in Reo MacGregor's mind. And there has to be a photograph, even if it's lost or forgotten, because one after another the graduating students stand next to the Dean, who hands each one his or her degree as their picture is taken together. The Dean doesn't let go until the photograph is taken, because the school gets paid for each snapshot the student buys. So, there is always a photograph.

Reo MacGregor, sweating in the May afternoon sun, waited in a long line snaking its way around the esplanade outside the steel building. Like many plazas in New York, it was an area of concrete dotted with benches and small trees planted in square, wooden boxes of dirt in an attempt to make it seem a natural environment. Envisioned as a refuge from the dangerous streets of the city, it extended across Amsterdam Avenue a full story above the backed up traffic, incessant honking, and daily hustle right below them on the sidewalks; but from here Reo could only see the upper floors of nearby buildings, slivers of blue sky between them, and, imagine, far off in the distance, the skyscrapers where his classmates were headed to extremely well-paying work, where they would forever be protected from those streets below.

This was the Columbia Law School in a nutshell, he decided: deliberately unaware of the real world, concerned with finding an acceptable niche for its privileged graduates, most of whom would go directly into the best law firms, eat at the best restaurants, have beautiful apartments and vacation homes, and never know the grinding, aching poverty of the neighborhood which surrounded their school. Its tall, rectangular shape accentuated by full-length vertical steel stripes, it was known to students as "the Toaster" for the high twin balconies of the Dean's office that stuck out like handles on a giant kitchen appliance. To Reo, it stood in proud defiance of the community around it, cranking out graduates who would gladly serve and become captains of American wealth by inventing new ways to skirt tax, liability and environmental laws, and feather their own nests.

Reo's assessment of the school and its graduates was undoubtedly harsh and probably unfair, considering that some graduates would also become top criminal and constitutional lawyers, not to mention leading advocates for minorities, social causes and progressive change in the legal landscape. But it served him well, for he had already decided he wanted no part of any of it, and it steeled him for the decision he had made.

The line snaked across the plaza as each name was droned out and applauded, as each student stepped forward and received his certificate from the Dean, a prematurely balding, bespectacled man in a dark suit. The Dean and the student would smile, the flashbulb would pop, and the graduate would go forth into the world, forever a graduate of Columbia Law School. He or she could then purchase this memento at a price that was not, Reo noted, particularly cheap; this fact, he decided, accounted for the Dean's willingness to stand there all afternoon, flashbulbs popping in his face, holding the diploma as long as possible, for probably in some earlier year there was a mere professor or secretary to give the diplomas and no one had bought the photos. Somewhere, somehow, it always came down to money.

From out of nowhere a gray-suited man appeared at his side.

"MacGregor. You showed up for graduation at least, I see," he said quietly.

Reo smiled. Within the school he was known as some kind of rebel, the least likely to enjoy the trappings of success. Among those trappings was a good job, and Harold Snyder, the school's placement officer, had been after him all year. He was young and friendly, perhaps in his thirties, a rising star in the administrative world. Reo had once had a beer with him and thought he was a decent guy.

"Well, I did graduate," he replied.

"I don't suppose it would do any good to ask you one more time to come and see me," Snyder continued. "It's not too late."

"I'm just not interested."

"You've ruined what would have been a perfect year for my office," Snyder went on, clearly frustrated. "I've placed every other student, but you."

"You know, it isn't personal, Harold. I'm sorry if I've screwed up your statistics, but I can't help you."

Harold Snyder sighed.

"I've never had a student like you, MacGregor. Never. I don't suppose it would do me any good to find you an offer."

"No, it wouldn't."

The placement officer extended a hand.

"Well, then, let me be a good sport and wish you good luck wherever you are going. And if you ever change your mind, my door's open."

Reo smiled and shook hands with the man.

"Thanks, Harold. I appreciate it."

A few yards away the parents waited, perched on folding chairs in the shade, watching the slow parade move forward in alphabetical order to receive their rolled parchment certificates. Most of the parents were proud, some fiercely so, for their offspring were advancing into realms of American society hitherto only dreamed of, coming from immigrant or small-town families far removed from the skyscraper offices of New York City. And somewhere in the crowd were parents who, like his roommate Jeff's, were Harvard graduates, who thought Jeff a disappointment.

And then there were his own parents, so proud of the first member of either side of the family to graduate college—and now law school—waiting quietly in the far corner of the esplanade, somewhat confused by their son's admission he had no interest in pursuing a legal career.

At last his name was called, his parents were standing, and Reo MacGregor stepped forward to meet the Dean. He and the Dean knew each other well, for Reo had been called into his office many times for absences from class and for articles he had written in the school newspaper, articles criticizing the school's highly obvious bias toward producing lawyers for the wealthy downtown law firms. Reo had called the school, in print, a "factory for privilege."

The Dean smiled and offered a handshake, just as the cameraman spoke up.

"Can you hold that a moment? I have to change film."

"So, MacGregor, we meet one more time. I often wondered if you'd make it to graduation."

"I'm a stubborn guy."

"Yes, I'd have to say that's true. I'd even say some of your criticisms around here were heard. You may have had a positive effect on us all, however slight."

"Thanks, I guess."

The Dean looked at the cameraman, who still wasn't ready. So they stood, holding the handshake as they waited.

"Harold tells me you're the only one he didn't get a job for. Ruined his perfect year. He says you never even came to see him. Why?"

"Why what?"

"Why didn't you go see him? He could have helped you. Do you already have a job?"

"No." The cameraman had changed his film, was almost ready.

"That's crazy," said the Dean. "Columbia Law School graduates get some of the best places everywhere. Your grades weren't so bad. Don't you want a job?"

"No."

The cameraman took aim.

"Are you ready?" he asked, but the Dean barely heard him.

"What *are* you going to do?" he turned toward Reo, suddenly curious.

The student looked the Dean in the eye. The cameraman focused.

"I'm going to be a folksinger," Reo MacGregor said.

"Huhh?" recoiled the Dean, straightening up, his mouth open wide. The cameraman shrugged, hit the shutter, and the flash popped, capturing the moment.

The Dean's priceless expression almost made Reo want to buy the photo. But he would never know, nor care, what happened to it. Instead he released the hand, took his degree, and slid away into the crowd.

3–Making A Living

Reo walked his parents to their car. They were not sticking around New York City, not even to celebrate. His mother, who had grown up in Boston, probably would have loved to soak up some city lights, but his small-town father, who had spent most of his time worried someone would steal his car, couldn't wait to leave. Columbia University is on the northern end of Manhattan, and that was fine with him, it took less time to drive back to northern, rural Connecticut. And if they had been inclined to celebrate, that idea had entirely been forgotten once they had learned, about a month ago, that after all the years of school, the thousands of dollars in tuition, and the pride of having the family's first graduate of either college or law school, he was not going to use that education and become a lawyer.

Reo had always worked, delivering newspapers, bagging groceries in his teens, office jobs, and even as a newspaper reporter, and paid more of his bills for school each year. If it was a cause of concern that now Reo was turning his back on it, his parents would not make it an issue, for the decision had been long in coming, and easy to foresee, through the countless arguments and conversations about what Reo called "society's materialism." He was young, he was driven, and most important, he was tired of being an apprentice to life. It was time to live it, and he was not going to spend those years learning to be a lawyer.

They walked in silence the two blocks of city streets. Finally his mother took his hand.

"What are you going to do now?" she asked.

"I'm going to find a place to live and get a job. And start singing wherever I can."

"Why not get a law job, just til you got your feet on the ground? You could play music in your free time, til you got known and could make a living at it," she tried.

"It doesn't work that way. When you start as a lawyer you work 16 hours a day til you get anywhere. And that anywhere doesn't interest me."

His father stood quietly by.

"I hope you know what you're doing," she said quietly. "We worry about you, all alone in this city with no money."

He turned to face them.

"You know, I'm going to be fine," he said with a smile. "I've always worked, and I will now. But I'm going to work for what I believe in, not something I'm going to hate myself for."

They hugged and kissed cheeks with him, proud, concerned, disappointed perhaps, but probably not surprised. All the same, they weren't going to stick around New York City. He held out the rolled up degree.

"Here," he said. "Don't lose it."

His mother opened her purse, put the document inside, and snapped it shut.

"I won't," she said. And then they were off to Connecticut.

It was left to Delfina Worman, 18, a freshman at NYU he had met at one of his coffeehouse performances, to join him at a small, bustling Middle Eastern restaurant just off Broadway. Six years younger than he, slender, pretty, her long blonde hair flouncing along in a pony tail behind her, she had seemed so natural and unaffected he had been drawn to her at once. And she said she liked his music. He liked that, it was the first time anyone had said that to him, at least anyone like her.

"What are you going to do?" she asked him soon enough, smiling through a glass of white wine. No one had even asked for an ID.

"Get a job," he said. "I need to have some income."

"Doing what?"

"I have an interview tomorrow with a neighborhood newspaper, as a proofreader. Something I learned to do in college."

"Can I ask you something?" she munched through some rice.

"What?"

"What will you do if it doesn't work out?"

"If what doesn't work out?"

"You know. Your music. A career."

"You sound as if you don't believe me."

"Me? Oh, it doesn't matter if I do or don't. The music business.... well I don't know much about it. But neither do you. What if you can't make it?"

He found himself twirling the beer bottle, edging the label with his fingernail, then sat back against the wall and thought a moment.

"You can't think like that. It's not a question of making it in a set period of time. You have to be committed to making it your life's work. I'm an artist. At least I intend to be, a professional musical artist. You don't approach it expecting to fail."

"But so many people do. What will you do if that happens?"

He took a bite of his shish kebob before answering.

"Why do you ask?" he looked at her.

"I don't intend to be poor," she replied, staring at her food. "I've been poor all my life, and I don't want to live that way for long."

He smiled at her in spite of the thoughts going through his mind.

"What you're saying is, you're not interested in some guy who's chasing a dream instead of raking in the dough?"

"Don't be crass. It's not that simple. But I want to live well, have a family, have a real life. Could I be happy living without those things? I don't know."

"You've thought about this, I see."

"Haven't we all?"

He nodded.

"Look, Delfina, I don't want to ignore what you're saying. But I have to give this my best shot."

"I understand that. I support you completely. I just want to know if there's a plan to make sure your life doesn't fall apart."

They ate in silence for a few moments.

"There's something else," she said.

"What?"

She took a long breath.

"Back in the winter, before we met, I applied for a transfer to another college in Pittsburgh. I just heard yesterday that I've been accepted."

He studied her face, which at that moment was studying his. He looked at his plate, his hands slicing open a brown, crunchy ball of falafel.

"Are you going to go there?"

"I don't know. They have a much better pre-med program. What do you think?"

Watching his own finger, he traced the edge of the flower pattern baked into his plate, chewing slowly, taking his time.

"What does your mother say?" was his first question.

"I haven't told her yet. I wanted to ask you first."

Delfina's mother, her sole parent since she was too young to remember, hated Reo. She had taken one look at him and told her daughter, "He'll leave you just like your father left me." But Delfina did not listen to her mother, and though they shared an apartment, they were not close.

"I think you should go where you'll get the best education."

"Meaning you might not be around anyway."

"I didn't say that. But if this is a real opportunity for you, you should take it. I'll be around or not, for reasons having nothing to do with location."

She threw down her napkin and cried softly.

"I thought that's what you'd say."

Now he was angry.

"You mean you want me to ask you to stay here even if it means giving up something you really want?"

"I want to know so much that you will never tell me," she whispered through more tears, and he softened, saw in a glance how they both cared.

"When do you have to decide?"

"Two weeks."

He said nothing for a long time.

"Delfina, I want to do right by you."

"What does that mean?"

He shook his head, wondering, which one of us will be first to let go?

"You have to do what's right for you."

She sighed heavily, nodded, wiped a tear from the corner of her mouth, and seemed to toughen right before his eyes.

"I will, then," she said, as if to herself.

The next day Reo applied to a neighborhood newspaper as a proofreader. A tall patrician man in a brown tweed sport coat with elbow patches, gave him some copy to read and correct. He did it quickly and well, missing one punctuation mark. But his grammar was excellent, the publisher told him over the top of his glasses, introducing himself as Raymond Talleyrand, the publisher of the *Westside Courier.*

"Talleyrand, as in the famous writer?" Reo asked.

"The same, no relation, however. Anyway, they tell me you have some experience at this?"

"I was an editor of my college paper, we learned everything from writing to production. And a lot of proofreading."

"It says here you're a law school grad. Are you studying for the bar?"

"No, I'm not taking it."

Talleyrand studied him for a long moment.

"Well, that's your business, I guess. Do you want a job?"

4–The Road To Ruin

Reo and Ted watched the next few performers, talking quietly but mostly listening. Some performers walked on stage before their name was finished, as if in a hurry to start; a few even started playing their guitars before they got to the microphones. Sonoma Sal was mixing the sound from behind his console, trying to keep one step ahead of the wide variety of guitars and voices, some strumming as hard and frantically as they could one moment, barely touching the strings the next. It seemed to Reo that the louder they played and sang, the quieter Sonoma Sal mixed them, so that the ones who actually projected into the crowd were usually playing quietly and singing in a normal tone of voice. The crowd, mostly other singers waiting to go on, was enthusiastic enough, giving almost everyone a good sendoff, even the bad ones; and a few were good, though Ted seemed unimpressed. And a few numbers were called but not answered, so before long they were at number 7C, a short, large-nosed, Arabic looking man. Ted sat up.

"I love this guy!" he said out loud. And it seemed everyone else did too, as shouts of "The Dragon!" rang out. The singer began strumming his guitar, a very cheap-looking instrument with a row of blinking Christmas lights strung along the neck, and launched into a voice that was pure Brooklyn nasal whine:

> Bagging the Dragon
> that's for me
> I only take him out
> when it's time for tea
> I say 'ok little dragon,
> if you're so tough

why don't you get me a doughnut
instead of eating me?'

The crowd roared its approval. Reo clapped, looking around the room, watching the scene; it seemed as if everyone changed their seats after each singer, sitting with friends, going out to tune their guitars. Ted shouted "Great!" and bounced back against the vinyl bench, then grabbed Reo's wrist.

"Okay, now we get going," he said.

The next performer was one of the young men who had been standing around the blond woman. Her little group had edged into the wide doorway between the two rooms, not coming in to sit down, but clearly about to pay attention to the music for the first time.

"You can tell when someone's really good," Ted whispered, "because they start getting quiet in the bar."

The singer was a tall, dark-haired man with a Gibson like Reo's, slightly larger but equally dark. He began finger-picking at a quick tempo, and soon was singing in a clear and very pleasant voice:

I never knew I loved you
til I went into a store
and bought a rose to hold in my hand
I never knew what a rose was
until I saw you
and still I don't understand

"That's Eddie Astor," Ted said. "Not bad. Kinda sentimental but not bad."

Reo watched the young woman in the doorway, who was in turn absorbed in watching the young man singing; behind her another member of the group stood talking to his other companions while watching the girl watching the singer.

Eddie was followed by another member of this same group, a shorter blond man, wearing glasses and a tweed jacket with elbow patches. He was named Franklin Something, Reo missed his last name. Also finger-picking, but much more slowly, he launched into a solemn oration with a voice that came straight out of prep school, enunciating every word with perfect diction:

One day by the river when I was buying water
I spied a young maid who looked sad and forlorn
'What is it?' I asked her and she began crying
'Kind sir,' she said sadly, 'my lover has gone.'

Says I, 'Well, young lady, why not take another?
I'm sure there are many as handsome and strong.'
Says she 'he would never forgive me betraying
I'll wait by this river until he's come home.'

Reo's mind drifted away as the song droned on, nearly devoid of melody or excitement. He noticed one couple kissing in a dark corner, and saw again the young woman standing in the archway between the bar and back room. The thought occurred to him that she was very interested in the story of the song, as if she imagined herself a part of it. He nudged Ted.

"Do you see that girl in the archway?"

"Yeah. Why?"

"She seems to be studying these songs as if she's trying to figure something out."

"Yeah. So?"

"Well, I don't know. It's as if she thinks they're about her or something."

Ted studied him for a moment.

"They probably are," he smiled. "All those guys are in love with her."

Reo laughed.

"What's so special about her?"

Now it was Ted's turn to laugh.

"You'll have to see for yourself," he said. "She's on next."

"I'll wait by this river until he's come home," Franklin finished, bowing low with a great sweep of his hand, as if he had just won an archery meet. Sonoma Sal leaned forward and spoke the next name.

"Okay music lovers, number 10A is the lovely and talented Callisto Maya." There was a sustained burst of applause, and all five of her retainers drew forward into the archway, jockeying for prime standing space. Clad in black jeans and black sweater, her wispy blond hair floating across her shoulders, the young woman moved with no great rush, actually walking her slim case onto the stage, where she took out a slender, shiny black guitar with an egg-shaped hole in the center.

"Someone said he wanted a song about household implements," she began. "Or maybe he didn't. But this is one. Or maybe it isn't. I don't know."

Into the waiting silence, she stroked the strings in a downward, chopping motion, not the alternating finger pattern of the other singers, but a percussive attack with the backs of her fingernails, quiet, repetitive, a droning bass note behind a moving line on the higher-pitched strings.

In my hand I hold a
pair of scissors
in a way they
remind me of you
the way you slice through a
conversation
dividing everything
in two

In my hand I hold a
pair of scissors
In a way it
reminds me of when
like thumb and finger, we
separated
all the way open and
closed again

Her soft voice soothed the audience, as she chanted the phrases rhythmically to the music. After the second verse, rising to a high note, exhaling a series of "ahs," each one descending in melody as if a bird were attached to it, she landed on the third verse with a slight pause for effect:

Should I cut something?
My hair my nails?
My hair my nails
aren't ready just now

what about my
eyelashes
I know, I'll cut my
eyebrows

In my hand I hold a
pair of scissors
legs open, eyes
big and round
the way you look when you
want something from me
I think I'd better put
these scissors down

With a sustained, single "ahhh" sung over the chords, the song ended.

The crowd applauded steadily if not loudly, as if puzzled, or waiting for something. Several people settled back into their seats, finally abandoning the conversations they had let lapse. Shifting to a minor key, she opened her second song in a conversational tone:

You came to my island
for your own survival
I gave you shelter and
yes, I gave you love
You should go now
while the tide is rising
I can't promise to save you
or love you enough

Singing again, she raised her voiced to the chorus:

Oh, leave me now
Leave me now
I won't wait for your return

Then she was back in her speaking voice:

The men who serve you
who fought alongside you
I changed them all
when I saw their ways
They wait for you now
as your own wife calls you
as your kingdom needs you
til the end of your days.

Reo realized he was listening, for the first time all night, to all the words; was it just because she's pretty, he wondered? No, it seemed as if she were talking directly to him, telling him a story he already knew. And then it hit him.

Circe, you whisper,
when you want me
Ithaca, you murmur,
as you sleep in my arms
Go, before your salt tears
drown the ocean
and keep your sails
away from harm

The end of the song brought a diverse response, ranging from what seemed confused murmurs to sustained and loud applause. Ted turned to Reo with a sardonic grin.

"So, what d'ya think?" he asked.

"Pretty amazing," Reo shook his head. "Beautiful."

"She is that."

"No, I meant the song."

"Oh that. Yeah, I guess so, I'm not big on mythology myself. Well, here we go," Ted added, pointing toward the stage, where the sandy-haired man from the group by the arch was walking up to the mikes, as Sal announced "10B, Jonas Waverly."

"That's Jonas. He's working here, he opens the shows for the weekend headliners. Pretty cool, the first of the open mikers to get a gig."

Wearing a suede jacket, fringes running along the sleeves, he stood with a dark brown Gibson, watching his own fingers as the audience, now lulled into silence, waited quietly.

"Jonassss!" someone yelled, exaggerating the *sss*.

"What?" he replied in a rasping stage whisper, turning a tuning key, not looking up.

A moment passed, with nervous laughter from offstage.

"Play a song."

Jonas broke up, laughing.

"What did you think I was gonna do?" he shook his head, drawing a loud laugh from the crowd.

"Shut up!" someone else yelled, and Jonas snapped his bass string with his thumb. Standing up straight, his eyes watched his thumb rub his fingertips, as he began speaking.

"There are people who insist" he began, leaning on the last syllable, "that a folk song has to have a train in it. I don't personally buy it. But if there's anyone who thinks so and has been waiting for a folk song"—emphasizing the "folk"—"then this one's for you." And with that, he snapped the low string of his guitar, and plucked a slow, moody chord.

> You said you were a falcon
> and I saw you swoop down
> taking the prey in your mouth like
> a lost wounded dove
> but I must be an eagle
> for I'm still circling
> not at all ready to dive
> from my vantage above
>
> you move deep below me
> like a shadow on the land
> you're quicker than I
> at taking each meal
> I don't waste a motion
> or chase a false hand
> I'm waiting for the moment
> when your love is real

But oh, she wails like the midnight train
when the leaves lay on the ground
and I, I was only passing through
when I first came to her town

"A train song!" Ted whispered to Reo, sinking back against the wall. "Whaddya know."

You gaze out the window
as if scanning a field
til you're lost in your own
reflected stare
and I, with my arms
wrapped 'round your shoulders
drew the hood over your eyes
and captured you there.

There were hoots and whistles as the song finished. Ted turned to Reo, said "well, gotta go tune up now," and walked off toward the bar.

5–Disappearing Act

Reo MacGregor had spent his previous year in New Jersey, in a small house shared with four other law students, all males. They started the year driving in together, across the George Washington Bridge, down the West Side Highway to 125th Street, winding through the neighborhood to a parking space somewhere. Reo skipped classes after awhile, but rode into the city with them, and went to the school regularly. But at night, as his classmates studied below, he lived in the attic, outside the house's insulation, where he huddled before a space heater night after night, playing the guitar for hours with a fleece-lined coat draped over his shoulders. Once in awhile, one of his housemates came up and played the bongos for a few minutes. When exams came, they loaned him their class notes, and he studied well enough to pass. They said goodbye at graduation, leaving for jobs with firms in California and Chicago, and seemed in a different universe now, or rather, he had left their universe and traveled on. He was on his own.

Reo spent three days alone in the New Jersey house, whole days and nights strumming the guitar, his voice echoing in the empty rooms, where he imagined a great hall filled with people, conjuring drums, bass, guitars, keyboards, flutes, saxophones, and back-up singers. Strolling barefoot across hardwood floors in rooms with no furniture, he couldn't make himself stop, barely took time to sleep, then walked to a nearby diner late at night, after his best hours. Home at three, he grabbed paper and pen and set it on the black wooden stool, the only piece of furniture in the downstairs bedroom. He started strumming, and writing a line at a time:

If you could ride this train I'm on
You wouldn't miss your happy home
It wouldn't take too much to make you wander
Out there where the wind is free and there's
nothing much but you and me
and a whole wide world to believe in
You might hear the sound of people crying,
laying down a lifetime they've stopped trying
feeling everything they love won't be long
if you could ride this train I'm on
before it's gone

It was a strange sensation, to hear the words coming to him as he sang and strummed the guitar. He knew he had little experience "out there where the wind is free" and had never ridden the train anywhere but from Waterbury to New York. Still, it felt real, as if the song was speaking to him, trying to tell him something.

On June 1, he closed up the house and drove his car and belongings up to his parents'. The bags of clothes, papers, and mementos seemed to belong to someone else, or at least somewhere else, and he stashed them in a remote corner of the attic, a place where no one but himself had gone for years. He stayed the weekend, restlessly biding time, checking in with old friends, going out for a drink with his father and sister Jayne to a bar with a guitarist-singer in the corner. They settled around a corner table, as the small crowd clapped a thin round of applause.

"You could stay here and sing," Jayne said hopefully. "There are lots of bars in Connecticut." But their father shook his head.

"You could do that. Then one day some guy would come through from New York and everyone would go off to see him. You'd think you had your chance and didn't take it. Better you go to New York, do what you need to do."

Reo looked his father over and understood what it had taken for him to make that statement, to let him have his own idea for his life.

"Thanks, Dad," he said, smiling, looking his father in the eye.

"Oh, I suppose you're right," Jayne nodded softly. "But you have to play somewhere. And I miss you."

"I miss you, too," Reo returned, and he meant it. There were always just the two of them; while their parents worked she had taught him to read, taught him to dance to rock and roll, taken him for summer drives in the back seat of her boyfriends' cars, driven him for ice cream when they were supposed to be at church. She was one of those short but very curvy dark-haired girls with a pretty face, and he was nearly six feet tall and thin; but they were un-mistakenly brother and sister, his face like hers, yet a man's face, with even darker hair and eyebrows and lighter eyes, his blue-gray and hers light brown. All his childhood she had been there, through his early teens, when she finished high school, got married and moved out. She had a son the next year, and soon Reo was babysitting on Sundays so she could go bowling with her husband. She had a second son, then got divorced while Reo was in law school, and now lived alone with the kids in the same house; he sometimes stayed there during school holidays.

Now he was consciously choosing to live somewhere else. He wasn't coming home.

She'd been the first in his family to tell him she actually liked his music. He remembered it well: she drove to New York to watch him play at Xanadu, one of the west side coffeehouses he found in his last year of school. He expected her to seem out of place, with her bouffant working-girl hair and her small-town sense of humor, but she enjoyed the show and his friends and they had a wonderful time. He enjoyed showing her the city as he knew it, taking her to an Italian restaurant near the coffeehouse, basking in the glow of her understanding. Now here they were, back in their hometown, and she wanted him to stay.

"Well," she grinned ruefully, "I suppose I can always come to New York to see you."

"You liked it, didn't you?"

"I couldn't live there! God no. But it's fun, for a couple days. How are you going to live there?"

He studied the label on his beer bottle, thinking, whenever someone asks me a question that takes some thought I do this, I twirl the beer bottle and study the label.

"I'll just have to figure it out as I go along," he said.

"You're not one to back off, are you?" she asked suddenly.

"What?"

"I mean, once you set your mind on something you just believe it's going to work out, don't you?"

"That's how it is," his father interjected. "You do it or you don't."

The singer finished his version of "Fire And Rain." The audience clapped, and someone yelled "Cat Stevens!" The singer nodded, turning the pages on his music stand, obligingly finding the lyrics to a Cat Stevens song. He started in on "Wild World," and Reo leaned forward, whispering.

"They always yell out the names of singers, like they expect you to be that person. I want to play songs, my own songs, songs I can get behind, not just sing any old stuff and pretend to be some fragment."

"Well," she said, "that's fine, but you have to play what they want to hear, too, I suppose, if you want to work."

"You have to make them want to hear your music," his father said without looking at them, looking out over the crowd at the singer. "This guy's not bad, let's listen awhile."

The next day he took a train to New York, carrying his guitar, a sleeping bag and a backpack with a few changes of clothes, jeans and t-shirts mostly, and a sandwich made by his mother. He felt silly—going back to New York ought to be some rebellious act, shouldn't it?—and here was his mother sticking the homemade lunch in his pack. But he greedily ate the sandwich before the train left Connecticut, and arrived hungry in New York City on a wet, Monday afternoon. He came to New York, not for law school this time, or because he had to, but for himself, for his music. This time he had to find his way on a different path, starting with nothing, with no one expecting him, and nowhere to go.

He had told no one he was coming, and no one where he was going, because he wanted to step into this new life with no chance of being dragged back into the world of law students and safe havens. He wanted so badly to emerge into a new world of music and writing, of experience and ideas, that he walked slowly out of Grand Central Station onto Forty-Second Street as if afraid it would be a fake, an illusion, a dream one awakens from before it can come true. Standing on the pavement in the fresh rain, energized with the rippling currents of people hustling in every direction, that moment he had always wanted, sought for, longed for, that moment when he would know his very life was changing, came so stealthily it took him by surprise, as if from another side of the world, from somewhere else. He would have to shed everything that had come before, to disappear from the life he had been living as concretely as a family leaves a house they have always lived in and known and moves to a faraway place. Now he had done it. He had made it possible to go forward, and all the clichés, all the bad lines in a million songs, all the this-is-the-first-day-of-the-rest-of-your-life greeting card sentiments were his life, as he stood motionless in the street, people flowing around him as they hurried on. Not a single soul in the world was expecting him, for he was no longer following the path others had written for him. He was finding his own way, and the next step he took would truly be the start of a whole new life.

He set the guitar down on its fat end on the sidewalk and looked up, up to the top of a nearby building to the gray, formless void that was the rainy sky beyond, and he promised himself that he would never, ever quit.

6–The Weary Traveler

One Friday evening in May, Reo and Delfina had watched from the audience as Jonas Waverly sliced his finger across his upper lip, straightening out one side of his slender handlebar moustache so it framed the corners of his mouth. Tossing the long, brown hair back over his shoulder, he slid his thumb from under the low string of his acoustic guitar so it smacked back into place with a loud *thwack!*-ing sound. The murmur of conversation lowered momentarily, and Jonas stroked his guitar quietly now, into the space he'd created. People sat back on their chairs, waiting.

It was midnight in a Greenwich Village club known as Folk Life, and Jonas was starting his last set, opening for a five-piece band. He wasn't alone. There was also a very round, blond man with a large, mahogany string bass, playing it very well with a clean, deep tone, and always the right notes. The rest of the crowd—fifty or so crowded around the club's tiny round tables—wasn't listening, wanted the other, louder band to play; but it was Jonas' set.

Reo, who had brought Delfina with him to see the Jonas Waverly he had read about in the *New York Times* that week, was taking it all in. And what he saw was a singer at work, winning them over one song at a time, staying on course through his set. He had a raspy voice, a middle tenor that was clearer in the higher notes, rough in the lower range, but always musical, lilting out over the drone of conversation. He was lulling them, almost individually, into lending an ear—usually only one, however, as most continued to talk to someone next to them—while Jonas and the bassist swung lightly, playfully, through his lyric:

> why do I love you?
> I can't even say

why, do you love me?
it does feel that way
what do we do now
we lovers in love
why don't we make love
before it rubs off

A few people laughed, some hummed along. Reo wondered if Jonas was putting people on or thought this was a serious song. After three verses and choruses, it ended with a nice upward guitar lick, and the crowd burst into applause in spite of itself. Jonas bowed, sweeping his hand sarcastically across him as he lowered his head.

"That song has 47 times when it mentions the word 'love'," he stage-whispered in a high rasp. "Someone told me that's a record. I don't know myself."

"Well it damn well oughta be," a male voice called out, drawing a burst of laughter from the singer in return.

"I think he's boring," Delfina said, stirring her screwdriver. It had impressed Reo that Delfina was never carded, never asked for an ID. She was eighteen and looked 25, svelte, blond and lovely.

The swizzle stick was as tall as his hand and molded with a naked woman on the end, as if the bar had bought them as surplus from a strip club. The problem was, they were too tall for the drinks, and hers had fallen over, so she had to take it out of the drink and hold it.

"And this thing," she added, waving the stick in her hand. "What's this about?"

"Art," he shrugged. "Do you really, or are you being snide?"

"What?"

"Do you really think he's boring?"

She sighed, taking his hand, each fingertip in hers.

"No, I guess he's okay. I just have other things on my mind."

He nodded.

"I'd like to listen for now. Can we talk after?"

She shrugged and looked around. Jonas was beginning another song as she whispered.

"This is where you want to play?"

"I brought you here for the music. I play wherever someone wants me to," he said, crossing his legs, trying to silence her. He really did want to listen to someone who sang his own songs, in his own voice, telling stories he'd written, pieces of travelogues, almost all interesting to Reo in some way. There was sadness behind many of the songs, as if he'd seen too much, the weary traveler moving on one more time:

She said she always wanted
to have a man like me
That all the other men she knew
had fooled her eventually
what made her think I'm different
I guess I'll never know
but in the end, she always knew I'd go
if only down the road to Silverado.

"If Only" was its title, the singer informed the audience.

Reo had, in fact, had two singing jobs: one at the Xanadu, the Upper West Side coffeehouse where he had met Delfina; the other at a bar on the Lower East Side, a storefront with a small space in the corner. Each paid forty bucks, and he wasn't likely to do either again soon, since the coffeehouse rotated its acts over months, and the bar crowd didn't notice him much. Well, he thought, he didn't sing songs they wanted to hear, he only knew a few of them; as for his own, original songs, they stood no chance, for there was no sound system, and he showed up with just his guitar. The bar manager let him play and paid him while the bar crowd, forced to choose between silence and drowning him out, barely waited until the first song before choosing the latter.

"Allow me to introduce, on the bass, my brother, Jason Waverly." said the singer, indicating the large, blond man seated on the stool, who smiled and dipped his head slightly.

Jonas, out front standing at the microphones, continued.

"Of course, around the house we just call him Sparemee," he croaked, and someone yelled "Sparemee" back.

"What does that mean?" Delfina leaned over and whispered. "What is 'Spermy',? Is that like 'Spermy the Whale?' " He looked at her and laughed, suddenly glad she was there.

"I think it's with a long *a,* as in Spare Me," he whispered back.

Evidently it was well known in the club, as a few people shouted it out, and Jason Waverly beamed, stood up as if intending to go after someone, then sat down again. The crowd laughed, the loudest response of the set. Reo and Delfina laughed too, holding hands, then looked back at Jonas, expecting the next line. But Jonas was glaring at them, not amused.

They left during the band's set, sliding through the small crowd out in the bar. Reo had overpaid by two extra dollars, and the waitress approached him near the door with his change.

"Oh, that's ok," he said, smiling at the woman, a middle-aged Latin woman with dyed red hair and a missing tooth on the right side.

"You sure," she asked again.

"Yes," he said.

"Ok," she said. " 'Cause you got up and left without waiting for your change."

"Well, the band's loud," he replied. "We came to see the other guys."

"Him? Oh, he play Monday too. And then it's free," she said.

"Free?"

"It's Open Mike, you know Open Mike? Anybody can get up and play."

Reo and Delfina looked at each other.

"There you go," said Delfina. "Guess that takes care of Mondays."

7–Number 30C

The attention span of the audience perilously balanced between listening and socializing. Ted was floundering through his first song with the audience talking right in front of him. It wasn't that he was bad, thought Reo; but he didn't grab its attention, and so, like a thread stretched too far, it snapped. His songs, packed full of clever references to jazz and beat poetry, were a sharp contrast to the somber poetry of his predecessors, and he bounced through them with a big, round voice and a bit of swagger. Reo liked his set very much, even as the crowd overlooked it.

Alone at the back of the room, Reo waited as Sonoma Sal read off the names, and there were several numbers that drew no reply. Soon they were into the twenties, and one after another of the men seated in the audience, guarding their guitars and girlfriends with an air of wary territoriality, took the stage. None were as accomplished as the earlier performers, either as songwriters or performers, and a long time passed before several more numbers went unanswered, and Sonoma Sal spoke to the nearly empty room.

"Well, music lovers, here's the one we've all been waiting for, number 30C."

Taken by surprise, Reo MacGregor realized it was his turn. His second beer long empty, his legs asleep under the tiny cocktail table, he wobbled to his feet and bent down for his guitar.

"You know, it's late, music lovers, and we like it when the performer's ready. Let's just call it a night, shall we?" And Sal began to stand up, turning off the small lamp above the soundboard.

"No. Wait, I'm ready!" Reo spoke up quickly, his voice sounding to himself as if it was in the next room already. Sal stopped.

"Okay. Get a move on, please."

He opened his case right there, took out the guitar and weaved through three rows of tables directly to the stage. He turned and looked out across the scattered tables of people, none of them paying him any attention. In the distant corner of the bar he heard conversation.

Well, he thought, if no one's paying attention, I've got nothing to lose. He started strumming, a quiet, easy waltz-time excursion through the key of G, then slowed abruptly to a long, slow fingerpicking pattern.

> If you could meet a man I know
> lost an arm at Anzio
> and his life's been torn into patriotic pieces
> he's got a son who can't come home
> til he's ready to admit he's wrong
> to quit on Vietnam and follow his Jesus

He had just finished the second chorus when a slender man walked in front of him. Running his hand through greasy, straight black hair, he stepped onto the stage, picked up an electric guitar leaning on an amplifier, tossed the strap over his head, flipped a switch, and began playing soft, melodic notes right in the heart of Reo's song. Reo glanced over at the unshaven face, the mouth partly open around black teeth, the eyes squinting, seemingly lost in their own world; looking around, he saw Tony at the bar put his towel down, watching. The bar noise became quiet as the talkers drifted in, following the target of their choice, Callisto, who, quietly studying him, stopped just shy of the back room. To his right, behind the mixing board, sat Sonoma Sal, his arms folded across his chest.

Am I playing this song right? he wondered, looking at his hands, seeing the fingers go through the routine he had practiced, the same routine that had now became a circular passage of music, sustained by his hands even as his mind wandered. He stepped to the mike and sang.

> You might hear the sound of people crying,
> laying down a lifetime they've stopped trying
> feeling everything they love won't be long
> if you could ride this train I'm on
> before it's gone

As he finished the song, the skinny man took off the guitar, leaned it against the amp, flicked off the switch, and looked over at Reo.

"Thanks," he said. "You needed that." And without a further word he stepped off the stage, walked out of the room, past Callisto and her friends, through the bar and out the door, passing before the window and vanishing into the night.

"Well, music lovers, that was worth the price of admission. And you. You get two songs," he heard Sonoma Sal say.

For his second song Reo strummed his way through a lyric he was still making up, mentally thinking it needed something. But he made it, not really looking at anyone, suddenly feeling very alone. And then it was over.

"And that, music lovers, ends the open mike for tonight. Please tip your waitress, and remember: if you're driving home, don't forget your car," said Sal.

Out at the bar Tony pushed a beer across at Reo before he could walk away, then stood quietly, watching him with a bemused smile.

"Thanks. Who was that guy?"

"Oh, him? His name's a Mick."

"Does he do that often?"

"No, I don' think so. He walk in here, walk out, I don' know, by the time I stop him he's a gone, so why bother? He play good?"

Reo shook his head, not to say no but to clear the fog.

"I couldn't really hear him. But it seemed to blend right in."

"Oh, tha's a Mick all right, he blend a right in." And Tony laughed, and when everyone else laughed too, Reo realized they had all been listening.

"I think it's an honor to have Mick play with you, I never saw him do that before," spoke up Ted, extending a hand with a big grin. Reo shook it. He noticed Tony smiling, too, pleased in some way.

"You a not so bad. You a come back next week?"

One by one he met them all, for they were the only ones still in the bar. Ted, Callisto, Jonas, Eddie and Franklin asked him some pertinent questions: name, where he came from, where he lived, did he play anywhere else. He gave them some short answers without being very specific, Reo MacGregor, from Connecticut, staying in a coffeehouse on the west side, sure, a couple places. That left it to Jonas Waverly to administer the coup de grace, which he gladly took on.

"Methinks this one knows more than he pretends," he spoke derisively, waving him away with the back of his hand .

"Off with his head!" chanted Franklin and Eddie in unison.

"Too much," Ted said quietly.

"Ah, Imbonanti," Jonas weighed in, "always the compromiser."

"Ok, ok, go home now," Tony called from behind the bar. "Get outa here."

And so it was that the six of them exited as one, regrouping outside on the sidewalk just as the greasy-haired, black-toothed guitarist Mick stepped in front of them all.

"Ah Waverly, how's Granny? They let her out yet?" he tossed to Jonas, then zeroed in on Callisto. "And what's this? Helen of Tribeca? And you my friend"—this to Ted—"Never, ever let the truth get in the way of a good story." And to Eddie: "There's a job for you in Arabia keeping the king's harem." Franklin got "Your brother asked me to tell you not to wait." And last, to Reo, "They found your skin uptown, somebody needed it so I said go ahead."

Mick was gone so quickly that the individual gasps each statement elicited were still settling. They looked at each other in silence, stunned, unable to say the first coherent thought. Finally, it was Franklin who came through.

"Hey, I've got the car. Let's go somewhere."

"Where?" Callisto spoke up, her voice crisp, decisive.

"I don't know. How about Battery Park?"

"Great idea," said Ted. "Let's go." And so they walked the block and a half to Franklin's car. He opened the trunk, and they managed to fit four guitars inside, leaving Ted's and Reo's out. Jonas and Callisto got in front with Franklin at the wheel, as Eddie got in the other side.

"Come on," Ted smiled. "Hop in the back."

Reo squeezed himself in, yanking his guitar onto their laps. But nobody protested, and as they drove away he overheard Jonas at the other end of the car.

"It's already late," he whispered to Callisto. "I thought we were going to your place." Reo did not hear her answer, as Ted mused "Never let the truth get in the way of a good story; what the fuck does that mean?"

8–New York Nights

Reo and Delfina rode the subway back uptown, silent for a long time. There was nowhere they could be alone, since Delfina lived with her mother, and with a flash of inspiration he asked her to stay on the subway with him when they got to her stop.

"I'll come back with you," he said, "get you home safe."

And so she continued uptown with him, where they walked across the main plaza of Columbia University to the law school esplanade, a flight above Amsterdam Avenue. They sat on a wooden bench with long horizontal slats, talking about her day, her job at the pet store, as her green eyes drifted to his and back to her hands. Her long, soft blond hair framing her oval face in the faint light, she asked him, was he going to get an apartment? He said yes, as soon as I find one I can afford. Then they kissed, and began to fondle each other, and with a grin she helped his hands undress her so they could make love. The lights went on in a nearby room; they were still for a long moment. Then she kissed him again, ignoring the unseeing janitor and wrapped her legs around his waist. Reo kissed her ears, her chin, her neck, her breasts. Whatever it was she had wanted to say, to ask him, to talk about, she never brought it up. Later, he asked her what it was, as they walked from the subway to her mother's apartment building.

"Not now," she said softly, kissing him again. They stood outside her door, a thick glass with long rows of buttons on the wall, holding each other until she went inside.

It was nine blocks to Xanadu, where Reo MacGregor had shown up with his guitar and backpack, fresh off the train to New York, and been offered a bed in the basement. The coffeehouse had two floors, a performance space upstairs and a stone-floored basement below, connected by a single stairway. More like a half-basement, with windows that opened above one's head onto a street view of knees passing by, it was open to the public, so Reo had the choice of sitting there and helping out, collecting door money for the shows, making coffee, sweeping the floor, or of not being there. His sleeping bag and pack stashed in a locked closet, he'd gone out hours ago, for the first time since returning to the city.

It was late, he expected to go to sleep. But to his surprise, Xanadu had several people in the back area where a large clear plastic dome stood over a wooden pentagon of bleachers, three rows high on five sides, about fifteen feet across. Joseph, the leader of the group that ran the coffeehouse, used it in the evenings after the crowd had left. Tonight there were six people, Joseph, four other men and a woman. Reo took a seat.

Joseph Flanagan was a heavy man with glasses and long, greasy dark hair that fell across his eyes. He dressed like a rumpled office worker who never changed clothes. Reo saw him as a very smart man, and after playing there three times had sought him out. And when Reo showed up, unannounced, having nowhere else to go, taking the chance he would be welcome, Joseph put him in the basement. Days later, he was still there.

"So what have you been doing?" he asked, his eyes widening around the "you."

"Went to a show, in the village. They have an open mike Monday."

"Gonna go?" Joseph asked, exhaling a cigarette.

"Yeah, I think so."

Joseph nodded.

"You know you can't stay here forever. Sleep here, that is."

"Yeah, I know. I don't want to, either."

"You could rent a room upstairs."

"Got one?"

"Not right now, but that could always change."

Reo nodded. There was a lull in the conversation, and someone asked "good show?"

Reo nodded and said yes.

"Tell us a story, Jackie," someone said across the circle.

"Yes," echoed another, and Reo squinted across the dim candle-lit room to where a man with a shaven black head, smooth and glistening with reflected multi-colored light from tiny bulbs strung across the dome, gleamed back at him. The man was looking around quickly, caught everyone's eye, and grinned wide open.

"All right," he drawled through the grin in a velvet voice, soft and yet focused, clear and warm.

"Listen up, then. I'll tell you 'bout the time me and Diz got on a bus somewhere in Mississippi. Musta been twenty, twenty-five years ago."

Reo leaned back and relaxed, noticing that Jackie's left hand was doing something next to him, moving around, rubbing his fingers together, without looking, his eyes moving around in contact with his listeners.

"So there we was, the bus broke down, seventeen musicians in some honky bus depot, it's a hunderd degrees and everybody's got their jackets off, and this ...this....woman..walks by, all blond and shit, wiggling her little fanny like somebody oughta throw her a biscuit, you know, like you give one of them little curly-haired things they have on the East Side ("a poodle" someone said) yeah, that's right, a poodle, all covered with white curly hair and shit. You know how they walk. Anyway. So where was I? Oh yeah, this car pulls up, sirens screaming, guys jumping out, all sorts of shit going on."

Reo snuck a look around, and everyone was intently watching Jackie. But as he spoke, Jackie also produced—without looking at it—a small white piece of paper in his left hand, sliding it under a greenish spot on the table.

"So the next thing I know, some cop's in my face, and he's saying "What're you lookin' at, boy?', like spittin' and shit, like his mother taught him to puke before he could speak. I say 'nothin' sir,' in as low and calm a voice as I can ever—and I mean ever—remember using on anybody. He backs away and bumps right into Diz, who's leaning over listening to this. The cop pulls out his gun, pointin' it right at Diz with both hands, like it's gonna explode on him any minute."

Jackie paused, his fingers rolling the small piece of paper around some green-looking flakes, his eyes rotating horizontally around the audience. He had them now, and Reo felt everyone starting to laugh, before Jackie even spoke. It seemed as if no one but him was aware of the hand.

"What did Diz do?" someone finally spoke up.

"Diz? Oh yeah. Well, he took his hand out of his pocket, and damn if he didn't have his mouthpiece in it. He stuck it right in the barrel of the gun! Put his lips on it, like this, and played a little trumpet solo. Nice piece of music. I still remember it. Military song." Jackie made a mouthpiece with his hand and tooted a few notes, and when he took the hand away, a small, rolled cylinder remained between his lips.

"What did the cop do?" someone pushed on.

Jackie paused, took the joint out of his mouth.

"He saluted," he grinned. "No shit, he did. Then he said, 'Thank you, sir for that, I haven't heard that since I was overseas,' or some shit like that."

Everyone chuckled expectantly, as if there should be a bigger punch line.

After a few seconds, a plaintive voice asked "that's it?"

"Wait a minute," Joseph interrupted, shaking his head. "That isn't a military song. That's the theme from F Troop!"

Jackie lit a match with his right hand.

"You know that, and I know that, and I believe Diz, he knew that too. But that cop," he said, then touched the small flame to the joint, took a long puff and hacked twice, exhaling a miniature cloud, and held it out to Joseph.

"He didn't know that," Jackie finished with a cough. There was a small burst of applause and real laughter this time.

"You're truly an artist," Joseph said through the smoke, shaking his head side to side. "An artist of bullshit."

"You got that right," Jackie agreed, grinning his white teeth into the laughter all around.

9–Battery Park

They got out of the car just as a swift breeze blew in off the water, and one by one they closed their thin jackets, bent over, stepping quickly to the railing that overlooked the faraway Statue of Liberty.

"Ever been there?" Ted asked, his hands buried in jacket side pockets, his elbows swinging like a piston engine twisting back and forth.

Reo had to laugh.

"No."

"Me neither. Oh, wait, I went once with my parents when I was six."

"You grew up here?"

"Queens. Ever been there?"

"No. Oh, wait, yeah once, I went out there to interview someone."

"For what?"

"A magazine. *Newstand.* I would interview someone for them once in awhile, send it in, maybe they'd use a quote, or not." He was aware of Ted studying him.

"What is it you're doing?" Ted asked him.

"What do you mean?"

"I mean, what's your trip? Why are you here?"

"I thought we were a bunch of songwriters hanging out together."

"Like songwriters do, huh? No, I mean, why? What are you about?"

"I want to tell people my story...their story...I don't know...make music...play the guitar....is there really supposed to be an answer for this question?"

Ted laughed.

"Where do you live? How do you live?"

"Uptown. You?"

"Belmont. It's like the suburbs."

"Do you sing for a living?"

"Nah. I teach school. You?"

"I'm working in a print shop a couple days a week. And I have a couple coffeehouse gigs."

"You do? That's great," he said, smiling happily at him. "Good going! I have one night booked at the Folk Life, with my band."

"You have a band?"

Ted nodded, looking out over the water, seeming to come to some small decision.

"Hey," he said. "We're having some people over Monday, for a small party, we play our songs for each other, sit around and make music, eat some food. Want to come?"

Reo turned toward him

"I'd like that very much," he answered. Ted was looking out over the water, imagining his parents pointing upwards toward the tall torch above them as they stepped off the boat. How proud they were, that's what they had always said.

"What do you think of America?" Ted said evenly, his voice trailing off as if it were a statement, rather than a question.

"America, where opportunity knocks you down" interrupted Jonas Waverly, who arrived with his moustache fanning in the breeze, a big smile on his face, Callisto, Franklin and Eddie in tow. Unlike the rest of them in their thin jackets and denim shirts, he wore a black cape spread across his shoulders.

"And the mailman can't find his bag," Ted rejoined, snapping his fingers twice as if it were a jazz riff.

They both stared at Reo.

"Bats got your tongue?" inquired Jonas, running a fingertip up Reo's chest to his chin. But his voice, scratchy and venomous, betrayed no interest in a response.

"I was just thinking."

"What, pray tell?"

"What if America could talk?"

"Well," Jonas exhaled, turning to Ted for a second opinion.

"What would she say?"

Jonas burst into a laugh.

"'She'd say, 'What do you mean by that?' " he crooned in a soft, coquettish voice. "Just who do you think I am?"

They all laughed. Jonas was a funny guy, Reo thought, very quick, and liked him for it immediately. But there was a deadliness to him too, like a loaded gun looking for a target, and no one spoke until Franklin, with Callisto's arm in his, coughed.

"I was just saying how we could make some money."

"I told him it'd never work," Callisto interrupted, but Franklin was undaunted.

"We all play together some evening, each play a few songs."

"We just did," protested Ted.

"No, I mean charge to get in."

They all recoiled as if at once, and that led to a round of laughing. But then Jonas help up a finger, pointing straight up in the air.

"One dollar," he said. "'Buck night.'"

"That sounds like guys with antlers."

"Ok, 'Dollar Night,'"

No one protested the change.

"Why not?" asked Ted, raising his eyebrows. "I'll play."

"Me, too," said Reo, and now, as if for the first time, everyone looked at him, and he wondered if this was a private party.

"That is, if it's ok with you," he added, looking around. Callisto smiled at him, as did Ted. Franklin and Eddie, however, looked toward Jonas, who turned to the Statue of Liberty.

"I'll talk to Tony," he said, his pointing finger still extended as he lowered it toward the distant, spotlit monument, hazily aiming it like a pistol through the misty night air. He spat the sound of a small explosion, then sidled along the rail without even looking at any of them, as if expecting them to follow. Eddie and Franklin did. Callisto and Ted stayed behind.

"Off he goes," she said quietly.

"He'll be all right," said Ted.

"Oh, it's not him I'm worried about," she replied. The breeze picked up, and in the pre-dawn chill of the waterfront they began walking slowly toward the car.

"Have you ever been anywhere else?" Callisto asked in her soft, firm voice, looking at Reo.

"You mean out of the country? " Ted put in.

"No. You?" None of them had, except she had been to Puerto Rico, to her father's hometown, she said.

"But I'm sure there are singers there, too," she added.

"Of course. But there's nothing like there is here. No place where writers come together to do this," Ted broke in.

"You mean the Village?" Reo asked.

"Yeah. Well, all of New York, but this type of music seems to come together in the Village."

"What type of music is it? I get asked that sometimes, I never know what to say," Reo asked.

"I know! it's not folk, it's not really rock and roll either, and it definitely ain't that country sheeyit," said Ted, and they were laughing now. "So what the hay-ell is it?"

They arrived at the car to find Jonas sitting alone in the front seat. Franklin was standing outside, the door open, one foot in the driver's well. Eddie was in the back.

"So Jonas, here's one for you. What do you call this music we make?"

"It's folk music, boys and girls."

"No it isn't, you know that," Ted dismissed the idea.

"It's our music, and don't you forget it," Jonas said, sounding serious all of a sudden. "You have to believe in yourself, Chuck."

They drove away, caught up in getting comfortable, Callisto in between Reo and Ted, with Eddie and Jonas in the front seat, staring straight ahead until they stopped on a narrow street in the Village.

Franklin opened the trunk and handed Jonas his guitar as he stepped out of the car. Jonas set it down and gathered his cape in both hands.

"Well, goodnight, all," said the raw voice, as he made a low sweeping bow, then whisked away.

"Where do you want to go?" Franklin asked the rearview mirror.

She sighed.

"Subway, I guess."

"14th Street? I need to head east."

"Okay."

"You sure that's a good idea? With your guitar and all?" Franklin wanted to know. Perhaps he had somewhere else in mind.

"I need to go home," she said simply.

Sizing up the situation, Reo spoke up.

"If you're going up the West Side I can ride with you."

"Thank you, that would be very kind of you," she said with distinct politeness, nodding her head with a smile. "I'll be fine, Franklin." Soon they arrived at the subway, where Franklin got out and opened the trunk so she could get her guitar. She kissed him on the cheek and said goodnight through the window to everyone, by name.

Reo and Callisto went down the subway stairs, bought tokens and walked onto the platform, lifting their guitars over the turnstile. For once the train came right away, and without a word they boarded it. There was one empty seat amid the thin crowd, and he extended a hand toward it, signaling her to take it.

"Thanks, I'll stand up," she said.

"So, your name is Callisto?" he asked.

"Yes. And you are?"

"Reo."

She nodded, and he wondered if she would even remember it the next time they met.

"Callisto Who?"

She laughed, suddenly breaking the ice as if a breeze had blown in the car. The subway started forward, and they lurched together, clutching their instruments like parallel lines.

"That's me, Callisto Who," she replied. "Actually, it's Maya, Callisto Maya. It's Puerto Rican."

Now it was his turn to nod.

"You think because I have blond hair I can't be Puerto Rican."

"Let's just say you're the first I've ever met."

"My mother married again, my real father is probably blond and big-boned, since I am. Built for babies, my mother says, she's slim and small."

"You don't look big-boned. Certainly not heavy."

"Thank you. I dress simply." Now she studied him. "So where are you going?"

"We just passed my stop."

"Are you walking me home?" she asked in her matter of fact voice.

"I think it's a good idea. You'll be safe, I'll feel better."

She regarded him quietly.

"Hey, I'm not going to hurt you."

"I know that."

"Okay. So. Tell me about yourself."

"What do you mean by that?" she asked in her soft voice, and he knew now that Jonas had been parodying her earlier.

"I don't know. Always live in New York?"

"Yes."

"Are you singing professionally?"

"Not yet, but I want to be."

He waited, letting her talk, looking vaguely at the soft, fine blond hair falling around her fair face, with its pale eyebrows and unpainted lips. Instead, he noticed her clear blue eyes were studying him.

"I'm graduating Barnard. I have a job lined up doing office work a few days a week."

He nodded silently, still watching her.

"See anything?" She asked very directly.

"I see someone very special," he said. "Not like everyone else."

"Is that your line? I want to be like everyone else."

"Well, you're not. Tough."

She bit her lip.

"Neither are you," she said quietly, as the train banged to a stop.

"Oh, we're here, " she started, quickly grabbing her guitar. He followed and they walked upstairs to the street. A block later they stopped at an indented doorway under a single light bulb. There appeared to be no one around. She took out her keys and stood sideways to him.

"Well, goodnight," she said, and stood there without moving. He wondered if she was afraid to open the door, that he might try to charge in, or was she waiting for him to kiss her. But before he could say "goodnight," she stepped forward and kissed him on the cheek.

"Thanks for walking me home," she whispered, and turning, opened the door and went inside, smiling back through the glass.

10–Lost Days

He went to the open mike the following week, but none of the group he had gone downtown with showed up. He took a number, got 8B, played his two songs and was about to leave without even getting into a conversation with anyone, when two young women chased him down from behind, just inside the exit door. He stopped and turned around.

"Hi. Um. Got a sec?" said the closer of the two, dirty blond hair shaking over her forehead and eyes.

"Sure," he said, setting down the guitar on its fat end, so it stood up in his hand.

"We saw you play. It was....um...good, don't you think, Mol?" she finished, drawing in a frail, brown-haired woman with a face that struck Reo as ageless, the face of an old woman in a young woman's body.

"Yeah," the second woman replied. Was that it?

"You liked what I sang?"

"Yeah," they both answered simultaneously. "We want to ask you if you can play a few songs with us Friday night."

"We have this gig Friday night, they need three sets, but they don't have a piano. We don't have three sets without a piano. We were wondering if you could play a set between ours."

"We'll give you $20."

"Yeah, we're getting $60, so that will be an equal share."

"Ok," he said, looking from one to the other. "Where is it?"

"It's called Xanadu, on the Upper West Side."

"Ok, I know where it is."

"Just show up, we'll tell the guy there you're coming, and we'll pay you ourselves."

Reo studied the two faces before him. They were both quite pretty, slim, about the same height, long hair, with something intangible in common, though very different from each other.

"I'm Reo MacGregor," he said, extending a hand to either of them. "What are your names?"

"Micky Fresh," said the one on his left, the rounder-faced, lighter and straighter-haired, more cheerful of the two.

"Molly Fresh," said the other, frizzy brown hair curled around a genuine pensive smile, looking into his eyes as if she were really trying to figure him out.

"Well, cool," he laughed, "Glad to meet you. You play guitars?"

"Yes. Yes we do."

"This is on? Just show up?"

"You bet."

"Ok, see you there," he said. They shook on it all around, and he lifted his guitar case and left.

The days were hazy outdoors, amid afternoons at the print shop, reading and rereading newspaper pages, sometimes into the evenings. He fixed typos and corrected punctuation, spelling and capitalization errors with ease. Sometimes he would actually read the articles, finding yawning gaps in syntax, grammar, or logic. Incomplete non-sentences, lacking a verb but full of nouns, adjectives and subordinate clauses, were one writer's specialty. After two days the writer was coming to his desk on a regular basis, asking him to polish his thoughts into coherent sentences. But mostly he drew little proofreader's marks in the margins of the printouts, so the typists could enter the correct information before it was published. It occurred to him he was one of the last lines of defense before it went to the public, and for a moment he felt a responsibility to pay attention he had not really expected in himself. It was a distraction; this job was supposed to be just to make money.

Talleyrand visited him once in awhile, and later in the week offered him a promotion to assistant copy editor.

"No, thanks" he responded immediately.

"You're not even gonna think about it?"

"I don't want the responsibility."

The publisher looked down through his spectacles at him.

"Ok, have it your way," he shrugged, and walked away.

In the meantime he lived in the Xanadu basement, where he met

Jackie Fro one other time, a hot mid-summer afternoon in the dome while playing the guitar by himself. Jackie dropped by and sat down without a word. He took out a small pair of three-inch discs, then another, and stuck the four cymbals on his fingers, long slender fingers sliding through the black ribbons attached on the back. He smiled at Reo, who was strumming and humming quietly to himself through all this, as Jackie Fro began playing along with him, adding little syncopations to his rhythm.

"Mm hmm," Jackie nodded. "I got it."

They continued on like this for a few minutes, Reo wandering through various chord progressions, Jackie punctuating the rhythms with clear notes in patterns tied to his chord changes. It was a transparent sound, the tiny brass cymbals rippling through the melody.

"Have you ever tried Indian music?" asked a voice from Reo's left, and he turned to find Adam G standing there. Slowly the trance ended, the guitar and cymbals wound to a stop.

"I don't think so," Reo replied. "Have you?"

Adam G was a short, wiry man with a narrow face and gray crew cut. It was rumored he lived upstairs in one of the single rooms, but Joseph had said "No, he just sleeps in one of the closets."

"Sure, I can show you," he said. He opened a narrow case and took out a shiny chrome pipe, four feet long with a steel piece at each end to support a single thick gut string. He twanged it with his thumb once, then took a chrome bar from his pocket with his index finger inside it. He lay the bar on the string, slid it up and down about a foot and plucked the string so it rang out, long enough for him to slide the note up and down for a full octave.

"It's like this," he said, and began playing a simple, repetitive stroke, one-one-one-one-one, as he moved the bar with seemingly random music in mind, just running it over the spectrum of pitch with no real organization or structure of any kind.

Reo, holding a flatpick in his right hand, whacked his low string. Adam slid his bar to the exact same pitch, holding it right there as he pounded the time. Reo whacked his string again, this time in time with Adam's beat. He picked up the same pattern, one-one-one-one-one. Jackie Fro closed his fingers and began hitting the cymbals on the off beat, an entirely new feel that made it suddenly come alive, pulsing with the exchange of rhythm among them. They never once changed a chord or even a melodic note, holding the E the entire time, as Jackie occasionally burst into song with a mellow, deep voice.

> goin' down Louisian'
> gimme a mojo hand
> going' down Louisiana'
> gimme a mojo hand
> tell everyone you unnerstan'
> I'm gonna be your mojo man

sang Jackie, and Reo laughed, loving it.

"Sing that again," he called to him as the single notes pounded onward. When Jackie did sing, Reo sang a harmony, and Adam took a solo.

An hour later, they sat back and relaxed against the benches, laughing, digging the music. Then Adam G looked at his watch and said "gotta go," and was off.

"Joseph says you're a jazz drummer," Reo asked.

"Was," nodded Jackie Fro. "I don't have a set no more. That's what the man will do."

"The man took your set?"

"Long time ago. I had my day, all right."

"What are you doing now?" Reo asked. Jackie Fro looked him in the eye.

"Little of this, little of that," he said with an easy smile. "I can still hear the music."

It was early in the week, the cafe was closed, and Reo found himself at a chess table, absent-mindedly moving the pieces alone, reflecting on the fact he had told no one he was supposed to play Friday. He hadn't spoken with Delfina since Monday; she'd asked him not to call, it caused a fight with her mother when he called, she said. There was a pay phone on the wall, and she had the number, but it hadn't rung for him all week.

He told no one, not at work, not even Joseph. Reo wanted to let the Fresh sisters tell Joseph. It would mean something, he told himself, that they had hired him after seeing him play at Folk Life. And so, his hands vacantly lining up the knights, bishops and rooks as he thought the situation over, he had all the pieces clustered around the black queen as

Turk Gowen, a regular at the late night sessions, walked in. Turk studied the chess table for a moment.

"Feeling trapped, are we Reo?" he laughed in a deep, resonant voice.

Reo laughed too.

"Can you help me do something, Turk?"

"Maybe. What?"

"I want you to call this number and ask for Delfina. I don't want to have her mother answer, she hates me."

Turk called the number and had a brief conversation that told him Delfina wasn't home and wasn't expected home at all that night. When her mother asked who was calling, Turk said "Oh, just a friend from work," and said goodbye without leaving a message.

On Friday, Reo was sitting on his bunk in the basement when Joseph walked in with Turk and Josiah, a slender man Reo knew from the late night sessions. Josiah had a long curly black beard he wore in ringlets like a rabbi's, and liked to sit stroking it and make cryptic pronouncements Reo could almost figure out. Turk, on the other hand, was a music professor uptown and a tremendous ragtime pianist who would sometimes pound the beat-up old upright in the back corner while they stood around and marveled. He had a pointed, black goatee and moustache all the way around his mouth, and was setting down a square, open brown paper bag on the table.

"We need your help," said Joseph.

"Sure. What for?" asked Reo.

"We're going to move the piano upstairs for the show tonight."

Joseph took off his jacket and walked over to the big, hulking upright, a faded brown beast with streaks of what once was paint still barely visible in the grain. No one ever played it except Turk, who made the place rock on it late at night, after the show upstairs was over. Turk was a natural entertainer, with a big-hearted laugh, and Reo loved his playing.

"That piano?" Reo blinked at it, his eyebrows raised. "It's massive."

"That's why we need you," Turk laughed through a cloud of cigarette smoke, a staccato huh-huh-huh that was contagious. But Reo looked at the piano and could not imagine being able to move it.

"Upstairs? You have to be kidding."

"We have an act that needs it tonight," Joseph said. "The Fresh sisters, really good, I read about them in the paper and worked hard to get them to play here tonight. And they need a goddamn piano."

Joseph took a corner of it in both hands and gave it a tug. It didn't move.

"Help me out here," he said, and the three others stood up. Each took a corner with both hands.

"One, two, three," they chanted, then leaned into it, away from it, over it, under it, and with arms, legs, hips and knees, tried to get it in motion. They yanked it forward, forcing it out of the recess in the wall, dragging it with great effort about two inches, when Josiah lost his grip and recoiled across the room, smashing into a floor lamp by the far bookshelf.

Joseph stood and watched as Josiah slid down the wall onto the floor.

Turk helped him up, put his arm around Josiah's shoulder and said in a serious, deep voice, "It was a pleasure working with you on this project," even nodding as he spoke, as if they had just landed a man on the moon. Then he started laughing, and no one could stop dissolving into it.

Joseph eventually regained his serious self and looked at Turk and Reo, hands on hips.

"Ok, OK. Never mind. We'll think of something else."

Turk pulled a beer from the bag he had set down and handed it to Josiah, again seated on the floor. The sound of pop-tops and laughter filled the room, and before too long there was a knock on the windows that faced the street at the top of the basement wall. Joseph unlocked the door and Molly and Micky Fresh walked in, each carrying a leather guitar case.

"Hi. We're here for the sound check. Hi, Reo."

Joseph turned and looked at Reo, then back to the girls, their faces flushed and sweaty. They were still breathing fast from walking.

"You know this guy?"

"Yes, we meant to call you but we forgot," Micky spoke up. "He's gonna play our middle set. You said three sets, and we only have two."

"Oh? He is?"

"Yeah. That's ok, right?" Molly sang, bending forward to set down her guitar.

Joseph looked again at Reo. Turk slapped him on the back, a big grin on his face.

"Sure," said Joseph.

11–Slow Dissolve

It was a night he would often remember, if only because he was to meet a person who would change the way he looked at the world, a person with whom he would spend countless evenings in the coming years. Strangely enough, Reo didn't remember meeting that person on that night; it was only much later, when they had been friends for some time, that he would learn they had met that night. What Reo would first remember of that night was walking on stage in front of the Fresh Sisters' audience, just after they had played and sung beautiful, close-knit harmonies with really difficult, demanding melodies, wrapped around clever words that made sense in a way you couldn't explain because you couldn't describe it better than the songs described themselves. Reo, in fact, was overwhelmed with the music he had just witnessed, and walked out on stage believing he couldn't possibly follow what they had done.

His guitar was in tune. Also, he liked how it sounded tonight, soft and full, with the good ring on the treble strings. So he stood on stage, and blankly started strumming a quick tempo, thinking of what to sing while his fingers wandered the strings. Finally he came up with an idea, so he stopped his strum and looked up.

"Hey," someone yelled from a corner.

He stared out into the spotlights. He had played this coffeehouse twice before, but didn't remember such blinding lights.

"What?" he replied in the general direction of his questioner.

"Does that have words?"

"What?"

"That guitar piece you were playing."

"Oh." He realized what the man meant. "No."

"Too bad," the voice called out and a few people laughed.

"Play something!" someone else said.

"All right," he said softly. He started strumming and immediately saw the shadows of three or four people head for the stairway to the floor below, down to the half-basement where he lived, where they hung out between sets. And before he could start singing he heard voices talking, laughing loudly, filtering back up the stairs as the enthusiasm from the sisters and their backstage fans spilled into the room.

But a few people remained, and he sang for them, sang from his heart, words he had written that week, words he would not even remember himself after very long, but his own words. Until he was between songs, the room was quiet. A husky male voice called out "Hey!" from the corner. But this time he heard a softer, woman's voice whisper, "Please don't," a voice he knew from somewhere. He leaned out into the crowd, getting just enough in front of the spotlight that he could see a few faces. In the far corner, along the wall to his left, about twenty feet away, was Delfina, sitting next to where the voice came from. In the dark, she could not tell for sure if he spotted her.

"Hey," the man persisted. "Do you take requests?"

Reo finished checking his tuning, and spoke into the mike.

"Such as?"

Joseph popped up in front of the stage.

"One more," he signaled with an upraised finger. One more song.

"Fragile," said the voice.

"That's one of my songs."

"That's the one."

"All right."

The song was a quiet, intense, slow dirge in a minor key, built around a repeating picking pattern that ascended up the lower strings; hypnotic and moody, it required a tightly-focused vocal in a fairly high key. It was one of Reo's newer songs, and had to be sung with real feeling or not at all.

> The finest piece
> of crystal glass
> will tear my hand if it breaks
> And a clumsy hand on
> your fragile love
> will shatter whatever it takes

I've got nothing
I've got nothing
I've got nothing
without you
I'll keep singing
keep on singing
this song
that can't go on
without you

He sang another verse and chorus, droning the guitar notes until he realized he was running overtime. He finished one of the ascending lines and let the song trail off, exiting to a sincerely mesmerized eruption of applause from the crowd.

Near the door he met Molly Fresh, seated along the wall on a bench, her eyes wide open.

"That was..... amazing!" she whispered loudly to him, indicating the stage with her hand.

"Really? You, you liked it?"

She nodded and mulled it over.

"Really beautiful."

"Wow. Thank you so much for asking me to do this. I really loved your set."

"Oh, that. We had our problems. We should be better this set."

He excused himself and went downstairs, putting his guitar in a safe place out of sight. Micky Fresh was still downstairs, talking with a taller man in a brown sport coat, who seemed to be doing most of the talking, murmuring at a volume Reo was able to ignore. But he heard Micky cut in.

"I can't go with you tonight," she said firmly. "And I need to go on now." And then she was passing Reo near the entrance to the stairs.

"Thanks, Reo, you sounded very good."

"Thank you, Micky," he said. "Thanks for asking me."

"Hey, anytime we need a set, you're the guy." She had a beautiful smile and a clear bright voice.

"Okay," he smiled back, and watched her turn and go up to her own set. She had just gone when Delfina emerged from the opening.

"Hi, Reo," she said softly. She looked very pretty in a white silk blouse, her long hair loose around her face, obviously dressed for a date.

"Delfina."

"I'm sorry if my friend was rude."

"Your friend?"

"I didn't know you'd be here tonight. But you were wonderful. And that's such a beautiful song, Reo, I hope you always sing it, no matter what. When you sing it, it transforms you, like it's singing you, and you're that sensitive, passionate man I always knew. You become it in your music."

He exhaled and said nothing.

"You're upset," she whispered.

"Shouldn't I be?"

"I'm glad you're doing what you want to do, Reo. But I don't know, were we going anywhere?"

He took her chin in his hand and kissed her on the lips. She put her arm around his shoulder and pulled him toward her, returning his kiss, then pulling away.

"I have to go," she said softly. "Bye, Reo." And quickly, as if she might change her mind if she stayed, she stepped onto the stairs and was gone, just as the first notes of the Fresh Sisters began again.

Reo heard a laugh from across the room, realizing the other man had listened to their entire conversation.

"Yep, that's women for ya," the man said.

12–A Free Meal

His name was Zeke, and to hear him tell it, he was Micky Fresh's boyfriend, except now he wasn't so sure. By the time they rode the subway seventy blocks and walked through the downtown streets to a Mexican restaurant, he had gone from anger through sadness to weariness. But along the way he had defused Reo's own confusion about Delfina.

"I don't understand how she can change so suddenly," Zeke lamented, as they sat in a narrow wooden booth, dipping chips into salsa. Zeke had lured him downtown with the promise of buying him dinner.

"Why not," he had replied, "that way I won't feel like a total loser."

"Maybe she really likes you but just wants to hang out somewhere else tonight?"

"Oh, and where's that gonna be? No, I'll see her later with another guy, is what you mean."

"Well, Zeke, if it's that easy for her to change guys, why work yourself up over it. She's not worth caring about, if she doesn't care about you."

"Oh, that's easy for you to say."

"What's that supposed to mean?"

"Girls don't look at me like they look at you. You'll have no problem finding someone else, probably several different someone else's. Me, I'll have to wait until the next one comes along who gives a shit."

Reo leaned back and shook his head.

"Well, look," Zeke persisted. "My hair is thinning, I'm obviously going bald soon, yours is thick, dark stuff girls love, all wavy and messy around your face. You've got bright blue and green eyes, and I'm wearing thick glasses over light brown ones. And then you've got those, those cheekbones."

The waitress appeared out of nowhere, a short blue skirt and black leotards thin enough so her skin showed through, topped by a tight tee shirt. A round, soft face leaned into the radius of their candle.

"Oh, hi, Zeke," she said with a shy smile. It seemed to Reo she was actually flirting with Zeke, standing there, twisting her long light-brown strands of hair between her fingers. Zeke, on the other hand, never looked up from the menu and didn't notice.

"I'll have the usual," he said.

She wrote something and turned toward Reo, assuming the blank waitress pose and looking right through him.

"I'll have the guacamole tostada," he said.

"Good choice," said Zeke.

They sat for a moment, looking around the crowded restaurant, mostly full of couples leaning low over dimly-lit tables. The bustle of plates, silver and glass was everywhere, and at least four equally nubile, willowy fair-haired young women worked the crowd, gliding between the tables with trays of food, followed in turn by various young men in splattered white shirts and aprons cleaning the tables, piling the plates on top of each other with great dexterity. It struck Reo there was very little uneaten food, a sign of a good restaurant. It also struck him that most of the young men were dark, not black but deeply browned, with ponytails and knots of wiry hair wrapped in scarves.

"Ever been here before?" asked Zeke.

"No."

"The quintessential Village restaurant," he said. "The guys in the kitchen staff are all fresh off the boat, they stick around a year or two and get better jobs."

"And these waitresses?" Reo mused as one wriggled by.

"Oh, they're straight off the bus," he laughed. "Dancers, actresses, singers even. Don't get them started, whatever you do."

"You know, that's what happened to me."

"What happened?"

"Tonight. I looked into the crowd and what I thought was my girl-friend was sitting there with another guy."

"Oh, that. Does that happen to you often?"

Reo laughed.

"We sure are a couple of losers."

The waitress arrived with two beers in frosty bottles. She set down a glass in front of Reo and moved to pour the beer into it, when he stopped her.

"Thanks, I don't need the glass," he said, and, just to set her at ease, gave her a big smile. She looked at him curiously, tilting her head slightly, then turned to Zeke as he lifted a glass.

"Renee, we're drinking tonight to a couple of losers. What do you think?"

"You two?" she squeaked, her voice a thin shadow of her full self.

"Drink up, m'boy,' Zeke said, and took a big sip. "Let's get it over with. On to the next phase!" The waitress went away, shaking her head.

"I know, you think she's pretty, but she's not for you."

"Who?"

"That waitress. She's got a boyfriend, not that he's not a loser too," he laughed out loud.

Reo took a long sip.

"Ok, then, Zeke, what's the answer?"

"Ah. Now we come to it. You and me. We're going to make some great music."

"We?"

"Yup. I'm buying some good equipment, recording gear, mikes, the works. I'll have it any day now. Ever recorded your songs?"

He had, once at school when one of his roommates had a job in the audio visual lab. They had gone in at midnight and recorded every song he knew. But that was three years ago, and he had written lots of songs since then.

"Not really."

"We'll do it then," Zeke said just as the salads arrived, their waitress not hanging around this time, sidewinding the round bowls onto their table and zipping back into traffic before they had stopped spinning.

It had been a long time since he had been with someone who talked so openly of his personal life. In contrast to Zeke, everyone else Reo knew seemed so guarded, so careful. His relationship with Micky, for example, had gone on for a couple of months, meeting on late-night rooftops, outside the back doors of music clubs, in fact, it seemed to Reo everywhere but where they might be seen by anyone else.

"Oh, she has the most beautiful breasts. I used to love to feel them, put my face into them," Zeke reminisced. "Listen to me. 'I'm already saying 'used to'."

"Yeah, you don't know anything yet," Reo said through a bite of salad, thinking at the same time what Delfina had said. "Me, I know. It's over."

"It's good you know. She'll never say anything to me. When I find her with another guy some night, she'll just say, hey Zeke, that's how it goes."

Reo looked at Zeke and knew the man was hurting. Simultaneously he realized he was going to move on, forget Delfina, get on with his own life.

"Women, they're like Chinese handcuffs. You know those little bamboo things you stick your finger in, and the harder you try to pull out the more it hangs onto you. Then you relax, forget to struggle, and it slips right off." Zeke took another sip of beer, but Reo didn't interrupt his monologue.

"Making love with her was so amazing," he went on. "She just got so into it, so passionate, I wanted to give her everything, just totally drive her over the top, you know?"

Reo waited, but Zeke was looking at him then.

"So. Did you? I mean, get her over the top?"

Zeke smiled, his eyes widening.

"Boy, did I. Drove her wild a couple of times, ooh, that was sweet. That's why it's so hard when they turn on us. We think it means something to them, to get them so far out, but they just think of it as, well, that was great. Thanks. Don't call me, I'll call you."

"I've heard women say that about men, that we don't care."

"Why should we? Look what they do to us when we do care! I should know better, after all the women I've had."

Reo was not a fan of guys who bragged about their conquests, but at this point was willing to make Zeke feel better.

"So, if you're so good with the girls, why are you sitting here thinking she's the last one who'll ever want you?"

"Oh, she's not, I know that."

"Do you love her?"

Zeke sat up, his fork paused in mid-air.

"Love her? Yes. I'm crazy about her. But I have to forget it. She doesn't love me, I know that." And the fork entered his mouth.

"Can you do that? Just turn it off?"

"Yes. No. Well, I guess we'll find out."

They finished the meal and left the restaurant. It was a Friday night, still early, and the streets were full of people out enjoying the warm summer air. Reo recognized the greasy-haired man who had played guitar with him at his first open mike, huddled in a doorway across the street, smoking a bent cigarette.

"Do you know him?" Reo indicated.

"Mick? Everybody knows Mick. He's got quite an act."

"What do you mean?"

"I don't know. An acid casualty, that's what they say. Gets a check for it every month."

As they watched, Mick stepped onto the sidewalk, spinning around on his heels and directing a diatribe at a couple who had just passed him. He spotted Zeke and Reo across the street, crossing quickly over toward them.

"Well, look who's here," he sneered.

"Hi Mick," Zeke said. Reo just studied the skinny, gap-toothed man in the dirty striped shirt.

"Got a cigarette?"

"You're already smoking one."

"Can't be too prepared."

"No."

Mick turned to Reo.

"Give me a dollar, I'll tell you something you need to know."

"We gotta go," Zeke said, starting down the street. But Reo took out his wallet, dug out a dollar and handed it to him.

"Very good, MacGregor," Mick said. Reo wondered how he even knew his name.

"Okay, here it is. Don't fall in love with the same woman."

But Zeke was already down the street, out of earshot.

"Thanks. I'll keep it in mind."

"Good. Got another dollar?"

But Mick turned and was off without waiting for an answer. Reo caught up with Zeke at the end of the street.

"MacDougal Street," Zeke shrugged, as if that said it all.

"You hang out here?"

"It's where you can usually find me," he said. "Right in the middle of the block, like all the other nut cases."

"Why here?" Reo looked around. "It's just another city street."

"No, it isn't. Really. I can't explain to you, but it's home for people who don't even live here."

They reached Folk Life, looking in through the window at a healthy crowd. The music sounded good, too, a full-sounding band with a strong, deep female voice. As if drawn by a string, they walked inside. Tony was standing at the door, talking with the man taking the cover charge. He looked them over and nodded with some level of recognition, and waved them right past the doorman.

But two steps inside Zeke pulled up short. Through the crowd they could see Micky Fresh, seated at a table just inside the bar from the main seating area, talking animatedly to Sonoma Sal.

"Alec," Zeke said quietly to himself. He put a hand on Reo's shoulder.

"Thanks for joining me for dinner. I gotta go."

"You okay?"

"Yeah, sure. Look, you should sit at that table. They need you more than you need them, believe me. But I'm going." And he turned and was out the door so quickly that Reo would have been left behind even if he wanted to go with him.

By the time he got to the bar Tony O was standing there.

"How you do?" he smiled, wiping the bar off with his ever-present towel. "You wan' somethin'?"

"Sure, I'd love a beer," he said. Instantly Tony reached down and popped out a small, squat bottle of something cold.

"Here you drink-a this. On me. You want something else, two dollars."

Reo grinned. He'd love to know why Tony was buying him a beer, but Tony walked away, and he meandered over to the archway, where the big round table was recessed into the wall in the corner of the bar. It was the first time he'd seen anyone sitting there, but he knew everyone: Micky, Molly, Sonoma Sal, and in the back corner, Jonas Waverly and Ted. There was one empty seat.

"Reo," Molly waved her beer at him. "Thanks for helping us out."

"Yeah Reo, sit down a minute," Micky said, and waved at the empty spot next to her on the bench, to Sal's evident displeasure. He retaliated by getting up and going to the bathroom.

"How are ya?" Micky said cheerily.

"Okay, I guess. Thanks for the job."

She unrolled her fist and handed him twenty bucks as if she had been waiting for him.

"Thank you. Did you have fun?"

"Yeah. Well, it was a little weird, my girlfriend was in the audience, with another guy. I guess she wasn't expecting to see me there tonight."

"So what happened."

"We broke up, I think."

"Do you feel bad?"

"A little. But I'll get over it."

She gave him a great smile and nodded confidently.

"Can I tell you something?" she asked with a downward inflection, as if making a statement.

"What's that?"

"You're trying to do something difficult. It requires all your attention, all your effort. If the people around you don't support you, you'll never get there. So if they make it harder for you, you have to let them go."

He waited, but that was it.

"I know that," he replied quietly.

"Do you? Do you really? That's good. You can't let people close to you drag you down. Even if it means pushing them away. It's tough, isn't it?"

Sal reappeared at her side. She clinked her glass against Reo's, then stood up.

"Remember that. It's important," she tapped his glass again. Then she took Sal's arm and walked with him from the bar.

13–Chance Encounter

In late July he went to Rhode Island to see his sister, who had rented a house with her two kids and husband for a week at a beach town just across the State line. So it was that Saturday night after a cook-out of hamburgers and hot dogs, corn and potato salad, after the coffee and the dishes and the kids to bed, Reo found himself alone on the public beach, watching the flat waves drift to shore and out again. It was the kind of night he loved: a dark, but warm and fragrant evening, with salty air and slight breeze; before long a large black bird descended from the night above, standing purposefully at the water's edge, staring out to sea. Reo stopped moving and waited, wondering which way the bird was headed: toward, or away from, home?

They stood together for some time, as if friends on a quiet outing, before the bird took off without warning, disappearing into the darkness. Eventually he found himself at a picnic table facing the ocean, a few yards south of some waterfront bar, listening to a band play the current crop of radio hits, a half-finished bottle of beer in his hand.

To his left a sandal spiraled into the dark beyond the umbra of the barroom. A girl stepped into view, flinging her other sandal outward with her other foot, spinning into the night.

"Hey," he called.

She spun and looked right at him. Clearly she had heard him.

"What?" she said, her hands on her hips. She faced him calmly, almost his height, slender and finely-shaped, a tan denim skirt halfway to her knees exposing slim and pretty legs, a tee-shirt and shoulder-length light hair, and a softly-lit face with kittenish eyes and mouth. About ten feet away, she waited for an answer.

"What's your name?" he asked her, unable to think of anything clever.

"Who wants to know?" she replied, stepping closer, trying to see his face where he was seated, out of the direct light from the bar, in the dark. "Do I know you?"

"My name's Reo. I was in the bar there, too." She was really very pretty, he thought, and maybe a little drunk, swinging a long-necked beer bottle by the throat.

"I'm Diana," she said. "I'm from New Britain."

He looked at her for a second, and she hopped on one foot.

"Can you help me find my shoes?" she asked him. "I threw them out here somewhere."

"Sure" he said, getting up. They headed onto the beach, beer bottles in hand. She had flung the second sandal a good distance, and by the time they reached it the bar seemed far away, and they were near the surf. She straightened up and held the sandals in her hand, still not putting them on.

"Want to walk down to the water?" he asked, beckoning them on with a nod of his head. She nodded, and without a word they went toward the ocean, silently crossing the very sand that would be covered by hundreds of people in a few hours, lying on towels and blankets, listening to radios and eating ice creams in the warm summer sun. Now it was quiet, just the sand and soft waves landing ten yards out and skimming over the beach to their feet.

They stood there, two strangers, not knowing what—if anything—to say to each other, and she shivered, leaning against him. There was a warm breeze, and without asking her, he unbuttoned and removed his shirt and wrapped it around her shoulders. She smiled at him, and they sat down on the beach, drawing up their legs in their arms.

"Are you from around here?" she asked him.

"No, I live in New York."

"New York. Wow. Why?"

"I'm...playing music there in clubs. I'm up here visiting my sister."

"What's New York like?"

"Big. Crowded. Exciting. Dangerous. Expensive."

"Do you have a girlfriend there?"

"No."

She stared out at the water, its six-inch waves lazily drifting along the beach.

"I remind you of someone, don't I?" she said quietly.

"Not really," he replied. But now that he thought about it, it was true, she did remind him of someone, although he couldn't place who it was.

"Do I remind you of someone?" he asked her, thinking that might be her reason for asking.

"Yes," she said right away. "I thought you were him when you first spoke to me. That's why I stopped to talk to you."

"Someone important to you?" he asked her, watching a small bird walk by six feet away, a dark shape against the shifting foam.

"Not any more," she answered.

A moon of sorts floated hazily over the water, about half full, loafing its way across the night sky, and when he finally looked at her it seemed as if she radiated in its light, her fine hair and pale eyebrows aglow with its soft brilliance. She had a lovely face, clear and flushed with the fresh night air and bathed in moonlight, and without warning she turned to him with a quiet, unhurried smile.

Neither one spoke, and then Reo MacGregor leaned forward and kissed her, right on the lips, taking his time, giving her the chance to turn her face away. But she did not—instead returning his kiss easily, not breaking away, until they lay horizontally facing each other, still kissing, their mouths open and their tongues exploring the taste of beer and desire. It was a kiss without end; as he felt her hands moving down his back, he slid his hand under her thin tee-shirt and deftly unhooked her bra. She gave no resistance, her hands unzipped his jeans, as he caressed her bare breast, a soft, full-roundness with its hard nipple in the center.

She rolled onto him, sliding her panties off with one hand, still locked in their kiss. He held onto the sand with his fingers as they made love, until she shivered all over with a muffled cry. The endless kiss finally dissolved into breathlessness as she pressed her lips to his cheek and kissed him again and again. As their breathing returned slowly to a normal rate, he heard a voice, and saw a flashlight beam on the sand.

"Hey," the voice said. He looked up, where the shadow of a policeman stood behind his flashlight, shining it into their faces.

In that instant he thought of the girl in his arms. What was her name? Diana. She did not look up, but lay on him as if dead, breathing quietly.

"Yes?" he asked, not moving.

"You're not supposed to bring the bottles down here," the cop said. He had a distinct accent, Haitian, Jamaican, an island cadence. Reo could see he was grinning, enjoying himself; the cop did not really want to bust them, was probably just having some fun.

"Unless those bottles ain't yours," he continued in his sing-song patois. "But then, how old is that girl?"

"Old enough to drink that bottle," Reo said.

"Well, take it back to the bar before one of the other guys comes along. Someone less, oh, shall we say, open-minded than myself."

"Yes, sir."

The cop stood there.

"Now," he snapped, forcibly.

Reo jiggled the girl carefully. He didn't want to have the policeman see his open jeans. He removed himself slowly and zipped his jeans shut, then fumbled around until he found her panties on the sand, hidden by her skirt. He closed his fingers around them and let her slide off, blocking the man's view, staggering to their feet. Reo spotted the offending bottle and picked it up.

"Go on, now," said the cop, waving the flashlight.

They walked back to the bar, stopping just outside the door, from where they could see people milling around, lights on, no music. The show was over.

"I have to meet my friends," she said.

He faced her.

"I know this is crazy, but could I call you sometime?"

"Okay," she smiled after thinking it over for a second. "Come with me."

He followed her inside to her friends, found a pen and paper and wrote it down without introducing him to the young man and woman who took her aside. To his real pleasure she was as lovely in the harsh bar light as she was by the ocean, pretty and fine, and he wondered why she was alone and why he was so lucky to have met her.

"I gotta go," she said, handing him the folded paper. "Call me if you want to." And without another word the young woman he had just made love to was gone, trailing after the young couple she had come with, her lithe body disappearing into the crowd of rock and roll fans leaving the club for the parking lot.

The paper said "Diana" and a number. He folded it in half and half again, put it in his wallet, and went out the back way, dancing the hundred yards to his car along the edge of the surf, letting the warm summer waves soak the ankles of his jeans.

14–Back To Basics

On the way back to the city, Reo lost his wallet. He had no idea how, or what had happened, he simply reached into his pocket in Grand Central Station and it was gone. He had no credit cards, a drivers' license and very little cash, and knew he could replace what he had lost, except for one thing: Diana's phone number. He would have called her sometime, he thought, but now he knew he would never see her again.

He went back to work three days a week at the newspaper, and as the summer wound on through July, he got a new license, saved some money, and rented a room upstairs from the coffeehouse in the small warren of single-occupant loners who shared one kitchen and bathroom. He spent a whole night in there alone, quietly working out a new song to remember the girl he had met at the beach; he wanted to describe her, but his mind kept returning to the smaller, dark image of the bird at the edge of the sea, until he decided she would be best remembered if he let it happen that way in his song:

> Chances come and chances are
> we do not linger long
> dancing down the water's edge
> the waves break castles down
> I will take you in the sand
> as the sunlight fades away
> and you look just like a raven
> a raven out on the gray

he sang in a whisper so no one in the rest of the house could hear. The tune had a fine, descending guitar line, and he was excited to think he could play it at the open mike next week.

He was wandering the streets of the Village late one afternoon when he met Ted Imbonante, lugging his guitar case around. Without saying where he was headed, Ted fell into step, and they spent more than two hours walking, talking, discussing the music they loved, the books they read, the other singers at the open mike. Ted liked to snap his fingers and considered himself a devotee of bebop, and Reo heard him quote two Dylans, two Wolfes, a Simon and a Presley before they arrived at a doorway. Ted pushed a small button.

"Come on," he said, pushing open the door at the faint buzz, and left Reo to hurry inside before the door slammed shut again. Upstairs they entered a small apartment through a door next to a kitchen sink, adjoining a bathtub with a large round-cornered sheet of plywood over it. There was a small wooden table with a candle in a wine bottle, surrounded by streaks of multi-colored wax from past candles, and a few photos on the walls.

"And the cat drags in whom?" a voice croaked from the far couch in a second room, and Jonas Waverly stood up, walking toward them.

"Let's go eat," Ted said in reply, setting his guitar down beside the table. But Jonas stopped in front of Reo.

"What's that on your shirt?" he said, stabbing a finger into Reo's chest, and, as Reo looked down at it, sliding it up to his chin with a laugh. It was the second time Jonas had done this irritating thing, Reo remembered; apparently Jonas thought it was real funny.

"Come on," Ted said, grabbing Reo's arm, and soon they were heading downtown, Ted and Reo followed by Jonas, in a buckskin fringe jacket, and the larger, even blonder brother named Jason. In contrast to the earlier part of the afternoon, Ted hardly spoke, and it wasn't until they were on the way back after a very tasty Chinese dinner that they were walking four abreast, when Reo heard someone call his name.

"Hey Reo," the voice repeated, and out of nowhere materialized Al Mays, one of Reo's best friends in law school.

"Al. Hi. How are ya?"

"I'm great. You?"

"I'm fine. What are you up to these days?"

"I finally got a job, with the Bronx D.A.'s office, I'm an assistant DA, so watch your ass." And he flexed a muscle, parodying a bodybuilder pose.

“That’s great, I’m happy for you.”

“How about you? Are you taking the bar exam?”

Until this moment Reo, absorbed in meeting his old friend, had forgotten his new companions. But it was Ted who spoke first.

“Bar exam?”

Al, who had been Reo’s first roommate in New York, was a year older than Reo and had graduated law school a year earlier. He stood confused and waiting for Reo to reply.

“Al and I were roommates when I first came to town,” Reo told them. “In fact, he took me in when I had nowhere to go.” But that wasn’t really an explanation, and he turned to his friends.

“Al and I went to Columbia Law School together,” he said simply.

“Not only that, we were in college when he helped get me elected president of the student body,” Al Mays enthused, giving Reo the impression he had always wanted to say that.

“Law school!” interrupted Jonas. “Methinks our young friend has been hiding something from us.”

“Not really. I just never thought you’d be interested.”

“Well, here we have been thinking you’re a train ridin’, cow ropin’, hard lovin’ sort of guy, and all the time you’re really a lawyer,” Jonas sang in a voice raw with irony, a parody of being wounded that made Jason laugh out loud.

“Actually, Al, I’m not taking the bar exam, or studying for it. I’m not going to practice,” Reo said to his old friend, ignoring Jonas’ taunt.

“Well, I am,” Jonas said. “I’m going to practice.” He started moving on, followed in turn by Jason and a flustered Ted, who was insisting “it doesn’t matter, you can be who you want to be.”

“What was that about?” Al asked when they’d gone.

“I’ve been playing music,” Reo said “Those guys had no idea I went to law school.”

“So?”

“I don’t know. Maybe they won’t take me seriously now, if they think I have some other thing to do.”

“I get it, “AL said, shaking his head as if he didn’t. But they stood and talked for several minutes. Reo was glad to see his old friend. He realized that, other than by accident, they would not be likely to meet, for he had lost contact with his school friends after graduation; dropping out, and into the world of music he had chosen meant, to him, getting past his own history into a future where he could start fresh and make his own life. And he knew that his school friends were now immersed in an entirely different world of law firms and bar exams, and had no time for him. Still, they had been good friends, and Reo was glad to see him, if only for a passing moment on the street. They shook hands and parted without any pretense they would "get together," and Reo thought how easily he might never see him again, like Diana. Here in the great city, he thought, you can disappear and never meet someone again, not even accidently.

Later he meandered uptown, running into Ted just as he came out of Jonas' apartment. The summer evening was still bright, and they fell back in step, drawn by the reddening sun to the river, where they sat on a rotten beam and stared out over the murky water. If it had bothered Jonas that Reo went to law school, or if it were merely ammunition to use against him, it seemingly made no difference to Ted, who, upon hearing the brief summary Reo made of his background, returned to a theme from earlier in the afternoon.

"So you went to a private high school, the University of Virginia, and Columbia Law School, and never read *Moby Dick*?" Ted inquired in disbelief.

"That's right."

"How did you manage that?"

"I was in an advanced placement program, and skipped it. I guess you could say I was so advanced I didn't have to learn anything," he joked.

"What are you, a fucking genius?" Ted stared at him, his eyebrows up, running three fingers through his woolly mass of curly black hair.

"Yeah, that's why I'm sitting here, talking to you," he replied. Ted didn't answer, and Reo started thinking out loud.

"You know, I don't even know what day this is. The sun's going down over the river. It could be any of a thousand days. And that's what I like about it, that we can sit here and talk with all the time in the world. Why would I give that up to be a lawyer."

Ted didn't answer.

"And you know, the bar exam is expensive, and if you're not going to be a lawyer, why bother?"

Ted kicked the beam with his swinging foot.

"Are you here to hang out or to play music?" he asked.

"Play music, definitely," Reo said without hesitating. "But I do enjoy hanging out. I feel like I have so much to learn."

"Yeah, I know what you mean," Ted nodded, suddenly enthusiastic again, his old self, the self that made Reo feel there was someone else who shared his passion, the need to do what he was doing, to devote himself to it without looking back.

"I'm teaching English in high school," Ted continued, "I don't know if I can do that anymore. I have to get into my music, let it carry me forward. So here I am."

"Are you making a living from it?" Reo asked.

"I wish! I have some savings, and a few gigs here and there. I'm playing the Folk Life later this month."

"That's great, I'll come see you."

"How about you? What are you doing for money?"

"I'm proofreading three days a week for a small newspaper."

"But no law job."

"No."

"Good. Hey listen, we're having some people over tomorrow night, make some music, drink some wine. Want to come?"

"Sure."

They met the next day at Jonas' building. Jason sat beside Reo in the back seat of Ted's car with an enormous wooden string bass spread across their laps. They got stuck in traffic on a long bridge incline in Queens, and Jason sat there, singing the bass notes one at a time-dum…..dum….. dum.....dum....as Peter Frampton wailed through a guitar solo on the car radio. Eventually they arrived in a quieter neighborhood, parked on the street and went inside, where Ted introduced Reo to his wife, Veronica, a thin brunette with a long narrow face and a big laugh. She took Reo by the hand and dumped him in the center of the living room, where a dozen people were sitting around by candlelight, softly singing along with a song he'd never heard. After a round of appreciative applause, Veronica pointed at Reo.

"New guy has to sing the next song," she sang across the crowd.

Surprised, he steadied his guitar on his lap. He stroked the strings, trying to imagine what to do, when he remembered the piece of paper folded in his shirt pocket.

"I've got this thing I've been working on," he began.

"New song!" someone called out, and was quickly echoed by a couple other voices. Reo looked around the room, vaguely recognizing one or two faces from the open mike, and spotted Jonas in the hall, talking animatedly to a red-headed girl, waving a glass of wine in his wrist as he spoke.

"Okay, here it goes," he said, and started strumming an Am chord, pulling his fingers off to syncopate the beat.

> Late last night a stranger came calling
> crawling down my fire escape
> came to a gate bolted in my window and ripped off the
> entire frame.

From across the room came the sound of Jason's bass, deep and resonant, throbbing in time with his strum; and from a different direction, the sound of Jonas picking lightly on a mandolin. In a different part of the room Veronica was playing a violin, and there were three other guitars trying to keep up with Reo's strum, only one of them with much success.

> Now there's boards on the floor and I'm twenty dollars poorer
> and the living room's got a breeze
> and on the window he broke, he left me a note
> sayin' 'there'll be others just like me'

Jason was good, Reo realized, the song was taking off, and by the time it kicked into the chorus the room was rocking.

> And there's hard times a-coming
> hard times over the hill
> you can't buy 'em off
> you can't shout 'em down
> if hard times are coming they will

Ted came over and sat next to Reo, reading the words and singing along on the chorus.

> You got to stand in line to get somebody
> to say there ain't enough to go round
> you better tell somebody about it 'cause hard times
> is out on the edge of town.

By the time the end of the song came, and Reo read the last phrase, Ted was totally on top of it, singing with him in his full tenor voice:

> You better get your shotgun ready 'cause hard times
> is out on the edge
> out on the edge
> out on the edge of town.

There was a blast of applause, and someone yelled "Great song!" before Jonas stepped into the center of it.

"I don't know about that," he croaked through the din. "Hard Times 'is' on the edge of town? Shouldn't it be 'are' on the edge of town?"

Ted jumped in immediately.

"Nahhh," he waved Jonas off. "It's right as it is, hard times is a thing, a concept, a singular thought, like human rights or something."

"So you mean," Jonas pursued him, "it really should be 'The Times They Is A-Changing?'"

"How about 'These Is The Times That Try Men's Souls?' " another voice piped up.

"It Was The Best Of Times, It Was The Worst Of Times," someone else countered.

"This Time They're Real," a woman spoke up, and Veronica laughed so hard her violin banged into a lamp, nearly knocking it over.

"What's that, the Boob Job song?" she burst out, effectively ending the argument. Someone else launched into a song, then another, and Reo joined in when he caught onto the song, listened when he didn't play. Everyone seemed to know everyone but him, and it was two hours later when Veronica sat down next to Reo and asked if she could look at the lyrics to his song.

He handed her the paper.

"You can have it," he said.

"Why, you're not gonna sing it ever again?" she teased him, her large brown eyes twinkling with mischief.

"No, it's not that," he laughed. "I know it already."

She squinted at it for some time, making sure she could read his scrawl and the phrases he had written over those he had crossed out. Finally she handed it back to him.

"If you're giving it to me," she said, "you have to sign it."

"Really? You want me to sign this thing?"

She stood up and went to a nearby desk. The music was between songs, and by now she had attracted the attention of the people around the room with her contagious, rapid laugh.

"You never know, maybe you'll be famous someday and I can finally make some money from music," she joked, handing him the pen.

He wrote in big letters across the top, signed it, and gave it to her.

"I hope this makes you rich," she read. "Me too!"

15–The Threat

"You're no fucking saint," Zeke intoned over his plate of guacamole, salad, rice and beans.

"What?"

"I said, you're no fucking saint. Everyone thinks you are. You act like you are. I know better, that's all."

Reo chewed a mouthful of rice.

"Who says all this? I don't think I'm a saint. Whatever that means."

"I said, a fucking saint."

"Right, Zeke. Whatever."

"Yeah, sure, go ahead and act like you don't know what I'm talking about."

"I don't know what you're talking about."

He stirred a forkful of salsa in a spiral toward the center of his refried beans.

"You don't have a girlfriend. You aren't seeing anyone. You're just letting them talk."

"Letting who talk?"

"The girls. Around the neighborhood, in the Folk Life. Even in here." Zeke flagged down the passing waitress, a willowy blond in black leotard and a gray skirt, her legs black to the toes sticking out through her sandals, bearing a tray with two beer bottles swaying perilously with every step.

"What are you talking about?"

Zeke sat back and folded his arms across his chest.

"Look at me. What do you see?"

Reo studied his companion. This was their fourth dinner together, spanning three weeks.

"I see a guy trying to say something, but I'm not getting it."

"You see a guy with thinning hair, glasses, not a bad face but nothing special, average size, someone who can walk through a roomful of women unnoticed."

Reo shrugged.

"I don't know, I thought Micky was pretty cute," referring to the girl he had been with when they met.

"Oh, that one," Zeke mused aloud, his voice suddenly melodious and high. "She had the most perfect breasts. I could kiss them all night."

Reo exhaled a laugh and took another bite of his dinner. Zeke suddenly got serious.

"No, I mean look at you. That's what women do, they look at you. They want you. You're a good-looking guy. You know you are. You don't have to play dumb or act as if you don't know it."

"I do all right, I guess."

"You do better than all right. You could have your pick of these girls anytime."

"Well that's nice of you to say, but probably not true. I don't feel that way about it myself."

"Does anyone ever turn you down?"

"Sure. Lots of times."

"But you're not afraid to ask. Most guys are afraid to ask. They know it isn't gonna happen."

Reo sat back and stretched his arms across the back of the wooden bench. They were across from each other in one of the narrow booths along the wall of the Mexican restaurant, right under the rod iron candlesticks topped with six-inch blocks of burning wax, their flames constantly changing the shapes reflected on the walls. The way the ocean never looks the same twice, Reo thought.

"You know, Zeke, I don't know if what you say is true. Maybe it is. I've had some pretty nice women come my way. It's hard to care about somebody and have them not care enough about you. And it's easy to hurt someone if you don't care about them as much as they care about you."

Zeke nodded.

"The problem for you," he said, "is you'll want someone, want to have them, then not want to stay with them after."

Reo shook his head.

"I like being with a woman. It just has to be someone who can be with me."

Zeke laughed.

"That sounds like a greeting card. Okay, here's what I mean. Some of the guys are a little suspicious of you."

"For what?"

"They think you're after their women."

Reo put down his fork.

"What do you mean?"

"Because they see their women looking at you. I can tell you this, because I don't have a woman myself right now."

"I don't believe this. I'm minding my own business, just trying to play some tunes and hang out."

"I believe you. It's not what you're doing that makes them wonder, but their own fear. It's just something you should keep an eye on."

"So what am I, some pretty boy?"

"Not at all. You're a good guy, I know you. But look at it this way: you're going to take who you're going to take. They know that. It scares them."

Reo watched the waitress wiggle toward them with another round of beers. She had a pretty face framed with fine, wispy blond hair, and a sweet figure underneath her official demeanor. She parked herself next to their table, arching her torso so her skirt edged onto the table and bending forward so her leotard lowered just enough to demonstrate some cleavage without really showing anything. She placed two beers on coasters.

"What's your name?" he asked her.

"Kiersten," she replied in a professional tone.

"And you are a Dancer? Actress? Singer?"

She slung the tray against her hip and snapped her gum, regarding him with a squint.

"That the best you got?" she chewed, turning back into the stream of waitresses and busboys in perpetual motion around the booths and tables.

Zeke laughed.

"You'll get nowhere with that one anyway," he said. "Boyfriend."

"Then what are their boyfriends afraid of?"

Zeke tossed a lump of guacamole onto his tongue.

"You ever notice," he began, "how girls always have to blurt it out. 'Boyfriend,' " he blurted, blasting out the first syllable, "like they just have to get it off their chests. I suppose it's a way of saying they like you, they'd consider you worth the time, but they're off limits, cause they got a, they got a, got a ...."

"Boyfriend," they sang out together, laughing and temporarily stopping conversation at several adjoining booths and tables.

"Well, I've been a boyfriend," Reo said conspiratorially.

"Me too, and had my girl fuck me over."

"Yeah, well, not the right one, I guess," Reo finished, thinking of his own recent breakup. "At least I can say this, Zeke."

"What?"

"I miss Delfina, but don't want her back."

"Did you love her?"

He nodded.

"Yeah, I think so."

"You don't know?"

"Oh, I loved her. Still do. But she wants a different kind of life. It's better not to fight it."

"So who do you love now?"

The question took him by surprise.

"No one in particular."

"How about Callisto? Everyone's in love with her."

Reo laughed.

"What makes you think I'd be in love with her?"

"Well, I've seen you look at her. But then everyone looks at her that way. Except me. Doesn't interest me, not as a lover anyway. She's okay as a singer, nice girl, woman, whatever, but not my taste as a lover. You, on the other hand, she's very attractive to you."

Reo finished his rice and beans, saving the last mouthful of guacamole for last.

"She is somebody who interests me," Reo said. "She's beautiful, very smart, very direct when you speak with her. It's just that there's always this scene around her."

"Hard to get in there."

"I'm not sure I want to. It's a bit strange, I don't know why she likes to surround herself with those people, it's like she's playing the queen or something. It makes me think I don't really know her."

"Maybe you don't. Would you like to?"

"Yeah. I'd like to get to know her, just as another person, without all the bullshit that goes on around it."

Zeke should his head.

"You'll never get near her with an attitude like that. Whoever gets that one will have to claim her, in public, right in front of everyone."

Reo polished off the guacamole and took a slug of beer, brandishing the bottle as he spoke.

"Somehow I think she will choose for herself who that is," he said.

"Yeah," Zeke nodded. "But you, on the other hand, have to be careful you don't want to grab somebody too easy and then be stuck with them. Or dump them, and hurt their feelings."

"Thanks, Zeke," Reo answered with no trace of sarcasm. "I'll keep it in mind."

The waitress swung by, letting the check float down to the table in her wake. Zeke, who said Reo "wasn't making any money, and would pay him back someday, but don't worry about it," took the check and counted out the bills to pay it, as he did each time. Reo took out three dollars and put the tip on the bare table.

"For the lovely Kiersten," Zeke said, waving at Reo's money. "With the boyfriend at home right now, living on her waitressing money, watching her TV, drinking her beer, and waiting for her to come home so he can get laid and go out. Be generous."

Reo put another dollar on the table.

16–Number 13c

On Monday he went to the open mike, arriving in time to get a number. There were ninety slots, two songs each, and to get one, you had to be one of the first ninety people to pull a card, face down, with a number written on it in magic marker. There were many weeks when all the numbers were gone before then, and only the first ninety got to play.

Reo was choosing a card from the deck when Tony O. walked over, wiping a glass clean with a small white towel.

"Give him his own number," Tony O said. Sonoma Sal took the card from Reo's hand and put it back on the deck without looking at it.

"You sure?" he asked Tony O.

"Sure, I'm a sure."

Sal scanned the list.

"You're number 13c," he said. "What's your name again?"

"Reo MacGregor."

"Reo MacGregor. Okay, 13c it is."

Tony finished polishing the glass.

"That's a you number now, from now on," he said. "When you a here, that is."

Reo looked at Sal, who raised his eyebrows and nodded.

"Well, well," Sal mused.

So it was true, what Ted had told him, that they saved "numbers for people who are good to play when it's crowded. I'm number 12b myself. Jonas is 10A. Brad is 9b. There are a handful of us."

Ted had smiled and shrugged his shoulders—Reo could still picture it—and said, "It's all about selling beer, and you still don't get paid, but hey, it means somebody's listening."

Reo stepped aside to allow a short, heavy man in denim coveralls walk past, carrying a large, solid guitar case. He didn't see Ted or anyone he knew; he went into the main room and found a seat in the back.

Number 8b was a woman in her thirties with shaggy blond hair and an even blonder guitar, which reflected a beam of the bright spotlight into the room in front of her. Did she see it herself, he wondered, as it cruised across the front row, following where she looked, until it zeroed in on him, hidden in the back corner, momentarily blinding him as she sang, bouncing in place, wagging her blue-jeaned hips back and forth in time, staring straight out over his head. She had a pouty mouth and lips that turned down at the corners, as if they never could be satisfied with anything, especially herself. But then she smiled, and an audible murmur went around the room. As she finished, three men got up from their tables, each making his way to the corner beside the stage where the singer was exiting.

Reo wondered what each would be saying. The first to reach her approached her politely, as if introducing himself; but before he could get started the second man, a burly figure in a tweed sport coat, barged in front of him and was embracing her, as if claiming her. The third arrived more slowly, biding his time, but was the one she opened up to, reaching for his embrace. The boyfriend, Reo figured, as they exchanged a quick peck and settled into each other's arms. The first two men backed off as the next act was introduced, someone's "ssshhh" silencing conversation for a moment.

Number 9C turned out to be a slightly balding man in a denim jacket and blue jeans, who strummed his way through a song about the subway in a serious New York accent, an attempted folk song:

> Dis is da way I go to wuhk
> go to wuhk
> go to wuhk
> Dis is da way I go to wuhk
> early in da moanin'

just as Reo leaned back against the wall and burst out laughing, soaking it up, thinking there was no place in the world he'd rather be than here listening to this guy. It was so true he felt like a fraud, a faker trying to be someone he wasn't, some sort of rustic poet with a twang that would lend authenticity to his writing. But, suddenly in a flash, he saw how brilliant it was, to just be oneself, and how difficult to even know who that is.

"Hi Reo," said the waitress, a round-faced young woman he'd seen here a few times, but didn't know her name.

"It's all right, I'm Lila," she said.

"Hi, I'm Reo," he answered, extending a hand.

"I know that," she said. "That's why I said 'Hi' to you," she smiled, taking his hand. "Are you gonna play?"

"Yeah."

"Oh good, I'll be listening," she said over her shoulder, moving away. Then she leaned back and swung a heavy glass of beer onto his table.

"Here," she said, "some guy ordered this and split."

During this conversation the act onstage had gone, replaced by a pony-tailed man with a tiny guitar, who played with bare fingers, stroking some very sweet notes. Just as he was about to sing, the prior entertainer walked up to Reo, dragging his guitar case on the floor.

"You laughin' at me?" he squinted at Reo, obviously not pleased about it. Reo opened his eyes and put up his hands.

"No, not at you. I was laughing at something that happened to me, something I realized while listening to you. I'm sorry if I distracted you."

The young man in denim didn't seem convinced.

"Really, I liked what you did."

The man set down his guitar.

"I don't like being laughed at."

"I'm really sorry if that's what you think. It isn't what I was laughing at. It was something else."

"What?"

"You want to know what it was?" Reo found this hard to believe.

"Yeah."

"Okay. But look, there's somebody singing right now, and we're having this conversation. Want to sit down?" He slid over to make room.

The man stepped over his guitar case and sat down.

"What's your name?" Reo whispered.

"Jack."

"Reo."

"Huh?"

"Reo. That's my name."

"So fuckin' what."

Reo laughed quietly.

"Exactly. So fucking what.."

"No, I said 'fuckin,' not 'fucking' like some prep school asshole."

"What is it you want?" Reo said quietly, turning to face the man directly.

"I don't like you," the man said in a strange undertone.

"You know, Jack, I was just sitting here enjoying your singing, and now here you are busting my balls. You're not gonna make many fans that way."

Jack stared back at him and for once didn't say the first confrontational thing that came to mind.

"You like my singing."

"That's what I said. I did."

"You're fulla shit."

"Nope. I meant it. I like your singing. In fact, I would like to ask you for a favor."

"What's that?"

"I'd like you to sing one of my songs."

Jack scowled.

"Why? So you can laugh at me?"

"I'll tell you what. I'll sing your song if you sing mine. Fair enough?"

Jack was temporarily speechless.

"You'll learn one of mine?"

"Deal," Reo said, sliding his right hand under his left arm, offering a handshake, getting a grudging smile in return.

"All right," Jack said at last. "You got a deal."

A few minutes later Reo sang his two songs, the first, the one he had slaved over all the previous night, being immediately forgotten. The second, which had come to him as if unasked, was based on a simple guitar line he had made up late one night, doodling around in a quiet apartment. The notes descended from the highest point of his middle G string, moving down the scale in a syncopated rhythm to the main chord:

> Every time I think of you it almost makes me listen
> songs may come and songs may go but you keep right on
> singing

you make a man feel bolder
to see you stand so proud
and you look just like a raven
a raven out on a cloud

It was a hypnotic, quiet song that settled the crowd down after some of the previous, more chaotic, performers. When Reo finished there was a respectful applause that lasted until he was well off the stage.

Jack, his erstwhile assailant, met him at the bar.

"I can't sing that," he said. "Too many notes."

"Sure you can. Do it your own way."

Jack looked him over.

"Give me something else. We got a deal."

"All right," Reo said. "Meet me here next week."

17–Hanging Out

Reo sometimes felt as if he had no home and could go wherever the wind blew him. But it did not blow him far; a chance meeting with Allan, Delfina's former employer, resulted in an invitation to use a spare bedroom on the fourth floor of a Chelsea brownstone, coming and going pretty much as he pleased. From there he zeroed in on the Village, walking on a nightly basis, taking his guitar if there were somewhere to play; within a few days he was being invited from one club to another, from one apartment to another, to sit around and make music. There were dozens of songwriters like himself circulating around, and a few were dedicated to it, working on it every day and evening.

"You got it," Zeke told him over a plate of guacamole one evening in early October. "You thought you were doing something unique, something inspired by guys who've done it, but not thinking there were a lot of others beside yourself. A real lot. Every one of them like yourself, wanting to sing their little songs, make their money, win their fans. It's why I never went for it. Too competitive. I just want to make music."

Reo dipped a chip in the salsa. It was spicy, lemony and all tomato all at once, like a quick trip to another place and time.

"The question is," Zeke went on, "what do you do now?"

"Me? I'm not going to do anything."

"Nothing?"

"Different, I mean. I'm not going to do anything different."

"Oh. Well, it's not like anybody is noticing, have you seen there are 30 songwriters for every civilian in the audience on open mike nights? What does that tell you?"

"That a lot of us stink."

"No, not that. That the ones who can bring in a crowd are the ones who end up playing on the paying nights."

"Right," Reo mused. "It does come down to that, I guess."

"You bet it does. Now what are you going to do about it?"

For the time being Reo was taking it all in. Tony O had let him know he was welcome to hang out at the bar anytime, even the weekends. He didn't go there every night, but when he did some of the "civilians," the business guys hanging out into the evening, would buy him a beer. None of these men ever asked anything from him for it, he noticed; sometimes he would try to strike up a conversation, but for the most part they just bought him a beer and went in to watch the show. Tony O certainly didn't mind.

About once a week there was a gathering at the MacDougal Street apartment of Tim Marcek, a swashbuckling dude with a black mustache and a flat-brimmed black hat. There were seven of them, seated around a large wooden picnic table with their guitars. This was a completely different group than Ted and Jonas', more western and southwestern than urban; the music was more basic too, simple melodies played with big open chords to a straight four-four beat. He sat next to Renaldo, a slim man with a lilting way of speaking who was an Apache from Arizona; each played a song in turn, starting with Marcek himself, who had a very strong, driving rhythmic strum and a deep voice that sounded like something you would expect to hear over a desert wind.

> She said we would always be lovers
> No matter how many more lives
> It would take til we were together
> And I, I, I watched her walk down the aisle
> Wearing a smile
> And I said I'll see you baby
> in 3005.

At first it seemed Tim Marcek was trying for satire; then the song went on for two more verses, describing a time of great civilization, with widespread psychic wisdom and universal peace, a glowing sun, prosperity and foods for every plate, and tolerance for every point of view, in short a fantasyland where, of course, he and she would be together. And no husband this time to mess it up, he finished, concluding each verse with an invocation to 3005.

Reo started to laugh but realized the others were all taking it seriously. He held it back, wanting so badly to bust out when it finally ended that he couldn't let anyone see his face. He didn't want to offend his host, and he was pretty sure he had gotten over it without anyone noticing, when he heard Renaldo speak in a spacy voice.

"Wow. That was something."

There was a murmur of soft "yeah, yeahhs" in assent, with a red-haired woman at the end of the table going "Yeaaahhhhhh" real slowly to finish them all off. Then everyone laughed, and Tim shrugged it off, turning to the woman who had spoken last.

"Okay, then, let's hear one from you," he taunted her.

"Okay," she said immediately, suddenly focused and ready. She flicked her bangs out of her eyes with a quick wave, shook her long red hair free in the back, and plucked a string.

If you don't love her now
you will never know
all the things she told you
were really so
If you don't love her now
you will never see
all the time she lost
when you weren't free

The slow, swinging blues chords drew them all in, several guitars picking up the changes behind her easy fingerpicked guitar notes. It sounded like a small band, all acoustic guitars at one time. Reo settled into a simple three-note chord he could develop under her voice, and she looked at him approvingly as she went on.

Most of all, you'll never call
her love your own, and when alone
you'll roam the wild empty land of your soul
dreaming of the story untold

If you don't love her now
you will never find
all the ways to her heart
and your peace of mind

You don't have to love her forever
You don't have to take any vows
Who knows where you'll find her tomorrow
If you don't love her now

The wave of approval that came on with the song's end was genuine and spontaneous, a mutual smile fest that was, no doubt, enhanced by everyone's having learned the simple chord progression before it ended, playing quietly together.

Her name was Brandy something, and true to her name, as the whiskey bottle got passed around the table a third time, Reo watched her take a big swig, toss her head and laugh with glee. She could sure sing, he thought, as the freckled, baby-faced male singer on her right squinted and launched a quavering burst of raspy syllables:

Long train late tide
Big station I'm inside
Baby I won't be coming back this time

Reo's mind drifted off. When it was his turn he felt unprepared, had nothing he had confidence in to play for this group. But it was Brandy who saved him, calling for a song she had heard at the open mike.

"Why don't you play 'Hard Times,' " she smiled across the table.

"How was that received?" Zeke asked him later, when he had described the gathering.

Reo smiled.

"Well, you had to be there."

"Don't pull that on me."

"Okay, it was fun. I think they liked it."

"Did Tim invite you back? Who invited you this time?"

"Renaldo. I met him on the street, we started talking, had some coffee, next thing I knew we were climbing the stairs to Tim's."

"And?"

"Yeah, Tim said come anytime, he's cool."

"Wow," Zeke shook his head. "Actually they're a very cliquish bunch, they must have liked you."

For his part, Reo saw no reason not to get along with everyone, and tried to turn a deaf ear when he heard someone in one clique talking about someone in another. Before long he felt he was in no clique, more or less welcome in different gatherings but not necessarily of them. This had its advantages, to be sure; he was able to choose when he would, or would not, show up; but it also had disadvantages, in that the warm support the members of each clique gave their comrades was more reserved in his case. Reo thought that over and decided he was going to keep it in mind, that he had to win them over every time.

One Monday he ran into Callisto on her way to the open mike, and after walking together for a few blocks they entered the club separately. She walked in a few steps, stood in the middle of the bar area, and within seconds Brian, Jackson and finally Jonas Waverly had found their way to her. Reo gravitated toward Ted, who was having an animated conversation with another singer, who wandered off just as Reo arrived.

"Hey, what's going' on," Ted nodded.

"Yeah, what," Reo shrugged back.

"Trouble," Ted said quietly.

"What do you mean?"

"I don't know, things are changing. Could be good, though."

"You and Veronica?"

Ted simply nodded.

"Not that it's my business," Reo began. "But what is going on?"

Ted turned toward the stage and picked up his guitar. He looked once at Reo and said "they just called my number," and disappeared into the crowd. Reo watched over some shoulders as Ted took the stage, extracting his guitar from its hard-shell case with one motion, dropping the case on the stage. It took him a minute to tune, as a few listeners drifted off into the bar, and by the time he got going the moment seemed to have passed. The bigger surprise, however, was that Ted had nothing to say—in song, anyway—relevant to what he had just told Reo. For Ted was not a writer, he was a singer, one of a rare breed in the open mike scene, someone who wasn't there singing his own words. Ted had music of his own, set to lyrics written by two old friends from high school, songs about wanting to get away from New York City and head to a mountain stream somewhere, that he sang as bebop in a big, round voice.

Reo's turn came a little later, and after a set that barely seemed to register on the crowd, he met Ted in the bar again.

"So is that what you want to do? Leave New York and go to some mountain stream?"" he asked him.

"Not a bad idea," Ted agreed, "but not right now. I was thinking of learning that song of yours."

"Which one?"

"'Hard Times.' I like it."

Reo let that sink in before answering.

"Sure," he said. "Go ahead."

As the open mike was ending Reo saw Callisto heading out the door alone. Quietly he came up beside her, lightly touching the sleeve of her jacket. She turned and saw him and stopped, and suddenly he was at a loss for words.

"Yes?"

"Are you going?" he finally asked.

"Why, yes."

Reo studied her for a moment, trying to read her expression.

"May I walk with you a bit? I'd feel better if you weren't alone on the streets."

She smiled, as if she knew it was a line but was going to let it slide.

"Come on."

They wound through the narrow streets to the 7th Avenue subway station at Sheridan Square, their guitar bags across their backs, striding side by side.

"I'm surprised to find you alone," he said after a few yards.

"Oh? Why is that?"

"Well, you're always with your gang. Jonas and his friends."

"You don't like Jonas, do you?"

"Oh, he's all right I suppose."

"You suppose."

"Is liking Jonas required or something?" he inquired testily.

"No," she said, stopping and facing him. "But you brought it up."

She was right, he'd been a fool. He managed a smile.

"Well, I won't make that mistake again. Let's talk about something else. Whatever you like." And he started walking toward the subway, which, in any event, was on the way to his Chelsea brownstone room.

"I'm sorry," she called from behind, walking briskly up. He stopped.

"I'm angry at him, and I took it out on you. Will you forgive me?"

He faced her, nervously wondering if he should go away and leave her alone.

"Yes, sure," he said. "You don't have to act like I'm stalking you or something. If you want me to go, I can do that."

"No," she said. "I want you to walk me to the subway." And she encircled his arm with hers, put her head against his shoulder, and took a step forward, leaving him no choice but to follow.

18–Tools Of The Trade

His first capo was a simple strap with a curved steel band, so it clamped down on the frets when you pulled it over the top and hooked the knubs into the slots. On the other side of the metal band a hard rubber slab 1/32" thick held the notes in place. But he left it on stage one night and later, when he discovered the loss, couldn't find it anywhere. He ended up at the music store, where Sonoma Sal was holding court from behind the counter, a worldy-wise grin placidly holding up his long, blond handlebar moustache. Even the tips were shaped perfectly, twisting upward and outward.

"Ah, MacGregor, is it? What brings you here? Decided to play in tune after all?"

He set his case down on the fat end.

"I need a capo."

"A capo. How splendid. They're over here, behind me on this wall."

His gaze followed the hand to the display, zeroing in on a plastic package containing a rubber tube wound around a steel pin, fastened by two elastic straps wrapping around the guitar neck, as tight as you could pull them. There was also a spring-loaded clamp that clipped into place, but had a lot of metal edges. And a brass model, two pieces hinged together, one wrapped by a flat rubber sheath that snapped shut against the other, was below it, the most expensive at $12.

"Can I try one of those?," He asked, pointing to the brass version.

"Gee, I don't know," said Sal, his raised eyebrows forming a skeptical burlesque.

"Well, do I have to buy it first? I just want to see if it works."

Sal eyed him professorially through rimless glasses.

"Your guitar?" he nodded at it.

"Yes."

"Let's see it."

Reo set the case down flat, opened it and took out the contents without saying a word. When he straightened up, he simply presented it across the counter with both hands.

Sonoma Sal drew his breath, reacting immediately as if he couldn't take it quickly enough. He twirled it adroitly so it faced him, looked down its length, and lifted it so he could see into the sound hole.

"Gibson. Nice. Country And Western. Trapezoidal inlay on the frets, possibly mother of toilet seat. Spruce top, mahogany back and sides. Uh huh."

He looked up at Reo, then glancing toward a card on the counter, he adjusted it and read the information he wanted.

"It's not hot."

"Didn't say it was. I was looking at the year. 1968."

"How do you know that?"

"From the serial number. Here. Don't tell me you never wrote it down."

He realized he never had written it down.

"Oh my. Here, allow me," and he wrote the numbers on a slip of paper and stuck it into Reo's shirt pocket.

Sal took the guitar in his hands and began to play, slowly at first, in a blues mode, snapping the bass string on an E chord, then working his way up the neck in jazz fingerings. Reo watched as he settled into a nice easy swing, moving through the chord changes with impressive fluidity. He seemed as if he were about to sing something when another man came out of the doorway behind the counter, snapping his fingers.

"What's happenin' here?" he bopped, curly dark head bending forward to make eye contact with Sonoma Sal, then swooped around to Reo behind a smile.

"A capo, wasn't it?" he addressed him, as Sal kept on working his way through the chords on Reo's guitar. Then abruptly he stopped, handed Reo his guitar and took the brass capo off the wall, tearing open the soft plastic packaging and handing the capo to Reo in one seemingly uninterrupted motion.

"Here you are. Try before you buy."

Reo took the guitar and placed it over his shoulders, then snapped the capo on.

The device had a long screw that determined the tension applied on the neck of the guitar. This was adjustable, so it worked where the neck was thicker, or nearer the nut where it was less so. It took him a few seconds to figure it out, but he managed to snap it shut on the second fret and have none of the strings buzzing within about a minute.

"Not bad, kid," the curly-haired man said. "But you could save a lot of time if you just faced it toward you instead of away."

He removed it and turned it the way the man had suggested, and snapped it shut. Again the strings all rang out without any buzzing.

"I'll take it."

Sal and the other man looked at each other. Except for Reo, there were no customers. It was that time of day when the sun reflected downward from above, back and forth across several floors of windows, yellow and streaked with dust particles floating on air, the color of good aged cheese, as it arrived in the ground floor.

"Play something," said the dark-haired man.

"Okay," Reo nodded, still mesmerized by the playing he had just seen. He stroked a G chord, quietly at first, then wacked the strings hard with his fingernails so abruptly that the salesman jumped. But the guitar didn't buzz, the dissonant notes rang out clearly.

"Good capo," he said.

He let his mind wander, and drifted into a piece of music he had been fooling with, a chord progression with a major chord, the same chord in a minor, then the relative minor and the major chord again, played as a waltz. He strummed it with his fingers, losing some volume when his nail snagged on the thinnest string, but kept the tempo through a verse, then stopped.

"Well, just something I was fooling around with."

"Nice piece of music. Can I ask you something?" It was more a statement than a question.

"Sure," he said, expecting him to ask what it was titled.

"Have you given any thought to learning to play better?"

Reo gave no reaction but noticed Sonoma Sal slide off his stool, grab the sides of it and hoist himself back up.

"Yeah. Lots. I practice all the time."

"I don't know, it just seems to be that, well, part of being a musician is always trying to be a better musician. Accepting the quest," he began and turned slightly toward Sal, who finished with him in unison, "hopeless though it may be."

"You guys think I don't know how to play."

"No, not that. We think you can play. Or at least I do, I can't speak for him. I just think you can also play better."

Reo understood, slowly, the way one understands a car coming down the road.

"You're right, I can play better. Got any ideas?"

"Lessons."

Reo, still holding the guitar, thought how little money he had.

"Hard to afford it at the moment," he said. Was he embarrassed to have to admit it, or proud of his hard-won poverty, he didn't know himself.

"Ah, the old catch-22. Before you can afford lessons, you need to make more money. But can you make more money before you have the lessons? Or do the lessons need to come first? Always an interesting question." The dark-haired man studied Sal and Reo momentarily, then skipped back to the door.

"Well, I'd love to ponder this fascinating topic all afternoon, but I have work to do," he said, waving his dismissal, wrist backward like some diva.

"That's twelve dollars and ninety-six cents," said Sonoma Sal.

Reo took out his wallet and fished for some bills, handing over a ten and five.

"Who is that guy?" he asked quietly.

"Him? Oh, he's my boss. The guy who owns this shop. Maron Laverov."

"Does he teach lessons?"

"Him? Oh, no, he makes guitars. Plays well enough I suppose, but doesn't teach."

"Oh." Reo heard himself answer.

"Say, why don't you stop by my apartment some time this week. How about tomorrow, seven o'clock? I'll write it down." Sal tore off the receipt, scribbled an address on it, and handed it to Reo with his change.

"Say, seven?"

"Okay."

"Good. That's settled then. Enjoy your new, improved capo."

The afternoon light had almost faded as he worked his way back through the people heading home from their jobs. He bought an apple at a sidewalk market, rested the guitar case on its end and ate it right on the street. The sun was setting somewhere beyond the city's looming skyline, and he felt, not for the first time, that he would like to follow it, see where it goes when it leaves here.

But today he had promised to go to Ted's house for a get-together, or, as Ted called it, "play a few songs and have a few beers." He headed down Bleecker Street toward Jonas Waverly's apartment, where they were to meet for another ride to Queens.

19–You Gotta Have The Girl

Reo came out of the subway on a cool, mid-summer evening, feeling as if everything was in rhythm today, the people on the train had all seemed at peace, riding along in their separate worlds. The sky was a faraway blue with pale pink ribbons of pointillist dots slicing across it in three wide stripes, and the air smelled fresh, so unusual for a New York evening that he noticed it right away. Even the old woman who stuck a cardboard box in his face, shaking the coins and looking into his eyes, seemed to smile for once, vaguely staring past his eyes toward his right ear.

"Money for food," she pleaded in her cracked, soaked voice. He fished in his pocket and felt a round coin, drew it out of his pocket and put it in the box without looking at it, seeing, when he removed his hand, it was a quarter.

"Money for food," the woman repeated, as if it were in an old comic routine where the woman just keeps asking for money until the man loses it and starts yelling, tearing out his hair and stamping his feet.

But Reo just smiled and stepped around her, crossing the street toward the Folk Life. That's when he noticed the sign:

"Tuesday: Dollar Night $1" it read, and listed six singers for that very evening: Jonas, Franklin, Ted, Eddie, Callisto and a woman from the open mike, Roxy Dexter, a blond and curvy young woman who sang with a high tremolo that somehow remained soft, never shrill. And her pitch was terrific.

It was sinking in as he walked inside that he had not heard a word about Dollar Night since the trip to Battery Park. He had been to the Folk Life since, sung at the open mike, seen Jonas and Callisto there and made a point of saying hello. He had sat with Ted on a back bench for a beer the previous week, and no one had said a thing about it.

It was not very busy yet, still early, and the only face he recognized was Eddie, who like himself had been there when the idea came up.

"Too bad we only had room for six people," Eddie said at once.

Tony walked over and wiped the bar in front of Reo, then wrung out the towel under the bar.

"You want somethin'?" he asked.

Reo looked at the bar owner and Eddie and figured it was as good a time as any to ask about a job. There was an empty bar stool, and he leaned over toward it, sliding his guitar along the bar until he reached it and sat down. Tony came down the bar, cleaning a glass inside and out with a small white rag.

"You want a beer?"

"Can I ask you something?" He began softly, not wanting to be overheard.

"Ok, you gonna ask me anyway," Tony replied, also lowering his voice.

"What can I do to get a job here?" he said quietly.

"Job? Doing what?"

"A singing job."

"Ohm," said Tony, nodding his head with a faint gleam in his eye. "I thought you wanted a job."

"You know, a booking. Would you give me a chance to sing here sometime?" It was so hard to put it into words, he exhaled when he finished, as if he'd been holding his breath.

Tony rubbed the glass and set it down, and fixed his gaze on Reo.

"You gotta the following?" he asked, simply. It was one of two phrases Tony always used that everyone quoted. He knew the other wouldn't be far behind.

"Well, I've been playing some other clubs uptown and in Brooklyn, coffeehouses, and stuff like that."

Tony studied him.

"You gotta the girl?"

There it was, just as Ted had mimicked for him when he had asked how Ted had gotten hired for his upcoming show.

"Why, is that necessary?"

Tony nodded, pursing his lips, rubbing the glass.

"No, I mean, I booka you, who's a gonna come?"

"Well, I'll tell everybody I know."

"Ok, that covers the guest list."

Reo nodded, aware he could not promise an audience. He hoped to play for an audience and do well, that Tony would give him that chance.

"What if you hire me some night when there's already an audience?"

"You mean like a opening act."

"Ok, sure."

Tony picked up another glass and inserted the towel inside.

"You gotta have a the girl. Otherwise, nobody's a gonna come."

"What if you already had a woman singer and I open the show? Don't you have some women headliners?"

"Well, then you gotta the girl and people gonna come. But then why I need a you?"

Reo studied Tony, stuffing the small towel into another glass, and started to laugh, realizing Tony was playing with him. Tony was enjoying this, he had probably had this very conversation dozens, even hundreds of times, and from Tony's viewpoint, it was going very well. At the same time, he sensed a twinkle in his eye, as if he liked him and wanted it to work out.

Eddie stood up and started toward them, and Reo modulated his voice to keep the conversation private. Perhaps he had been listening the whole time.

"Ok, thanks," Reo said quickly, thinking that was probably as far as Tony was going to go for the moment, and that if he was going to be turned down, it wasn't going to be in front of Eddie.

"So, you staying for the show?"

Reo looked away for a moment, noticing it was still light outside. He was about to leave, shake Eddie's hand, stoop down and pick up his guitar case and drift away, when he looked up and saw a short, squat bottle of beer on the bar.

"That's a for you," Tony pointed to Reo.

He set the guitar case down and sat on the stool again.

"Sure, Eddie," he said with a smile.

He nursed the beer for a few minutes when Ted walked in.

"Hey, Reo, glad you could make it," he grinned, extending a hand. "And drinking the house brand, too."

"Yeah, Tony bought me this."

"Oh, he's buying? That sounds good. Hey, can I get a beer?"

Tony walked down the bar to where Ted stood next to Reo's seat.

"You can't afford to drink here. I know," Tony said, rubbing the inside of a glass with his towel. He reached under the bar with one hand and popped open a beer, handing Ted one of the short, squat bottles and walking away.

"You see,' Ted said with a smile, "he knows great artists when he sees them."

"You mean, buys them a beer."

"Exactly," Ted beamed, took a sip, then grimaced. "Oh, well, at least it's free."

They were halfway through the beer when a tall, lanky blond man Reo had seen at the open mike sat down on his other side.

"Gentlemen," he interrupted their conversation, "it's time we met. I have seen you at the open mikes and enjoyed your work tremendously. May I buy you each a beer?"

Before Reo could reply, Ted said, "sure." And, whispering to Reo, "watch this."

Tony appeared behind the bar and was duly asked to provide some nourishment for "the fine artists sitting beside me at the bar."

Tony reached under the bar and produced two slender, green bottles with thick, foil labels on the front.

"Ah, the good stuff," Ted said to Reo. "It's good to have fans."

20–See You Around

It was a sweaty, humid evening in August when he met Ted on MacDougal Street, hanging out on the sidewalk with his hands in his pockets. It was 7 pm, a clear sky but still heavy air, as if it was going to be a long night.

They went for coffee and it turned into dinner, a slender plate of sausages and potatoes and Greek salad in one of the neighborhood falafel places. Ted told Reo that Jonas had left town for a month; Ted, not teaching during the summer, was hanging out at the apartment to be closer to the scene. But Jason had a girlfriend over, and thus, Ted had to go out.

"Are you staying there?" Reo, who was still crashing in the Chelsea brownstone until his friend tossed him, wondered out loud.

"Oh, it's just til Jonas gets back, probably," Ted smiled. He was an agreeable guy, a curly-haired Italian with a broad face and an ever-present cigarette. Nothing seemed to bother him in his daily life; the only things that bothered Ted were people who didn't get the music, who didn't understand it was a significant thing happening, who just walked on by or talked in the bar when people were playing. The rest of it, Ted was fine.

They hung around Folk Life for a couple of hours before someone invited them to a party somewhere else; the show at the club was boring anyway, some actress who'd been on television and could draw a crowd, but couldn't sing and had uninteresting songs. So they went to the west edge of the Village, to a small loft building overlooking the dilapidated wooden piers and torn fences by the Hudson River, and climbed three flights of stairs to a large, marijuana-scented apartment, where a single floor lamp with a towel draped over it was the only light. A slow, sultry jazz recording was playing as Reo gazed over the twenty or so people in the room and saw Callisto on the couch, leaning back, the seat empty beside her. He sat down next to her, and she opened her eyes and smiled dreamily, took a long sip of something from a large plastic cup, and handed it to him. She was humming along with the music. He looked into the cup, at the deep red wine almost to the bottom, and drank it in one motion. She fell against him, swaying in slow time to the music.

"Dance with me," she whispered in his ear, sounding more sober than he expected. He held her up, her head on his shoulder, stepping slowly to the smokey music in the distance.

Jason Waverly walked across the room with a beer in his hand, shaking his head at Reo.

"Oh shit," he said, then walked on.

Callisto was dead on her feet but still moving; a slow shuffle kept her from dropping off.

"I shouldn't be doing this," she said in his ear, sounding clear-voiced and serious even as she fell against him. She repeated it.

"Doing what? Dancing?" Reo replied. Finally, Ted walked over and said he was going; Reo asked him to help him get Callisto to a cab.

"I don't want to go home," she murmured.

They went downstairs. Ted flagged a taxi and dropped them off in Chelsea, where he snuck her into the four-story brownstone, entering at street level onto the third floor. He led her silently to his room on the top floor, where he lit a candle and stood watching her look around.

It was a child's bedroom, a small space empty except for a few bookshelves, with a tiny table holding a clock and the candle. She was certainly a girl child, leaving behind pretty, pink and purple stuffed animals, books, and homemade drawings, random shapes colored perfectly within the lines.

A sleeping space was built into the wall, a narrow bed with a thin mattress and a single blanket. Grateful to have a place of any kind to sleep, he had been here a month and had no visitors. Until now.

Callisto managed to get her light jacket off before falling on the bed. She stretched her legs out until they met the opposite wall, then pushed herself along the bed until she could extend them fully. With nowhere else to sit or lie down, he removed his jacket and sat on the bed. Callisto wasn't moving, so he gave her a light shove toward the wall and stretched out on the mattress, squeezing himself in over the wooden frame.

"What do you want from me?" she asked over her shoulder, her back to him, just when he thought she was asleep.

He felt a sadness around her, something there all night, and now weighing her down.

"I want to see you smile," he said.

She turned her face toward him.

"You'll have to work for it," she whispered, and began turning toward him, spiraling herself slowly around, until her lips were so close that neither would ever know who made the first move to kiss. It was a long, slow kiss, with open lips and tongues and teeth. A hand on her back drew her toward him, and before long they were undressed, sliding under the blanket with their hands all over each other. She was surprisingly substantial in his arms, strong and full-bodied in a way that belied her slim wistfulness in clothing.

"I don't have any protection," she said, wide-eyed and breathing hard.

"All right," he said quietly, catching his breath; then they were kissing again.

When he woke up, she was sitting on the edge of the bed, her clothes on. It was 8:30 am and gray outside the single window.

"I have to go," she said. "I have to go to work today."

"Saturday?"

"Yes. Can you walk me out?"

He got dressed and walked her to the subway, where she gave him a perfunctory kiss and went down the stairs. He asked for her phone number, and she wrote it down for him, then looked into his eyes.

"I'm not who you think I am," she said.

"No? Who are you?"

"I'm unprotected. I'm at risk. I'm isolated."

"I'm on your side," he said.

She smiled quickly, then looked away.

"I'd like to believe that," she mused. "But I do have to go."

That night he had dinner with Zeke, who asked him what was on his mind, he seemed distracted.

"I am trying to understand someone, I guess, not having a lot of luck."

"Callisto, huh?"

Reo looked at him with raised eyebrows.

"Oh, it's all over town. Everybody saw you leave the party. Did you sleep with her?"

"That's none of your business."

"Well I guess you did, or you'd say no."

He ignored Zeke, took a bite of his tostada and a swig of beer.

"She said she feels unprotected, isolated. What do you think she meant?"

"Her? Who ever knows what she means? I tell ya, there's lots better fish in the sea than that one. She knows I see completely through her. She'd never say something like that to me."

"She seems frightened, as if she's scared or something."

Zeke took a bite of his food and twirled his fork.

"I could see how she'd feel that way. She's been Jonas' project, he has been talking about how great she is to everyone, trying to get Tony O to hire her, making his friends sit and listen to her songs in his apartment. She's all right, I guess. I suppose you're thinking of being her boyfriend or something."

"Me? I don't know what to think."

"My advice is not think about it too much. But if you want her, you'll have to court her. She's been hurt very badly. Now's the time, if you're going to try."

"What do you mean?"

"Didn't you hear? Jonas has been overseas to England. He'll be back this week."

Reo tried once to phone her, got her machine and left a short message. When she didn't come to the open mike on Monday, he called Tuesday in the early evening, and found her home.

"What do you want from me?" she asked again in her clear, firm voice.

"I'd like to see you," he said simply.

"I don't think I can," she answered.

"What does that mean? You don't want to see me?"

"I can't see you."

"Why not?"

"I can't say."

"Why not?"

"I'm sorry, I know this is hurting you."

"Can we talk in person?" he asked her again, and she finally agreed to meet him the next evening for coffee. He got to the small Chelsea restaurant to find her already eating a sandwich. They made small talk about the open mike until a waitress brought his coffee, and the conversation turned.

"So what's the big secret?" he asked her.

She sighed.

"There's no big secret. But I'm in trouble."

"What trouble?"

"For being with you."

He sat back and folded his arms.

"What's wrong with that?"

"I was warned I shouldn't even try to be friends with you. I should have listened."

"I'm beginning to feel insulted," he said. "Like people are talking about me behind my back."

"They are. And about me, too."

"Well, I don't care."

"I have to care."

"Why?" he asked her, spreading his palms, leaning on his elbows.

"Because I love someone else," she said.

He hadn't expected this, although, he realized suddenly, he should have. He sat back against the booth and took a sip of coffee.

"I see," he replied, after it had sunk in.

"Do you?"

"Does he love you?"

"He says he does."

"What do you think?"

"Sometimes, when we're alone, I believe he does. I believe he thinks he does, too, which is different. But he has other girls, so I probably have to leave him soon."

Reo sat quietly, aware she never asked anything about himself, if he had a girlfriend, if he loved anyone. With a brief sadness, he understood she didn't want to know.

"Well," he said softly. "Then you're really a free woman, aren't you?" It was more a statement than a question.

"You're the person I'm not allowed to see. If he knew I was here it would be all over for me."

"Maybe it would be better that way."

"I thought you'd say that. I'm flattered. And you are attractive. But I'm not in a position to give you anything. Anything. Well, maybe we can be friends. If you understand that's all it can be."

He rested against the cheap vinyl booth, swirling the coffee in his cup with his left hand.

"I can't see you," she repeated quietly. "Do you understand that?"

"I understand, yes," he said, watching her spread a pool of ketchup on her dish with a fork. Abruptly, she stuck it straight into a french fry so it stood upright in the middle of her plate, and looked up slowly, returning his stare, her light blue eyes unblinking for so long that he felt he had to speak.

"So, as your friend, I should stay away from you," he said with a faint smile. "Is that what you mean?"

She stared across the diner, mostly empty in the mid-evening, and asked if he had any new songs. He said yes, he had some lyrics in his pocket. She reached out a hand.

"Let me see," she said. He fumbled through a pocket and found a folded page of lyrics scrawled in jagged lines. She read them out loud:

If I show up at 5 am
and knock upon your window
and you get up and let me in
then I will know
I will know
you love me too

She smiled and asked if he would sign it and give it to her.

"I hope the girl you wrote this for does love you," she said. "You need to be loved by someone who really cares for you."

He let that go by without a response, and when they had finished their coffee and paid the check he walked her home. It was late, and she had to go to sleep early because she was very tired, she had been up late the night before and had to work in the morning. Then, as he was about to leave, she surprised him, quietly took his hand.

"You can stay if you want to. If you keep your clothes on."

They lay on her bed, their jeans and shirts still on; she kissed him on the cheek and whispered "goodnight," nestled her head in the crook of his arm, closed her eyes and made no further sound or motion. He lay next to her, his arm stiffening after a while in its immobilized position, and found enough space on the single bed to manage a sleepless night. It seemed as if he had just, finally, drifted off, when she woke him very early, and made him wait as she changed into her stylish slacks and white shirt.

They walked together to the subway; she stepped off in midtown, ruffling his hair with her hand, giving him a big, warm smile as she left him on the downtown train.

"It was nice sleeping with you again," she said. "I'll see you around."

21–Dog Days

The summer deepened into hazy afternoons of sweat and blistering sun, before it darkened late one afternoon and unleashed a two hour thunderstorm on the streets. Reo was hanging out in a West Side apartment near Xanadu, apartment-sitting for a guy he barely knew from the coffeehouse next door, listening to old Eagles albums and drinking coffee, scribbling fragments of thoughts on paper, scattering them around the room on various surfaces, a desk, a chair, a table, the floor.

just as soon as the rain
stops beating on the glass
I'll walk you out to the garden
each word might be our last
you say it's easy for you now
I hope it's easy for a long time
what is there to say
that would ever change the way
that it's
in the morning I'll be gone
time

He went to the open mike and sang it; no one he knew was there, it was full of a different cast, summer kids with a guitar and a song. He sang it for the guys in the coffeehouse later that week, sitting around with beers in their hands after the customers had all left. Joseph Flanagan nodded slowly, beaming at him through rimless, round glasses. His friend Josiah, twirling his beard of ringlets into a tapered point, was the first to speak.

"Going somewhere?" he asked in a serious tone.

Reo gave it some thought.

"Not really. I mean, it's not a declaration or anything. It's a song,"

Turk, sitting at a chessboard across the room, exhaled a blast of smoke from a cigarette and burst into his big, hearty laugh.

"I'm so happy to hear that," he guffawed, nearly gagging.

Reo shrugged and grinned.

"Well, imagine it as a real song. What do you think?"

No one spoke for a moment, as Joseph Flanagan leaned forward on his lawn chair. He started to say something, then stopped and sighed. Then he tried again.

"I think you're wasting your time."

Reo looked around. Turk was staring at the chess figures on their board. Josiah sat eyes closed and palms together, pointing upward as if in prayer.

"You mean the song?"

"You know what I mean."

"No, I don't. What do you mean?" he said with a laugh.

"I mean you're wasting your time. You're wasting your life. I don't know what you should be doing, but this isn't it."

Reo didn't say anything this time.

"I know it's not what you want to hear, but that's not my problem," continued Joseph, and looked around at Josiah and Turk, slowly shaking his head. "You should use your education instead."

Reo saw Joseph lean forward and spread his hands out, palms up in the classic what-are-ya-gonna-do position, and thought about what Joseph was saying. It wasn't the first time someone had told him this; he thought it was some people's way of avoiding a new idea, or a new thought. But this was Joseph, who had taken him in when he had nowhere to go. He wanted Joseph to understand what it meant to him, to write a song.

"You know, you're right," Reo said, sitting back against his chair. "I am going to have to unlearn a lot."

"What do you mean?" Josiah opened.

"I mean I've been educated, but I don't know what people out there are doing. I have all this book learning, and no real experience in life."

Turk chuckled, a low, infectious sound that lightened the mood immediately.

"Experience, I've always tried to avoid experience. It's what you call it when you get screwed," he said with a contagious laugh. Josiah and Reo joined in; only Joseph stayed out of the laughter that filled the room.

Reo wasn't giving in, but he did have the feeling time was slipping away, as his first summer of freedom had yielded nothing but a part-time day job and few open mikes. He found himself looking through a newspaper someone left in Xanadu, reading an ad for a company called U-Drive-It that loaned you a vehicle with no rental charge, if you paid the gas and delivered it. Two days later, he promised to drive a small truck to a northern suburb of Chicago, signing a written contract.

The next afternoon a hot, sticky blast of mid-August gray lay over the city like an unwashed blanket, and Reo was wandering through the trails of Riverside Park when he heard his name, not loudly, as if escaping from someone's lips without prior consent. He turned and saw Delfina a few steps away, about to turn and leave.

"Delfina," he said quietly. "Hi."

She took a tentative step in his direction. She was wearing a white dress flecked with color, a modernistic pattern of pink, green, blue, red, yellow, purple and orange on white, open across the shoulders but fully pleated to below her knees.

"Nice dress," he said. "Very pretty."

She smiled, flattered.

"Thank you."

"Hey, can I ask you something?"

"All right."

"What did you decide about going to the other school?"

"The one in Pittsburgh?"

"That's the one."

"I decided to go," she said, sounding confident enough.

"Good," he said. "I always thought you should."

She bristled visibly.

"I'm sorry," he said, "I didn't mean it that way. I think you should get an education, the best you can, and the people who belong in your life will be there."

"You wouldn't be there."

"Well, as I remember you kissed me off," he answered. "So we'll never know."

She studied him for a moment but didn't move. She was as pretty as ever, slim and shapely in her summer dress, and wanted a real conversation.

"I hope you do really well. When are you going?" he asked.

"Next week. I have to move a whole lot of stuff. I have an apartment rented off campus, and I have to bring my own furniture."

"Wouldn't it be cheaper to buy it there?"

"I want my own stuff. I'm moving out of my mother's."

And then he said it, before it even occurred to think about it, the words escaped his lips in return.

"I'm driving a small truck to Chicago. Do you want a ride?"

From her initial recoil, to saying she wanted to think about it, to saying it was really a good idea if he was willing to do that, took only a handful of moments, once he told her it would cost her nothing. Two days later he pulled up at her mother's apartment building in a twenty year-old milk truck with a sliding door on the driver's side, and two tiny seats in front of an otherwise empty box the size of a small room. Delfina was astounded, confessed on the spot she had presumed it wouldn't work out and had been making other plans. But he opened the back doors wide, and, seeing the empty space and remembering he had said it wouldn't cost anything, she did the math and told him to put the hazard lights on, she would get some help to load it. Several phone calls and two hours later they were on the road, loaded up with suitcases and chairs, three cardboard boxes, a mattress, a desk, and a couch, all piled behind them. Still, it wasn't until they had left New York City, crossed the George Washington Bridge and fanned out into the open road that they discovered the truck would not do more than 40 miles an hour, floored, standing on the gas pedal.

They bounced along, perched on the hard bicycle-style seats of the local delivery vehicle.

"Normally, Pittsburgh would be eight or nine hours," he said. "Like this, a couple days."

"Did you know about this?"

"It never occurred to me. But hey, we'll get you there, me and this old truck. Let's check out the radio."

He turned it on, and soon she took over working the dial, settling on an oldies station with a lot of big chesty ballads; they drove through the early afternoon, squirming uncomfortably on the stiff seats that supported their weight, across New Jersey into the late afternoon sun. They stopped twice for bathrooms and once for gas, and found themselves a hundred miles into Pennsylvania as the night grew long, when a heartfelt voice throbbed through the speakers with a twang and a slide guitar.

> I was wondering where all the love had gone
> I was thinking of myself for way too long
> I gave in to thinking it was all remember when
> Then tonight I fell in love with you again

"Oh, I always loved this song," Reo said cheerfully.

"Really? What is it?"

"Well, listen to it. He's saying he always loved her, and still does."

She studied him from across the car, as he sang along with it, two full choruses at the end, until she was humming it herself. As the song ended she stood up and turned around, bracing herself by holding onto the framed doorway to the back of the truck. In the back there were two windows, both small and high up near the ceiling, and one had a slider to open it a few inches. Otherwise it was a box with a wooden floor and aluminum sides, rivets everywhere. All her worldly belongings sat in a pile in the center, hardly filling the room.

"I'd like to sleep sometime," she said.

"There's a rest area in two miles," he called to her. "I'll pull in there."

Conspiring to avoid being noticed, they parked the truck at the end of the parking lot under some low-hanging trees, uncovered the mattress, cleared off the floor and laid it down. Then they looked up, at each other.

"Are you going to sleep here too?" she asked evenly.

"I'm going to go use the bathroom. Want to walk with me?"

They went their separate ways into the brick doorways that housed the highway bathrooms, then met on the way back out. They walked slowly, sauntering toward the truck parked in the distant corner.

"Is it okay to stay here?"

"I suppose some cop could make us move. But I don't see anyone around," he replied. "So let's take a rest."

They stretched out on the mattress, both wearing blue jeans and t-shirts. He lay back and put his hands behind his head, staring at the brown-speckled ceiling.

"It's hard to believe anybody would bother to bring this rust bucket to Illinois," he shook his head.

She lay on her side, waiting for him to turn toward her.

"You know, I didn't have a lot of boyfriends before you," she said. She had a good voice, clear and full, even when she whispered.

"No?"

"No. You're the second guy I had sex with. The first one was late at night, he was the brother of a friend, I was at a party and we all stayed over, so I slept with him and had sex twice, and never saw him again. And then you came along."

"You waited a long time."

She didn't respond to that, and he rolled onto his side, facing her, extending his elbow to raise himself off the mattress. Quietly she met his eyes without making a sound or moving.

"It was worth it," she finally said.

He returned her gaze and they drifted effortlessly toward each other, meeting in the middle for a kiss. He felt her pressing against him below, and then her hands on his hips; as they flattened themselves against each other and ground their jeans together, he put his hand down her backside, grabbing her bare cheek, pressing her against him as their kiss deepened, open-mouthed and wet with desire.

And then they broke apart, leaned back and realized where they were, who they were, and what they were doing. He knew she would tell him to back off and leave her alone.

Delfina bounced up onto her knees and took the hem of her tee-shirt and twisted it right over her head. Wasting no time, she unfastened her bra and slid it off, then pushed her jeans down to her ankles and kicked them from her feet. She looked at him and smiled, biting her lip.

"Come on, then," she said, and lay back against the mattress.

22–Chicago By Storm

He hit Chicago two afternoons later, after leaving Delfina at her new apartment, emptying the van, helping to carry everything up the stairs of the small white wooden house on the little street. She asked him not to stay, she said she didn't want her roommate to know about him; then, she held onto him as he began to leave.

"Come see me when you can," she looked up and whispered. "Ok?"

He made it to Indiana before he stopped for the night. Delfina had taken the mattress, so he bunked down on the hard floor with his knapsack and guitar and wrote a song. He awoke early, drove toward Chicago through the morning, hitting the vistas of Lake Shore Drive in early afternoon, when the sun was lighting it all up and the glass towers glittered as brightly as the lake. He kept going into the far north suburbs, green and lush in the late summer, and followed the highway to Evanston. He found the address, delivered the truck, signed the papers, and walked out to the street with his guitar and a knapsack.

"Music clubs?" they had said. "Not around here." And so he headed out, walking two long blocks of houses and apartments toward Chicago, toward the lakefront skyscrapers and distant stations in neighborhoods and avenues whose names told him nothing. He found the elevated train and waited until the steel cars arrived, then boarded and grabbed a steel pole. They were riding slowly around a long curve, leaning to the left, as everyone grew silent and fixed their distant gazes on the backside of a row of tenements, where a naked couple was having sex on a porch table, the man on his back, the woman bouncing up and down on top of him. There were some snickers, and then some whispered "oh look," and then more laughter as everyone realized everyone else saw it, before the train sped up and left the couple behind.

"I hope she got off," a woman yelled, pronouncing it "awf" with great effect. A few people laughed, others went back to their conversations, their magazines, their headphones. Reo stood in the corner, holding the vertical chrome bar, as the train banged its way south, swinging him toward the window. A young woman was seated on a bench, reading.

"Excuse me," he said quietly.

"You're excused," she said without looking up.

He swung again toward the center as the train lurched, then straightened himself up.

"I'm sorry to interrupt. May I ask you something?"

The young woman, a brown-haired bundle huddled in the corner in a sweater and skirt, looked at him without speaking.

"I'm looking for some cafes or bars that have music. Where would I go in Chicago?"

She shook her head.

"I don't know."

"Where would you go?"

"I'd go to Lincoln Avenue, I guess."

"Lincoln Avenue. Where's that?"

"You should get off at this stop. Walk to your left. You'll find it." She turned back to her book.

He did get off at that stop, walked a long block to his left and found a well-lit restaurant on the triangular-shaped corner, where he spotted a rack of newspapers. Grabbing one of the free arts papers, he went inside and sat at the counter.

"What'll ya have?"

"Coffee, please."

"Like I couldn'a guessed."

He looked around and spotted two men in a booth. They were wearing short-sleeved shirts and pants, drinking beers. But, what interested him more was, each had a guitar case stretched out next to his seat.

The waitress set the cup down in front of him.

"Excuse me," he said. "Do you know those guys over there?"

"They play at Your Mama's Ghost, up the street, I think."

"Up the street? Which way?"

She pointed up the block.

"There are clubs all 'round here," she drawled. "You new in town or somethin'?"

"Yeah," he replied. "Any places looking for music?"

"Don't know 'bout that," she shook her head. "Seems a lot of it around already."

He walked the neighborhood and managed to sign up for two open mikes an hour apart; first, he signed up for a 10 pm spot at Your Mama's Ghost. But it was only 7:30, so he left before the music started and found a cavernous blockhouse down the street with a blue neon vertical sign from the 1950s, two letters missing. It said Canary Coalmines, but inside was a large room with a ceiling two stories high, and an echo that made the music seem far away from the small but enthusiastic crowd of 20 or so, mostly drinking beer and talking loudly. A young man with glasses and red hair sang and strummed a mandolin through a chorus of "I'm down to seeds and stems again," as two men seated at a front table raised their beer pitchers and cheered. The red-haired man was succeeded by an older man about Reo's height, with thinning brown hair and rimless spectacles. He wore a blue pinstriped shirt and a suede vest, and a pair of baggy khakis under which he bobbed up and down to his song.

Just a bowl of butter beans
Pass the cornbread if you please
I don't want no collared greens
Just a bowl of good old butter beans

he sang, and the crowd good-naturedly waved back at him.

Reo stepped over to the bar.

"Is it possible to sign up to play?" he asked the bartender.

"Sure, honey," she smiled, nodding. "You want anything?"

"I'll have a beer," he said. "Who do I see?"

She directed him down the bar to a clipboard, where a slender, black-haired man with a black mustache squinted at him. He looked either Asian or American Indian, or both, with angular eyes and copper skin, but spoke with an urban accent.

"You want to play?"

"If I can."

The man leaned forward and spun the clipboard toward him.

"Sign in, please."

Reo carefully printed Reo MacGregor on the sheet and handed it to him. The man squinted at it, and spoke without looking up.

"Reo MacGregor," he read, emphasizing the "Mac."

"That's right."

In the moments of silence that followed Reo decided he liked this guy, if only for pronouncing his name correctly. He had a voice that sounded sly and furtive, as if he were making sure no one overheard.

"Is it a long wait?" Reo asked him.

"You want to go on next?" was the reply.

Was he being sarcastic?

"Is that a question? Sure."

"Ok. Tune up."

And true enough, five minutes later he was on stage, a good five feet above the concrete floor, staring into the thin crowd scattered around a half dozen tables, not a soul looking in his direction.

> In a hotel room by the airport
> we will meet again, my love
> we'll fly in from our separate lives for a
> stolen night of love
> and you will kiss my fingertips and need to cry
> still afraid to break the silence

It was the song he had made up last night in the back of the truck, his image of her as he drove off into the afternoon haze.

"Hey, play something fast," someone yelled as he finished the song, earning a smatter of handclaps.

Reo strummed a couple of chords and launched into "Hard Times," trying to remember the words he had first sung at Ted's apartment party. It had a good, strong chorus, he thought, and he ripped into the words with a harder, more vehement vocal than he had ever attempted.

> There's hard times a comin'
> hard times over the hill
> you can't buy 'em off you can't shout 'em down
> if hard times are comin' they will

he called out. The crowd got visibly excited, sitting up and bobbing in place to the fast tempo of his strumming, and nodding their heads as if agreeing with the words. It was clearly a down message song, and in his own mind it didn't contribute much to the party. But he had rocked the crowd, he could feel the buzz in the air as he left the stage to solid applause and a ripple of interest. He was packing his guitar into the case when the bartender stepped over toward him.

"Ready for that beer?" she smiled at him, and held out an ice-frosted mug. She was almost his height, with long straight blond hair, a round face and the vague shape of a black t-shirt and black jeans.

"Thanks," he grinned.

"I'm Sarah," she said. "And that's on me." Still smiling at him, she went back behind the bar.

Your Mama's Ghost was the antithesis of Canary Coalmines, a new, fresh-smelling wood-paneled storefront with a carpeted stage and a long bar along the left side. A large sign behind the stage said

> Quiet
> This means you.
> Yeah, you!

in hand-written purple letters, and patrons would occasionally "ssh!" someone nearby. It was "a listening room" and said so in bold block letters out front, right under the wavy old-fashioned script of the club's name.

When Reo arrived about 9:30 pm the bartender wiped the bar in front of him and said "Where ya been?"

"I played another open mike," he said. "You didn't call my name yet, did you?"

"No, but soon. Do you want something?"

"I'll have a beer," he replied.

This time it arrived right away; he dug out four dollars from his wallet. The bartender watched the stage for a moment, where the same brown-haired older man in striped shirt, vest and khakis was singing and playing the banjo.

"In fact, you're on next. Where you from?"

"New York," he said.

"Really?" grinned the bartender, a tall, thin man with a black straightline mustache. "You working there?"

Reo set down his guitar case.

"You mean in clubs? Sometimes."

"I was in New York once. I'll tell you about it someday. What clubs do you play?"

Reo took a sip. It was much better beer than at the other bar.

"Folk Life, well the open mike. I also worked at some coffeehouses around the city."

"Ah. Coffeehouses. What music do you play?"

"I'm a songwriter."

The man stood up and nodded with an expression that was either approving or sarcastic, Reo couldn't tell.

"Oh, a songwriter. One of those."

"Is that a bad thing?"

"Not around here." There was a round of applause from the nearly full room, as the bartender appraised him.

"What's your name?"

"Reo MacGregor," he said clearly.

"Reo Macwhat?"

"MacGregor."

The bartender nodded.

"I'm Jim Holdman," he said.

Reo smiled.

"Good to meet you."

"You too. Okay, you're on. Follow me. Get your guitar out."

Setting the towel on the bar, Jim Holdman walked toward the front of the room, right onto the stage. He yanked the chrome gooseneck into a taller mike position, than pulled over a stool and sat down.

"Hi folks, how are you all doing?" he began to a murmur of approval.

"That was Martin Lehman, good stuff Martin, new in town. I tell ya folks, there must be some kind of word out there in America for all these new talents coming to town. Take this one, fr'instance, all the way from New York. New York! Says he's a songwriter too. There are some pretty good ones there, I know, I was there once, I couldn't compete against all the good songwriters that were already there."

"You got drunk" someone called, and laughter erupted around the room. Jim sat back and put up his hands as if in mock protest.

"I know, I know, I did. That's why this next act intrigues me. All the way from New York. Well here he is, Reo MacWhat."

He stepped onstage to the applause and sat on the stool. He didn't usually play sitting down, but decided to take the stage just as he found it.

"Well. It's Reo MacGregor," he smiled. "Nice to meet you folks."

> Marcie Jane says come on down
> to the river and walk me round in circles
> and please don't ask me why

The song played to a medium strum, the chords and lyrics building in pitch and power as he turned on his voice, filling the room with high notes.

> I want to follow every ocean wave
> play the symphonies I've never played and
> someday tell that Marcie Jane
> good-bye

It was a song he had written months before, during his early time with Delfina. It was not about her, and Delfina had loved it at first, told him it was beautiful; until she began to think he was "the goodbye kind," as she called it, and would tell her goodbye too. Still, he was proud of it, thought it a beautiful song, it's unusual melody and romantic passion giving him a chance to sing.

The applause was polite but nothing special. He took a deep breath and launched a full-speed guitar strum, the sound of an old folk song.

> If you ain't got the do re mi, boys
> you ain't got the do re mi

he sang, an old song he had learned in college. It was a song many recognized, and as he let his voice get rougher, lower and more open, the room got quieter, and he saw eyes looking at him, really studying him.

He looked at the floor, still strumming, then faced them again, finishing the words with a slight twang, hitting the last chord clean, taking a quick bow.

The crowd applauded generously, and as he left the stage Jim Holdman looked at him and raised his eyebrows, giving nothing away.

Reo barely heard the next intro as he put the guitar back in the case and walked the length of the bar to his beer, passing a table where someone called "good job" to him. Soon he was back at the end of the bar, behind the crowd, by the front window.

Jim Holdman walked over to him.

"Want another beer?"

"Maybe in a while."

"So is that what you sing in New York?"

Reo smiled, as if to himself.

"Sure, all the time."

"They like that first song at the Folk Life?"

He had sung it many times in Xanadu, sometimes by request, but didn't remember if he'd sung it at the Folk Life.

"Hey, do you ever hire people to sing here?" he asked.

"Sure, all the time," he said. "Excuse me." And he walked down the bar, taking a glass and filling it with draft. He filled several more glasses, poured a handful of shots and stopped to watch the singer onstage, who was telling a long story to the crowd, interrupted by bursts of laughter.

"Are you gonna sing a song or what?" Jim Holdman called to him.

The singer, a thin man with large eyes and a triangular-shaped wedge of brown hair, looked at the bar, then addressed the crowd.

"So we had it stuffed," he finished to wild laughter.

> It was winter
> when she came into my life
> oh oh
> that little dog of mine

he sang, simultaneously picking the bass notes of the melody. This guy is good, Reo thought, as the brown-haired man with the blue pinstriped shirt walked up to him at the bar.

"Hey, you just followed me at two open mikes. What's your name?"

"Reo. Reo MacGregor," he said.

"Cool. I'm Martin Lehman. What are you doing here?"

"I came to play this open mike," he answered.

"No, I mean here in Chicago, what are you doing? Are you on the road, or do you live here, or what?"

It was a question no one had yet asked him but himself. He had decided just to plunge ahead and go wherever it took him.

"I guess I'm on the road."

"Where are you staying?"

He looked at the older man, who stood waiting for an answer, watching him through rimless spectacles balanced halfway down his nose.

"I don't know," he replied.

"Do you need a place to stay?"

Reo took his last sip of beer. He didn't know what Martin Lehman wanted, if anything; maybe he was just being friendly. Reo remembered his performance as straightforward and old-fashioned, good time music.

"I do, actually. Why?"

"Well, you can stay at my place." Martin looked back at the stage, as if remembering something, and continued.

"Well, you don't know me. I'm a music professor here at a university. I just moved here, I have a big apartment full of boxes I haven't unpacked, and a big couch you can sleep on."

Reo stood wondering what to do, as Martin fixed his gaze on Reo, smiled, and held out a hand.

"It's okay, I heard you sing. I think I can trust you not to be an asshole," he grinned. "Come on."

23–Music Business People

Martin Lehman, who had just arrived in the city to teach Folklore and Anthropology at the State university campus downtown, made a large pot of coffee in a glass carafe and set a mug in front of Reo. They were seated around a metal table on two wooden kitchen chairs bought at a yard sale, the only furniture in sight. In the living room next to it sat the couch where Reo had slept.

"Well, the place is a mess, of course," Martin said. "My room upstairs is more or less ok, but there's not much down here."

"Thanks for taking me in."

"No problem, I kind of wanted to get to know you. I just moved here, I want to meet some of the local musicians."

Reo laughed at the irony.

"You don't live here, you're not local, I get it," said Lehman, taking a big slug of coffee. It was strong, serious coffee, and it filled his chest with warmth.

"Maybe you should be local, stick around. There's a good scene here, lots of work for the right people. What were you doing in New York?"

"Singing some. Working part time. Bumming around, I guess."

"Do you have a place to live there?"

"No, not right now."

"You're just livin' off the fat of the land, aren't you? Think you're Woody Guthrie or something?"

"I'm just wandering a bit," he replied. "I want to get out and meet some real people."

"Oh, well. Sleep on the streets a few nights and you'll meet all the real people you can handle. Well, look. You can stay here, I can use some company and I can always go upstairs when I can't. I'll give you a set of keys, you can come and go as you please, don't think you have to hang out with me all the time. Take a few days, try your hand at a few clubs."

Reo said ok, he would stick around for a while. He went back to the Coalmines and found the bartender, Sarah, who introduced him to a tall, bald man with a very large head, seated at a nearby table.

"Dirk, this is Reo MacGregor. He played here last night. He's good, well, I liked him. He wanted to ask if you have any openings."

The man leaned back in his chair, and stared at him with his mouth wide open. Then he looked down at his lap and produced an enormous black wig, which he lowered onto his bald head, dropping it into place. Taking a pair of black-rimmed eyeglasses from the table, he put them on his nose and looked at Reo.

"Thirty dollars a night," he said.

"Okay," said Reo. "When do I start?"

Dirk slid his hand across the table and reached a large, flat calendar. He pulled it close and stared at it.

"Sunday night. What's your name?"

Reo told him, had him spell it correctly, and when Dirk had written it into the calendar square for Sunday, he thanked him and walked to the bar.

"Sunday," he told her. "Thank you."

"That's good, I work that night," she smiled.

The Sunday gig went well. He played a solid hour of music for ten patrons, who listened and clapped in all the right spots. He sat at the bar and had a beer after, listening to Sarah talk to the customers in her sandpapery voice. But the bluegrass band played a two-hour set and he didn't want to spend more money on beer, so he said "good night" and went back to Lehman's. And there were other open mikes at other clubs around town, like Duke of Earl, a narrow bar with photos of performers who had played there all over the walls, many who also adorned Folk Life. This open mike, however, had only a handful of customers to listen to the half-dozen singers who showed up to play. The bartender, a rotund dark-skinned African-American with a big smile and even bigger, round eyes, had told him across the room "no more sad songs."

He was putting away his guitar in the back room, amid beer cases stacked from floor to ceiling, with an open hole in the floor to the basement. The bartender pointed down at it and said "don't go there." A large woman, with waving arms and thick, curly black hair, towered over him and said her name was Louise Gdansk. She asked if he wanted to "join her and Mick for a drink" somewhere else.

"Okay," he said. 'Why not?" And off they went, Louise driving a small, cramped box of a car, with Reo in front and Mick in the back. Mick had sung earlier than Reo—just before him in fact—had done a great set and been very difficult for Reo to follow. He was a rawboned kid from Nebraska, had a rural accent and a down-home quality, clean picking, and tried-and-true folk melodies. The small Chicago audience had taken to it, leaving Reo feeling hopelessly Northeastern by contrast, whatever that was. But he had gotten through a song that, for him, was his idea of being on the road, and what he might see:

> If you could ride this train I'm on
> you wouldn't miss your happy home
> it wouldn't take too much to make you wander

"So, you're from New York?" Mick asked, bouncing on the back seat with his hands folded on his lap, leaning forward.

"Oh, who cares? What was that second song you sang, Mick?" Louise cut into the left lane as they sped uptown.

"Oh, that was a little thing I juts been workin' awn."

"Well you juts keep workin awn it then."

"I juts will haf to."

They both burst out laughing, and she looked over at Reo.

"And you. Who are you anyway?"

"Yeah, who are you?" Mick echoed from the back seat.

She wheeled the car to the right lane at a light. They all sat there.

"My name is Reo. Reo MacGregor. I sang tonight at the open mike." He turned and faced Mick. "Right after you."

"I knew that," Mick said. "I knew that, didn't I, Lou?"

"You did. I'm sure of it."

Reo looked at Mick through the gap in the seats.

"'If I knew the way, I would come to you,' " he sang; it was a phrase Mick had sung earlier that had stuck in Reo's mind. "That was cool, I really liked that song," he finished.

"That's the one," Louise called out.

"If I knew the way, I would come to you, If I had the key, I would never do you wrong," Mick sang in the back, snapping his fingers, then stopped.

"You like that song? I'll teach it to you."

"I'd like that," Reo said. They went in reverse into a parking space. Minutes later they were upstairs in her apartment, a large all-purpose room with a stove and table and chairs.

"Ever hear of Barry Manilow?" she asked him.

"Sure. 'Mandy. You came and you gave without taking. And I sent you away. Oh Mandy.' That Barry Manilow?"

"The same."

"Louise, you got any bourbon?" Mick was rummaging under the sink.

"Not there, above the fridge," she called back.

"Anyway, I spoke to him last week, he is working on a new show."

"How about glasses?" Mick was working through the cupboards. "Oh, got it." He turned and set three shot glasses on the table, where Louise sat silent. She looked at him, as if it was his turn to say something.

"Does he write all his songs?" he asked.

"Who? What?" Mick sat down, poured each of them a shot and slapped the bottle down. He picked up a shot glass and held it to the light.

"Does Barry Manilow write all his songs?" Louise repeated for him. "I wouldn't know. Why do you ask?" And she lifted her glass halfway to her lips, her wide face breaking into a smile.

Reo picked up the shot glass and sighted the flame of the lone candle in it, swirling it carefully as he looked into the amber liquid.

"I have a song he could sing," Reo said.

Mick downed his shot in one gulp. Louise took hers slowly but in one pass. Reo downed his, too; it was good, smooth whiskey, a bourbon taste he had not often tried since he was 19, when he smuggled a pint home from New York and arrived half drunk at a dance, getting slapped in a friend's car by his girlfriend. He had stuck to scotch and beer since then.

This time, though, it tasted good, it warmed his chest and made him want more, and when the bottle went around the table it refilled his glass.

"You write all your own songs?" Mick asked.

Reo laughed, recognizing the absurdity of the question.

"Of course I do. But I know lots of other songs too, like yourself."

"You're serious about this, ain't ya?"

"Yes. Aren't you?"

"Me? Hell, no, I ain't serious about nothin', " Mick said, shaking his head, and they all laughed, a good feeling in the room.

"I know you," Louise said at last. "I have figured you out."

"Who, me?" Mick asked.

"No, him. Rayo, what's your name?"

"Reo."

"Whatever. You're the guy who thinks he's God's gift to songwriters."

"Naw, Louise, don't you think that's a little harsh?" Mick spoke up.

Reo was caught off guard, wondering what he could have said or done to provoke such a sentiment.

"I'm sorry if I have offended you somehow," he said.

"Me? Oh, no, not that."

"Then what?"

"You think you can write a song for someone like Barry? It's not that simple. Why should he listen to anything you might have to say?"

He folded his arms across his chest.

"Maybe he'd like it."

"Like what? Do you even know what he sings about? Ever sung one of his songs?"

"Sure," Reo said, breaking into a grin, remembering singing along with Delfina in the truck, just before they went in the back.

"I've sung 'Mandy' at least once," he said with a laugh. He had rarely been attracted to big, bombastic productions with waving arms and stage choreography; but like all those who listened to radio, he knew and liked some of them in spite of himself.

"Well, there you are then," she waved him away.

"So who are you? Are you in the music business or something?"

"You might say that."

"What do you do?"

"Whatever needs to be done. I organize things locally when people come to Chicago."

"Do you have a title?" Mick asked from across the small table, pronouncing it "tahytle."

Louise Gdansk shook her head.

"Not really. But I can tell you this."

"What?"

"Do you know how many people want to have Barry, or anyone like him, listen to their songs?"

"No. How many?"

"So many that he doesn't ever listen to them. He doesn't have to."

Reo laughed quietly.

"Of course not. He has too many songs to listen to any of them."

"Exactly."

"Unless someone like you played it for him."

"I don't do that."

"Why not?"

"I wouldn't want to jeopardize my relationship with him."

"Right. Why would anyone want to hear a song? What, you've never played a song for him or someone like him?" Reo asked. "Not even just sitting around, wasting time, hanging out? That's amazing."

"That's the music business," she said, as if that said it all, and was satisfied with her explanation.

"You know, when 'Mandy' was all over the radio, I was driving a milk truck from New York to Chicago. A girlfriend was moving to Pittsburgh to college, so I helped her. It was a drive-away truck, one of those where you deliver the truck for free and pay the gas. Anyway, this truck only went about 40 miles an hour and it took a long time, and that song kept playing on the radio. We were singing along with it like idiots, got all sentimental and had to stop somewhere and pull over. If you know what I mean. So I guess I should thank old Barry, if I ever meet him."

"There you go. Damn. Damn!" Mick slapped his knee, sitting upright. "Good story."

"Old Barry," she repeated. "Aren't you sweet."

Reo bent over and opened his case, taking out his guitar. He sat it on his lap and strummed a chord.

"Hey, maybe he's young at heart. So, what do you think?"

"About what?"

"Can I play a song for him?"

"No. No. Get over that idea now."

"Why not?"

"What, like on the phone?"

"Sure. Or on a tape."

Mick was looking from one to the other as if watching a ping pong match. He reached down and snapped open his guitar case, removing his aged Martin. Louise turned to him.

"How about you? Don't you want to play a song for him, too?" she addressed Mick, sarcastically raising her eyebrows.

"Me? Sure. Why not. What song do you think I should play for him?" He put the guitar across his legs and began to tune it.

"'If I Knew The Way,' " she answered immediately, and then released a long, loud sigh. Louise closed her eyes and shook her head from side to side as if trying to talk herself out of it. Reo strummed a chord for Mick, catching his eye. He was going to learn Mick's song, right then and there.

"Okay," she said at last. "Give me a tape of one song and I will listen to it."

24–Duke La Monte

"Do you know what the biggest single thing you have to think about is? What do you think it is? Getting a record deal? Money? Some girl? Hot sex with some waitress somewhere? No, it's none of those," declared the growly, cigar-smoking hulk parked on the hotel bed. As for Reo, he didn't have to say anything, didn't want to say anything, didn't want to interrupt; so he nodded, as if he understood every word, was taking it all to heart.

"It's none of those," continued Duke La Monte, waving the now-almost empty whiskey bottle in a large hand, a paw really, a gentle giant at the end of a hard night of partying.

"It's survival. That's it. If you can pick yourself up, make it work, and still look yourself in the eye and not hate what you see, you are truly a miracle worker."

Duke ended every such pronunciation with a big, gruff laugh, a whiskey-soaked burst of good humor, and Reo laughed easily, too, as the one-liners went on for an hour; it was some hours since they all left the bar, went to someone's apartment, got out the guitars and played songs for each other til the sun came up. Now Duke, the whiskey bottle, and Reo had ended up at Duke's hotel room, courtesy of the Chicago nightclub where Duke was playing later in the week.

"Hey, Duke," Reo spoke softly, his first words in a long time. "How do you look yourself in the eye?"

Duke LaMonte sat up and unleashed a grizzled burst of staccato laughter, unashamed and contagious.

"Why, painfully, I suppose," trying to squint at the tip of his nose.

Reo had never met Duke before, though he had heard of him, everyone had; he had one of his albums all through college and could sing virtually every song on it. But he could never sound like Duke; he tried imitating the raspy, primal voice and then gave up, occasionally singing one of the songs in his own way. As for his guitar, Duke was a legend, his finger stylings the best traditional treatments of many folk songs. Now here he was, one of the original Greenwich Village folk stars, holding court in a hotel room on the road.

Earlier, at the party, Duke sat there for an hour with no guitar, the only one in the circle who didn't play.

"Hey, Duke, give us a song," someone said from across the room. He looked up as their host handed him a beautiful Martin, big and blond with abalone inlay all around the sound hole. Duke's own guitar was a seasoned, round-shouldered Guild of a much older and darker vintage, and sure enough, Duke squinted at the Martin as if being handed a dish he hadn't ordered in a restaurant. Then he strummed it once and looked at all the other guitarists, nine of them, spread around the circle.

"I'll play," he rasped with a firm nod, "if no one else plays along. I don't jam." He plucked a few notes in a syncopated pattern, a slow, swinging beat, and landed on "Saint James Infirmary Blues," a minor-key progression known to musicians everywhere; the nine other guitarists in the room looked at each other and concluded he must be kidding. They all started playing along; Duke set down his guitar, then sang the impromptu band through seven full verses.

When the party broke up Reo tagged along, walking Duke back to his hotel; as Duke put it, "I need some help to kill the bottle of whiskey they gave me." Reo thus learned Duke was another sort of legendary, a non-stop fountain of hard-headed realism, a rolling analysis of the very things Reo was curious about, like getting paid serious money for singing instead of tips and beers.

"You know, I'm getting $600 and this room tonight, and a thousand dollars to play in Milwaukee tomorrow. Do you know why I'm getting four hundred dollars more to go to Milwaukee?"

When Duke paused, Reo reached across and took the bottle from Duke's hand, took a swig and handed it back to him without a word. He swallowed it down: good, smooth whiskey that put a bullet in your chest; then he settled in for the long haul.

"No, why?" he fed him the straight line.

"Because, who the hell wants to go to Milwaukee!"

Duke was also renowned for singing in a powerful, tender moan, :more compelling in that gruff voice than a sweet singer could ever approach. It was, Reo imagined, like painting with a different substance, oil instead of water, charcoal over pencil; and it came with this wonderful, funny litany of wisdom.

"So, Duke," he asked. "Did you ever compromise?"

"Me? I went out to 8th Avenue and 42d St, bent over and spread my cheeks with both hands," he roared, pausing to spread out his hands, palms up. "No one would have me."

Reo laughed along, feeling pretty loose himself. He took a swig and heard Duke lapse into a lengthy bout of wheezing, hacking coughs, before he recovered and reached for the bottle.

"So, kid," Duke asked him "Do you have to do this?"

"What?"

"This. Singing. You know, playing guitar, writing songs, all of it. What else do you do? Is there something else you do?"

Reo, who had been a professional journalist, received a law degree, and was gainfully employed as a graphic artist for the neighborhood paper in New York, nonetheless knew at that very moment he was there because it was the only thing he could do.

"No."

"That's good."

"Why?"

"In my experience, if there's something else you can do, you'll end up doing that anyway, so you might as well get it over with and go do it now."

Reo didn't say anything. Duke slugged down the last of the bottle.

"Well, then, you'd better get busy," he rasped. "There's a time limit to learn to survive in the game. And that's the key. Survival. Everything else, it's just what comes from that."

It was time to go, let Duke get some sleep. Reo said goodnight and let himself out. He never told Duke la Monte he could not go to the concert, he had a singing job at a hamburger restaurant in the suburbs that evening.

"Survival," he mused aloud, suddenly aware the other passengers on the elevated train were staring at him, the man in dark glasses humming and swinging around the pole in the center of the car, holding a case in his free hand. They would guess he was drunk and coming off a long night, while they were in the midst of their morning rush, to their jobs, their business suit world of telephone calls and office gossip, about the cute one over there by the computers, about the people on the trains. He lurched to the window, scraping a fingernail across the thin line of frost along the lower rim. Outside the brick houses flew by, making him dizzy and nauseous, and when he stumbled back to the center pole they were all still watching him, thinking, how weird, how exotic, or perhaps just how drunk, how serious a hangover awaiting; wait, he's got a guitar, is this just some guy with a guitar, or omigod is it someone we're supposed to know about?

25–Recording Session # 1

The apartment had a side bedroom with nothing in it but a pile of boxes: books, mostly, and some strange wooden objects, woven animal and fish shapes of hardwood. Martin Lehman said they were from a remote Pacific island where he had spent a year while studying for his doctorate. They carried the boxes upstairs, leaving a bare hardwood floor and a nice echo in the empty room. Martin showed him a tape recorder, an old reel-to-reel tape deck with a blank reel still sitting on the spindle.

"You can use this," he said. "There is a microphone in the box over there. There's a stand somewhere too, and blank tape. Knock yourself out."

Later, Reo set up the tape deck, microphone, found a pair of headphones and an unmarked tape. He hit the play button to see if anything was on it. There was no sound; he listened for a full minute, rewound the tape and missed the stop button. The tape ran off the reel, and he had to reload it. This time he hit the red record button first, then play, and the microphone squealed. He lowered the input knob and clapped his hands. The needle jumped halfway across the volume meter, in the yellow, short of the red lights that signaled distortion.

He picked up his guitar and put it on, strumming a chord. It sounded far away in the headphones, so he got closer, and it became clearer. The room had a great sound, too, an empty space with hardwood floors; he got comfortable quickly with the sound in his headphones, and went from one song to another, doing a one-hour performance on tape for the bare olive-green walls.

> You might hear the sound of people crying
> Laying down a lifetime they've quit trying

Feeling everything they love won't be long
If you could ride this train I'm on
Before it's gone

After singing this latest and last song he decided to get something to eat, and went for a walk. He sauntered through a pleasant stroll, the outdoor air fresh and clean, dark just settling in. He bought two tacos at the corner stand and ate them by the front window, then crossed the street and went under the elevated train track, finding a thin sidewalk to the left between two rows of houses. He followed the sidewalk past some wooden gates to an old wooden staircase beside a white wooden door. He climbed the stairs, two flights along the red brick wall, and reached a screen door atop the small platform. There was a faint movement inside.

"Hey," he called softly.

A young woman appeared behind the screen, an oval face with bright, pale eyes under a tangle of curly red hair.

"Hi," she said, as if pleasantly surprised. "Come on in."

An hour later, when he went back down the stairs, the scent of the night caught him again. He had asked her to come out with him after they made love, but she had to get up early. She didn't mind if he didn't stay over, she said. An so he went the other direction when he left her place, and by winding through the maze of alleyways connecting the backyards and diagonal streets of the north side, he emerged on Lincoln Avenue across from Your Mama's Ghost, where he encountered the personage of Louise Gdansk at the bar. He had been two months in Chicago, was singing regularly at the Canary Coalmines, and had not seen her in weeks. He told her he had a tape for her.

"No, that ship sailed, sorry," she said.

"What do you mean?"

"I'm not interested. Anyway, Barry has already picked the songs for his next recording." She turned and faced away from him, toward the stage, where the show was starting. As the lights came down, Louise Gdansk spoke to Reo over the introduction and aimed a hand toward the stage, a tiny hand for such a large body.

"Now, this," she said, "is a real folksinger."

Reo bought himself a beer and watched the middle-aged man, his hair down to the collar of his leather vest, finger-picking a well-worn blond guitar and singing in a stern, resonant voice.

> If you ever go to Houston
> Well you'd better walk right
> you'd better not gamble
> you'd better not fight

The singer was apparently a favorite of the crowd, but Reo got bored before he finished his beer. Silently, he went to the door and got out without making a sound, as the music droned on onstage.

Martin had returned home, and there was someone with him, a tall, elegant blond woman in a black dress, a string of pearls around her neck.

"Reo, this is Alice McAllister, an old friend of mine from New York. In fact, we were in a folk group together, remember that?"

"I remember," she grinned.

"Anyway," Martin continued, "Alice is here to play at the Duke Of Earl this weekend, we're going to go see her."

Three days later, Reo was in the back seat of a baby blue Cadillac with white leather seats and great sound. Before he had left New York, Reo had booked a date at Xanadu that was coming up soon; and so, after playing for her at Martin's, and catching two of her sets, he had taken her up on her offer of a ride back to New York. The car belonged to Joshua, who played guitar with Alice, or rather to his parents; and as they drove across Indiana Alice turned toward him.

"Joshua is heading back to Florida after he drops us off. I have a gig next week in a bar on the east side. I need a guitar player. Want to play with me? Fifty bucks."

He sat up, surprised.

"Sure," he said. It would be a first, playing behind someone else, but he liked her singing and liked her, she was not only classy but funny and smart. She could tell a joke and still come off as a lady.

"Chicago's fun, huh?" she said with a smile.

"Yeah," he said. "It's a hard place to leave."

"Yeah," mused Alice in a deadpan imitation of Reo. "It just isn't New York." She grinned, and Joshua turned to her and grinned right back.

When they hit New York at 7 am, he had no plan, no place to sleep. He had told no one he was coming and had nowhere to go. Alice took him back to her place, and before long they were in her bed, sleepless from the long drive, lying drowsily in each other's arms. It was late afternoon before he woke, and she was already up cooking something at the stove, a few steps away in the large one-room apartment.

He had some food and sat at a small table, stretching out the tired muscles from sitting in the car. She was fun to be with, making jokes all through their breakfast, while he wondered quietly what he was going to do. At last she stopped talking and stared at him.

"So, what do you want to do?" she asked gently.

It was a good question, a fair question. He didn't really want to move in with Alice, or anyone, and start a relationship too quickly. He wanted his own place.

"I can't stay here," he said.

She looked around herself and shook her head, smiling, as if to herself, as if relieved, he thought.

"No, not really. You can come visit, though. Can I ask you something?"

"Sure," he said.

"How old are you really?"

He thought about it a moment. He recalled Martin had told her he was 22, and if she remembered, she was now testing him.

"Twenty-two," he said.

She smiled again, that other smile, not the professional, open-faced smile she gave an audience, but a private smile that seemed a little wistful. It was when he thought she was most beautiful.

"You know I'm 37," she said.

"I did know that."

She looked down at her coffee cup, now empty, and swirled it around as if there were something still in it.

"I can't do this," she said. "You're too young for me."

He was all right with that, he told her, though he liked her a lot and would like to be friends. And he would still like to play guitar with her. She held out a long, slender hand, and he took it.

"You're on," she said as they shook hands. "And you can stash the guitar and pack here until you find a place."

He took the subway uptown, back to Xanadu. It was early evening and the streets were quiet in the stiff, wet breeze that pushed into his face. He knocked on the door and Joseph appeared, a large towel in his hand.

"Come on in, you can help me clean up," he said, drying his hands on his thick beard. "What's your story? Where are you these days?"

He told Joseph of Chicago, working for two months in the Canary Coalmines blues club, then meeting Alice and coming back to New York.

"Is that why you came back? With Alice?"

No, he shook his head. He had loved Chicago, the alleyways, the back streets, the girls, the clubs, the music, the singers and songwriters, the easy camaraderie between them. But it had one shortcoming he couldn't get around. It wasn't New York.

26–On The Road In New York Town

Xanadu was full, but Turk was going away for a few days and offered to let Reo apartment-sit for him.

"It'll be safer having someone there," he said, and then with his big, deep laugh added, "what could possibly go wrong?" And so Reo had a place to sleep in New York, five days at least, uptown at 122d Street and Broadway. He could arrive tomorrow at 3 pm, get the keys, move right in, Turk was leaving for the airport, going to visit a sister in California.

Still, he had no place to sleep tonight. So he headed back to the Village, walked past the Folk Life and saw the sign

Open Mike signup at 7

He went inside. It was hard to find a clock, and it wasn't until he was spotted by Sonoma Sal that he learned the time. Sal leaned against the bar and stroked his moustache, twisting the blond handlebar to a point.

"Ah, MacGregor. You're back from, where? What, no guitar?"

He stopped and shoved his hands in his pockets.

"Ah, no. I was just walking by and saw the sign."

"Just walking by."

"Well, yeah, I was on my way home from somewhere, that's why I don't have a guitar. It's probably too late anyway, isn't it?"

"Probably," said Sal with a sadistic grin. "But don't you already have a number?"

"That's right," the voice of Tony O leaned across the bar. "He's a number 13C."

Reo had to laugh.

"What, you think it's a funny?"

"No, no," Reo said quickly. "Number 13C is fine. Do I have enough time to get my guitar?"

"That depends. Where's your guitar?" Sal asked nonchalantly.

"Fifteen minutes away."

Tony O resumed washing a glass with a small towel. The matter was settled.

"That should be enough," said Sal. Reo hustled back to Alice's, found her about to go to sleep, wrapped in a nice green silk kimono and with her hair all hanging down, long and full. She's a beautiful woman, he thought, but did not let her see him admiring her, as he grabbed his guitar and headed back out. Arriving in time for his number, he sang "Marcie Jane," remembering he had been asked about it in Chicago, and a newer song:

> just as soon as the rain
> stops pounding on the glass
> I'll walk you out in the garden
> each word might be our last
> you say it's easy for you now
> I hope it's easy for a long time, and it's
> in the morning I'll be gone time

He'd already had two beers, and twenty-five singers had performed. There would be another fifteen or twenty-five; depending on how many actually stayed long enough to play, it could be 2 am or even 3 before they got to Number 30C, and Reo, with nowhere to go, stayed at Folk Life until it closed, not long after the last performer finished his song, a slow and quiet version of "Summertime, and the livin' is easy."

At last, Sonoma Sal delivered the coup de grace through the mike.

"And that, music lovers, is tonight's open mike. Time for my boot heels to be wanderin'."

One by one everyone left, as Reo sat and nursed a last beer. He still hadn't paid his tab, and was balanced on a padded stool by the window, his guitar case leaning against the wall next to him. Sal came walking out to the bar with his guitar case and saw him, still there.

"MacGregor." Sal said. He seemed about to say something more when

Tony O arrived, holding a thin slice of cash toward him. He turned and took the bills, then addressed Reo.

"What are you doing right now?"

"Nothing much. Why?"

"You need to come with me."

Reo stood up.

"Okay," he said, then looked toward Tony O.

"What do I owe for the beers?"

Tony O smiled at Sal and shook his head; then he said to Reo, "You can't afford a to drink here."

"Okay, thanks," he said with a smile, feeling silly from the beer. "Let's go, then."

He grabbed his guitar and followed Sal through the doorway and down the sidewalk, around the corner to the middle of the block. Sal walked fast, and Reo had to move very quickly to keep up with him, hustling through the late revelers on the street, through a glass doorway framed in polished wood, down an old concrete hallway, painted yellow and brown like a two-tone car from the 1950s. A left and right turn, a quick key in the latch and they were inside the apartment, entering on an angle into a kitchen. Sal set down his guitar and directed Reo inside to a small sitting room, waved Reo to the couch and sat down across from him in the wooden easy chair.

"Look at this," he said, and immediately handed Reo a small stack of papers, the top one a music score for "Nature Boy," as sung by Nat King Cole. The paper itself was stained brown by the years and had several pencil notes on it, tiny words scrawled by a subsequent reader.

'Wow," said Reo. "The real thing. What year is this?"

"1947."

"Can you play this?"

Sonoma Sal got up and went into the kitchen, returning seconds later with his guitar. He sat back on the chair, hunched forward to clear the arms and began to stroke the strings, the somber, eerie chord progression building as he went.

> There was a boy
> a very strange enchanted boy
> They say he wandered very far, very far

He sang in a tuneful yet mournful voice that reminded Reo of someone talking and singing at the same time, as if reciting a poem to the guitar piece. It was a stunning guitar arrangement with a slightly detached vocal, the singer observing the nature boy from afar. Reo followed the song on the sheet music, a hieroglyphic of scales and figures he could not fathom, until, just before it was to end, Sal chunked his fingernails across the strings and grabbed the neck, clamping down on the sound.

"Well, I know that much of it," he said, and put the guitar on the floor. He stood up, went into the kitchen and returned with a glass of water, and a second one for Reo.

"Let me ask you something," Sal said. "The song you played tonight, the second one, the slower one, it had six lines in the verse, right? Then there's a tag line, 'In the Morning,' something or other, it rhymes with the sixth line. So it's a seven line verse."

Reo listened and waited. Sal, however, was waiting for him.

"Okay, yeah, it's seven lines I guess."

"Shouldn't it be eight? Or six? Maybe you should write one more line for the verse, 'da-da-da-da-da and it's in the morning I'll be gone time.' See what I mean?"

Reo thought through the words in his mind.

"I kind of like it this way."

"Of course," said Sal. "Just an idea."

A few minutes later, after a brief conversation about Nat King Cole, Sal stood up and made it clear he expected Reo to leave.

"Well, music lovers," he said, as if there were others there, "it's been fun."

So Reo stood up and shook his hand and headed back out. It was 4 am, with nowhere to go, and it was getting chilly in the spring night.

> New York town and it's a quarter past 4
> Goodnight show's over, over here's the door
> You've sung every tune you know and a couple more
> Ain't there somewhere left you ain't been before
> You're on the road in New York town

He sang to himself, quietly moving down the block. It was good there were still people out on MacDougal Street, as the sign called it; he felt safe on the well-lit sidewalk with a few cars and couples still around, some waiting in line at a single doorway with a counter inside, backed up eight deep. A sign said "Falafel $2" and he checked his wallet, finding $21 inside. He bought a falafel sandwich, its chalky tahini sauce softening the crunchy ball of peas and herbs fried in deep fat, and ate it out front, not far from where a tuxedoed man leaned against a white limousine, eating the same sandwich. They exchanged a nod.

"Are you the driver or passenger?" Reo asked him. The man smiled, and then a policeman emerged from a nearby doorway, instantly recognizable in his blue uniform and hat.

"Is he bothering you?" the policeman asked the other man, who simply shook his head but did not speak.

Reo finished his sandwich in silence. He walked along, holding the handle of his guitar case like a suitcase; wary of losing it or having it stolen, he knew it would be difficult to sleep anywhere. When he reached the subway entrance he decided on the spot to ride a train, a train to anywhere, pay the fare and ride the system until morning. He caught an uptown train toward the Bronx, entering a car that appeared empty through the windows. Inside, however, a young man and woman sprawled across a seat, her legs extended out from under a black pleated skirt, his arm thoroughly up her dress. Teenagers, black hair and tight pants, Latinos in love, he couldn't say, as he walked past them and took a seat where he could not see them, behind the waist high barriers. But for five stops he heard the girl's cries, until he got off at 96th street and crossed over to the downtown side. He sat in a car with a dozen people heading south, no one speaking, the train rattling through the silence to the end of the line at Battery Park.

Oh Latin lovers, I wish I was you
Huddled in the subway makin' one out of two
Bright lights, splatter, screech, brakes drowning out
Old drunk singing can you help a fellow out
I'm on the road in New York Town

He walked the short distance to the Staten Island Ferry, alone in the hazy gray of the pre-dawn morning, a lone garbage truck finishing its rounds, pigeons pecking at the scattered trash on the patches of green.

He rode the great boat across the harbor in the quiet, salty morning air, one of no more than forty passengers, stood at the rail and watched the ship dock. He got off and got back on board, among at least three hundred passengers on the return trip, as the sun crawled over the low, scratchy squalor of the Brooklyn waterfront. Slowly it rose, as the boat steamed across open water, filling the windows of the approaching skyscrapers with a fierce yellow light, at first a mosaic of windowpanes, then at last coalescing into one great beam of fire, then two, then three, then again breaking into smaller pieces. As the crowd stood in near silence, the sun flooded the harbor with light, as the boat steamed into the Battery Park dock, another corner of the world.

Reo stood in the front of the boat, one of two dozen travelers hushed by the spectacle of the great city lighting up before their eyes. He knew he had to get off the boat now, walk into this city, now, sleepless and broke, and make it through the day.

He found a park bench along the railing overlooking the water, and sat down, his legs over his guitar case. He drifted in and out of sleep before the sun rose over the nearby buildings and shone directly on him. He got up and began walking, made it to Alice's. She was drinking a coffee and talking on the phone. He opened his backpack, with its slender collection of clothes freshly washed in Chicago.

"So where have you been?" she asked when she set down the phone a minute later.

"I was uptown. Hey, I have an apartment for a few days. House sitting for an old friend. I have to meet him uptown at 3."

"So, you have somewhere to go."

"Yes. At least for now."

Alice got up, found a clean mug and poured it full of coffee. She brought it back to her chair and sat down, then slid it across the table toward Reo.

"You're still going to play guitar with me tomorrow night, right?"

"I can do it," he said. It was good to know she still wanted him for it. She wrote down the address, then picked a guitar from the case open on the floor.

"Let's play something," she said. He took out his guitar, his Gibson Country & Western, set it across his knees, and waited as she leaned forward and looked it over, the fine blond grain of wood, the winged pickguard under the sound hole. Slowly, peering carefully through the strings, she touched a piece of trapezoidal white inlay on the fret board with a pale pink fingernail.

"You can tell a lot about a man by his guitar," she said with a knowing smile.

"Oh, yeah? What does this guitar tell you?" he asked, his left hand drifting into position as if on automatic pilot, as he stroked a fat A chord with his other hand.

She smiled and looked at her hands, then at Reo.

"It says, 'I need some sleep.'"

27–On The Job

Alice's gig was in a neighborhood bar on the Lower East Side, a place that regularly had live music and a discerning audience, according to Alice, who packed in a good crowd and gave them her most outrageous and real self, ending with a slow, moody paean to older women and younger men:

> Mrs. Jones Mrs. Jones I know that you see
> The woman in you is the woman in me
> our needs are the same wouldn't you agree?
> I'm in love with your son
> Hear my plea
> I'm in love with your son
> Tell me what will become of me

She sang, and the mostly male crowd cheered her on. Reo played a hot solo on one song and got a nice hand, and later when she paid him she sat down with a big smile.

"I have a question for you."

"What?"

"Folk Life wants me. Three weeks from now, Wednesday to Sunday."

He sat up and paid attention.

"You want me to play with you?"

Alice shook her head, the blond curls shimmering in the light..

"No, Joshua's coming up for that. I want you to be the opening act, do a thirty minute set, twice each night, three on Friday and Saturday."

As it sank in, he was about to speak when she interrupted.

"Well? You can do it, right?"

He blinked.

"Yes, sure," he said. Alice sat back and stared at him.

"Did Martin tell you how we know each other?" she asked him.

"No, I don't think so."

"We were in a group together. We toured all over the Midwest and Canada, until we got asked to be on a television show together."

"You and Martin?"

"And two other guys. We were about to go on when we found out there was this blacklist, this policy of excluding people for their political beliefs. It was all very carefully hidden, you understand, but it was real. Martin and the banjo player decided to boycott the show to protest the blacklist. The other guy and I went on the broadcast and did three songs."

Reo listened to her in silence.

"So. Martin quit the band and went on to become a university professor. I am very grateful we are still friends, I admire him for what he did. I, on the other hand, have remained a professional singer all my life, despite two marriages and a lot of things I can't remember."

He didn't interrupt as she laughed.

"So, do you want to open for me for a week at Folk Life? Yes or no?"

He said, "yes," of course," and "thank you," and she walked away with a smile. He started to pack his guitar and head back uptown to Turk's, when a stocky man with reddish brown hair, parted in the middle and curling around his ears, stroked his moustache and sat down.

"Got a minute?"

"Sure," Reo answered, positioning the strap in the case.

"I'm Bryce," the man said. "Bryce Waterburn."

"Waterburn? What kind of name is that?" Reo replied.

"English. Anyway, I want to ask you about something. The song you sang, was it your own?"

Reo thought back a couple hours, when Alice had asked him to do a short solo set. He had played three songs, and was trying to remember what they were.

"In the morning something," Bryce said.

""You like that song? I just wrote it."

"That's what I was wondering. You wrote that one?"

"Yes."

Bryce Waterburn nodded as if he was thinking of something. Reo wondered if it was to buy time, to act as if he knew what he wanted to say, but didn't have a clue.

"What's your story?" Bryce suddenly asked. "Where are you from? Where do you live? What are you doing with your music, with your life? That's what I want to know."

Reo looked at him as if for the first time. Waterburn sat back and crossed one leg over the other, his gray flannel slacks still creased.

"I just came here from Chicago. I'm playing music where I can and hanging out," Reo said, and added "and right now I don't live anywhere."

"Well, then," Bryce replied, "I might be able to help you there."

Reo discreetly asked the bartender, who had poured him a couple beers and watched the show with interest, about Bryce Waterburn. The bartender said he didn't know him that well but he was a regular, and seemed an all right guy. And so the next afternoon, Reo took the subway downtown from Turk's and met him for an afternoon coffee; they left the café and walked east into a beaten down neighborhood that seemed to darken as they entered it. Reo began to wish he hadn't taken the man up on his invitation, as they climbed a dim stairwell past a second floor with a broken overhead light, and four more flights to the top floor.

"It's a city-owned apartment, no one has lived there for months," Bryce told him. "You can move in tomorrow, write the city a letter, tell the lady on the first floor that you want to rent it, they'll contact you."

There were four doors, one at the end of the hallway. The middle two were boarded up with planks nailed diagonally across the frame. Right at the top of the stairs, however, the closest door was covered in aluminum foil. Bryce took out a set of keys and opened it, entering a kitchen with a small stove, a sink, and a wooden floor with a hole in the middle of the room, a foot long by five inches wide, above a well-lit room below.

"That's my place," Bryce said. "It's like having an intercom."

A kitchen door opened to a small toilet and rusty shower no wider than a person. There was a second room, with a bed alone on a faded blue and red splotch of old cloth barely thicker than a blanket. Two windows sat curtainless: one with a fire escape, protected from outside invasion by iron window gates bolted into the wall. The other looked into space, into the rare openness of an empty lot between this window and the nearest avenue.

"There was a building there. Burned down last year," Bryce said quietly.

Reo stood at the corner window and looked into the small rooms. It was more space than he'd had for months, and for the moment, it was free. He stepped to the center of the room and hummed a long slow, note, then a scale, listening to his voice resonate amid the bare walls and wooden floors.

"I'll take it," he said. "Friday ok?"

28–0 Please Don't Follow Me Home

It was a Monday, and he signed in at the open mike before running into Zeke on the next block, and before long they were eating chips in their usual hang. As Reo filled him in, Zeke stretched his arms along the booth.

"So you went to Chicago to deliver a car and ended up coming back to New York with Alice McAllister?"

"That's right."

"And you were hanging out in the club scene there, working in a bar singing?"

"A couple of them."

"Is that where you met Alice?"

"Not really, well, indirectly I suppose. This guy Martin introduced us, they were in a folk group years ago together."

"So did you sleep with her?"

"I played guitar with her last week."

Zeke nodded, grinning.

"I hear she likes younger guys. She's still pretty good-looking, too."

"I'm not really interested in her for that."

"And she got you the gig?" he asked Reo.

"I guess so. She's the headliner, I'm the opening act."

"Wow," said Zeke, leaning back against the hard wood bench. "Wouldn't it be amazing if you suddenly got famous or something?"

Reo laughed.

"Or something," Zeke went on. "Would that be so surprising to you?"

Reo shook his head, letting him rant; Zeke hesitated, then answered his own question.

"Yeah, I think it would," he mused, stirring his tea. "Oh, I don't mean that you're not good enough or something, that's not it. You're very good, actually, one of the most real around here. I think it's the market. You know, I hang around uptown sometimes, visit people in their offices, and I sense they are trying to move completely away from this kind of thing."

"What kind of thing?"

"It's unfortunate that the, the tradition, the line of music, what you call and they call folk music, that you are inspired by, that you are following, is exactly what they want to make a clean break from. They want a completely new direction and to leave that behind. So the question is, can you make that transition, can you move forward to the next thing, whatever it is, whatever it's called, and still do your music? That's what I'm wondering."

Reo was still pondering that when he got back to the open mike, negotiating the swinging doors of the second entrance without banging his guitar case against them. He stood inside the bar and caught Tony's eye. Tony poured him a beer and pointed to an empty stool.

"Alice a tell you?" Tony asked right away.

"Yes."

"Good. She tell a you the money?"

"Fifteen percent of the door after expenses?"

"Good. Okay, you got it," he smiled, eyeing Reo through a pair of half spectacles, rimless and smeared with steam. A customer signaled for a drink, and that was that. Reo would be the opening act for Alice McAllister in three weeks, for five nights, Wednesday through Sunday.

He sat at the end of the bar, nursing a stein of the latest brew; there were times when it had the slightly flat taste of cheap beer going stale if you didn't drink it right away. But this one tasted good. He was still sitting there when he heard Sonoma Sal inside the main room.

"And now, music lovers, the lovely and talented Callisto Maya."

There was a burst of applause from the crowd inside, and then a screech of feedback as she arrived at the mike. She stepped back, the feedback disappeared, and carefully she took half a step forward, humming softly. The room grew quiet for what now seemed the first time all evening.

> you step out of the shadows
> that look is in your eyes

your hands still in your pockets
I feel your hunger rise
heels clicking the empty sidewalk
your shadow shrinks beneath the streetlight
o please don't follow me home
o please don't follow me home
o please don't follow me home tonight

Her hypnotic voice had a low range for a woman, Reo thought, as she moved conversationally through the words with an edgy tone and a simple melody.

I have no money for you
even my icebox is bare
but it's not the money honey
you're looking for out here
what's missing that you have to
wait around looking such a fright
o please don't follow me home tonight

She sang the last line once the second time, a smart move, keep it from dragging on. Then came the middle part, higher in pitch, words flying more quickly to an emotional high point

there were times I wished somebody would walk my way
and say hey
you are who I'm looking for
but it's not one of those nights
and you're not one of those sights
you think you're looking for me
I just want you away from my door

Reo drifted toward the main room slowly, drawn by the music. He was able to find a vantage point without blocking anyone, just outside the archway, where he could see her on stage, leaning slightly backward but looking downward at her hands, strumming through a short instrumental chord section, her hair shaking as she bobbed, hair that, it suddenly occurred to Reo, was much shorter than he had last seen. She had cut her hair off, down to a length less than his own; wearing a black jacket and slacks, and playing a black guitar, she somehow looked brighter, and better lit, than he expected.

> I wish there were some way
> I could wave a magic wand
> have you be satisfied
> to keep on walking on
> my keys are in my fingers
> watch how quickly I slip inside
> o please don't follow me home
> o please don't follow me home
> o please don't follow me home tonight

She basked in the applause, her eyes sweeping the crowd from right to left around the room until they met Reo's and paused for a moment, giving away a small smile as she looked down. She looked up again and he was gone, headed back to the far end of the bar, where Ted Imbonanti had arrived with two beers.

"Wanta beer?" he asked, pushing one across the bar. Unlike Callisto's, Ted's hair was longer and thicker than before, a wooly mass of black curls around a face dark with day-old stubble. He was wearing gold-rimmed glasses with round frames on his wide face, with its dark eyes and big smile.

"Sure," Reo replied, and took it. "What number are you?"

"12B. Callisto is 9A., so I'm one, two, five, eight, ten spots away. You?"

Reo laughed, watching Ted count on his fingers.

"13C."

"That's lucky."

"I think it is," Reo nodded. He hadn't seen Ted in a couple of months; he looked different, a more relaxed version of himself.

"Where have you been?" Ted asked him.

"Chicago. I was singing in a couple clubs. How about you? Still having song parties?"

"No," Ted shook his head. "Veronica and I gave up our place. I quit my job too."

"Wow! Big change. What are you doing instead?"

"Right now we're staying at Jonas' place, sleeping on the couch in his living room."

"Both of you? You're all living in that apartment?"

'Yeah. Jason is on the other bed in the same room with us."

Reo thought about this for a moment.

"You gave up your job and apartment. Are you working?"

"I have a gig here Tuesday with my band. We have a little band out in Queens. We're playing here. Why don't you come?"

Ted smiled at him, his head cocked at a slight angle, his eyes giving off the impassioned glow of someone who has made a momentous personal decision and is very excited about it.

"I'm giving my self to my music one hundred per cent," Ted beamed. "Just like you, and everyone else around here."

Reo studied Ted, trying to imagine if it was a good move. He had done the same thing himself, and wasn't exactly setting the world on fire. But he was making progress, and so far was able to earn enough to live on.

"Next Tuesday? Okay, I'll be here," he said.

Ted turned and studied the main room, where Callisto was doing her second song. Neither had been listening, though it was familiar to Reo somehow, he had heard it before. Ted turned to him again.

"I want to ask you something. Our band is called Hard Times, and I want to sing that song. You know, the song you sang at my house. You gave Veronica the words. I could use the chords, too, if it's okay?"

Reo took a slug of beer and sorted it out.

"Sure," he said. "Want me to write them down?"

"Please." Ted walked across the bar toward a white guitar case and found a blank piece of 8 x 11 paper, took a pen out of his pocket and handed them both to Reo.

"Here," he said with a big grin. "Why don't you do it right now?"

Reo had sung the song several times in Chicago, and wrote the words from memory with chord letters above the lines. He had to turn the page over to finish it, writing the last three lines on the back.

"That's the trouble with long songs," Ted said when Reo handed it to him a few minutes later. "Now I have to turn it over."

Reo took the paper back and scrawled the three lines into a triangle in the lower right corner.

It was practically unreadable, even to himself.

"Well, that didn't help much, I guess."

"It doesn't matter," Ted waved. "I want to change the ending anyway."

"Why's that?"

"The last line, it should be 'You better get your shotgun ready 'cause hard times'. That's what you sang at my house."

"I did, you're right. I changed it later."

"Well, you sing it how you want. How about if I sing it how I want?"

Reo nodded.

"Okay, sure. Do your thing."

"Good. Anyway, it's the song that counts, not you. No?"

"It's okay, I may sing it that way sometime myself, who knows. Do what you want."

"Hey, here we go," Ted said, looking toward the stage, as Jonas Waverly stepped up to the microphones. He too looked different, clean-shaven and sporting a suede sport jacket of deep brown, thinner and more intense than Reo had remembered him. Two other musicians stood beside him; on the far side, a slender man with glasses held a guitar with long, thin fingers. Closer to the archway was Jason, Jonas' brother, playing a large string bass. They landed on a slow, rhythmic groove, Jonas snapping a guitar string to the beat.

> Give me one good reason
> why the color of her eyes
> ever mattered in the slightest
> anyway, they weren't the brightest
> no, those would be yours, my love
> those would be yours

Ted and Reo were a few feet outside the archway, from where Reo could not see the stage. But he could hear Jonas' dry voice reaching for a high note and getting there clean, opening up as he sang through the bridge. At the same time, the second voice of Jacob's smooth baritone sang a low, droning harmony that fit perfectly with Jonas' raspy tenor, filling the room with a deep, full vocal chord on the last lines of each verse.

There was a substantial roomful of applause after the song finished; Jonas swept his hand across his stomach and took a bow.

"Oh, shit," said Ted. "Now he's done it."

"Done what?" Reo asked.

Ted looked at Reo as if he were studying a stranger.

"He's saying one is better than another. Don't you see? It's all about jealousy, really, a statement about someone wanting reassurance. And there's no reassurance, not really, you can say it but you can never really promise it, and you certainly can't deliver it, you think you mean it but you are just saying it to please the other person, when the truth is you can't know. Not really. The danger is that another person might act on it."

Speaking rapidly, wound up, Ted then ran out of words.

"If they even know it's about them," Reo said quietly, and Ted sighed, as if letting out a lot of air, then relaxed.

"Or if there even is another person," he said through a laugh, and Reo caught it and joined in. Someone yelled "quiet," and they settled in for Jonas's second song.

29–It's Not About You

Ted went on a few minutes later, his first song a slow, melodic piece that started on a high note and worked downward to the end of a verse:

> America
> the scene of the crime
> the land that gave the world tomatoes
> the grand design
> the land whose only credo
> is more for me, less for you
> it's just what we do
> to change it would be unfair
> to who

Ted had a smooth round voice, and if he was unsure of the response he would get, he didn't let on, singing with total conviction, staring straight out into a blue, smoky haze of silence, the crowd in the big room for once transfixed on the man at the mike.

> What did she promise you
> A handful of her breast?
> A glass of wine and then it's down
> Down with all the rest
> On your knees in
> America
> Don't say please in America
> No one is listening

The strong melody reached its peak at the end, and the crowd exploded with applause.

"You got that right!" someone yelled.

Ted drifted back from his song and looked around, as if surprised by the intensity of attention, the focus so pointedly directed at him. He stepped back and checked his tuning, looked around the room and found his wife, Veronica, seated in the audience.

"Come on up," he said.

"That's ok," she said from the back wall. "I'm just gonna listen."

Reo wandered back to the bar, still holding his beer. Tony O came over and picked up his glass, then handed him a fresh one.

Thirty minutes later he was on stage, fumbling through the verses of a new song he was working on

> You've been on the highway and
> They're all your friends, they give you
> Rides, meals, highs, money
> Wave around the bend
> Now you look around, you're standin' in a mob
> Linin' up on Friday for a Wednesday job
> You're on the road in New York town

The song was fast, and its three verses took little time; Reo re-sang the first verse and then it was over in what seemed a minute or two. He stepped back and checked his tuning and heard a hoarse whisper from the back of the crowd.

"Play the horse you rode in on." There was a smattering of laughter in the crowd, and as Reo squinted into the lights he spied Jonas, Franklin and Callisto sitting at a rear corner table, laughing like school kids at a prank. He nodded and gave them a smile.

"How about this," Reo spoke into the mike, "You can call it the song I rode out on." He strummed a chord, once, twice, moved it up the neck two frets, slowed it down to a stately pace, and let the chord ring out.

> If I show up at 5 am
> And knock upon your window

And you get up and let me in
Then I will know
I will know
You love me too

Oh, what'll I do
If you say
that I shouldn't look at you that way
oh I
I will be lonely

It was too pretty, and realizing love was ultimately not on the horizon, the seductive song was headed for an ambiguous conclusion at best. But Reo felt a voice kick in, a voice he was learning to recognize, that felt true and spontaneous, connected to the song and the emotion without thinking about it. He drifted into the world of his song and felt something he couldn't identify, but it felt right, a certain honesty that at that moment he was doing exactly what he should be doing.

If I kiss you on the lips and
Look into your eyes
And you say you've been waiting
Then it will be all right
I will know
You love me too

Ending it, he had to collect himself for a moment. The crowd clapped quietly; as he stood there and slowly began to leave the stage, the applause deepened, and he was all the way back to the bar with his guitar before he heard Sonoma Sal over the house system.

"That was Reo MacGregor, number 13C. And now, number 14A, Vince Megabop."

Reo found his empty case and put the guitar inside, dragged it over to the bar and sat down. He wasn't looking forward to the long walk across town, to the sixth floor of the half-occupied building on the dark street. He had been living there three days and had heard people moving inside the other apartments, the ones whose doors were boarded up.

"They're junkies," said Dave, a thin bearded artist with a long face and a constant cigarette. Dave lived in the other occupied apartment on their floor, or more accurately, the other apartment whose door opened into the hallway. "They go in and out through the windows on the fire escape."

"Doesn't that make you a little nervous?" Reo wanted to know.

"I've never seen one in the hall," Dave replied. Dave's business was designing holograms, three-dimensional sculptures of people in various martial arts positions, hung from light cords, door beams, and shelves; but the best hologram was a free-standing one made entirely of focused light beams, right in the middle of the kitchen. Reo had been startled by it, stepped back, and Bryce and Dave had both laughed.

"Gets' em every time," Dave said.

Now here he was, facing going back there with his guitar, alone, late at night. So he had another beer, and before long Jonas, Callisto and Ted emerged from the music room and saw him at the bar.

"Good song, that first one," Ted said enthusiastically. "Is there more to it? More verses to come, I mean?"

"Inevitably," Jonas cut in with a dry laugh. "Whether it needs it or not."

Reo, about to reply to Ted, said nothing. Castillo stood apart, a few steps away, watching them and looking around as if she'd like to be somewhere else.

"Yeah," Reo answered. "I'm writing more verses for some friends."

Jonas smirked and looked at Reo's chest, poking his finger into his shirt, then up over his chin and nose.

"Got any?" he wheezed through a laugh. "Maybe one day you and I will be friends." Without waiting for a reply, he turned to leave.

"Don't forget my band is here next Tuesday. Please come," Ted stepped in, shook his hand and left. Reo rested an elbow on the bar. To his surprise Callisto did not follow immediately, but stood watching him, her hands clasped at her chest.

"Hey," he said with a slight grin. "Good song."

She was serious, unwilling to smile. Jonas' face appeared in the open window to the street.

"Come on," he called to her; but she ignored him and stood there.

"You seem so sad," she said softly. "I wish I could help." Then she reached out and handed Reo a slim, folded piece of paper. She turned and left immediately, a purposeful blur of action, gone before he could think of anything to say.

It's not about you

the note said. He folded it and put it in his shirt pocket. It was only 11 pm, and when Tony O offered him a beer, he accepted it gratefully, sitting on an empty bar stool where the bartenders washed the empty glasses. No one spoke to him for some time, until Lila began washing some glasses, bending toward him as she rinsed them under the faucet. She had her head down and her blouse hung forward; with no other garments underneath, he saw her breasts, soft triangles of tan and red exposed like forbidden fruit. He looked away at first, then, seeing no one else was noticing, carefully glanced there again, just as she walked away, clean glasses in hand. He drank his beer, as she kept returning to that spot, to that same stance, as if she knew exactly what he was seeing; he had another beer and quietly watched her walk the bar. A curvy young woman with round, dark eyes and a wild mane of curly black hair, she fit neatly into her snug jeans and cotton top. Before long it was closing time, and she was asking him what he was doing after the bar closed.

"Well, nothing really. What do you have in mind?" he answered in a conspiratorial whisper, met by a quiet, soft laugh that she instinctively covered with her hand, a beautiful and natural smile barely hidden behind it. Quickly, she glanced up and down the bar to make sure no one else was paying attention.

"You can walk me home," she whispered.

Home was a sixth-floor walkup in Soho with two roommates and a dog barking behind a neighbor's door as they passed. The dog sounded so vicious that Reo, drunk from the beers, took a step toward the door and said "shut up" to the mindless dog. Lila dragged him away, and then they were inside her place, kissing, and she pushed him onto a mattress and lay on top of him with her clothes still on, pulling a blanket over them both. It was October, and the night outside the open window was cooling down.

30–Folk Music

After two days it seemed like he and Bryce Waterburn were old friends, engaged in lengthy conversations through the hole in the floor, as Reo sat in his kitchen on his single metal folding chair.

"Why don't you come and talk to me? Bring your coffee and sandwich with you, here, I have two chairs."

It became a regular part of the day, coffee and a sandwich lasting through the afternoon. Bryce had no job; he said he was "living off an inheritance and a legal judgment against a financial advisor." He had some money and what he described as "some great ideas," including making a video of Homer's *Odyssey* with rock music. His apartment, less shabby than Reo's, was comfortably furnished with a loft bed by the windows overlooking the street, and a floor mattress in an alcove off the kitchen.

"You can stay there if you need to," Bryce said, waving at the alcove. "I know it's a little weird upstairs sometimes."

"You mean the movement in the walls?"

"Exactly. I hear it too."

Bryce dumped his cup and saucer in the sink, a five foot-wide cabinet of white painted steel with two bins.

"Hey, how'd you get such a great sink? Mine is the size of a book."

"It belongs to the guy who owns this apartment. Anyway, I want to ask you something. Have you ever done any recording?"

A slow moving cat, orange and white stripes rippling with each step, strode across the floor toward him. Reo put a hand down and extended the backs of his fingers toward the cat, pointing downward.

"Once or twice," he replied.

"I have a proposition for you."

Reo squared around, the flat wooden chair giving off a loud squeak. The cat moved with his hand, nuzzling his head against his knuckles.

"What proposition?" he asked.

"Well, I'm not exactly sure. I'd like to manage you, I think, and produce some recordings of your songs."

The cat walked ahead two steps and turned around, came back and gave the other side of his head a good scratch.

"That's Sam," said Bryce, nodding, and the cat ran off in a burst, into the smaller bedroom. "What have you recorded so far?"

"A few songs here and there. I made a tape in Chicago before I left there last month."

"Do you have it? Is it in Chicago?"

Reo took a sip of the coffee. It was bitter and getting lukewarm, but he took a second sip. It seemed to work, as if he suddenly remembered where it was.

"I sent it to someone before I left."

"Who?"

"Do you know who Jeffrey Harriman is?"

Bryce Waterburn sat down at the table again.

"You sent a tape to Jeffrey Harriman? Did he get it?"

"I don't know. Do you know who he is?"

"Of course I know who he is, he signed all kinds of famous people to record deals, produced their albums. You never heard from him? How did you get his address? How did you tell him to contact you?"

"My friend in Chicago had a Proust Wild LP."

It was unlikely the tape would ever have reached Jeffery Harriman, Bryce thought, the music business is set up to prevent that sort of thing from happening. He looked out the window toward a project of red brick in the distance, buildings a generation newer than this one, their flat walls set back from the avenue making a small city of its own.

"Did you keep a copy?"

Reo shook his head. Bryce fished out his wallet, scribbled on a 2 x 3 card and handed it to Reo.

"Does your friend in Chicago have this number? Give this to anyone who really needs to reach you. Not a problem."

Bryce Waterburn
Civic Affairs
Consulting

it said, with a different phone number handwritten below the printed one.

"That's my old office card," he said. "But it's this number."

Reo used the phone to call the print shop where he'd worked before, and after a short conversation, publisher Raymond Talleyrand offered him an afternoon a week with a new magazine.

"It's a journalism critique," he said, "sixteen pages each week. You'll put together the pages for printing." It paid eighty dollars a shift.

"Good for you," said Zeke, when they met that evening for dinner. "You can't live on that of course, but it helps."

"Don't forget I'm not paying any rent."

Zeke sniffed.

"Want to know how to make more money?" he asked with a look around the room. Their waitress, a slim blond in a very short skirt, red leggings and a beret, her lanky hair hanging straight down, set two plates of tostadas in front of them, holding them with potholders.

"These are HOT," she wriggled, yanking her hands away as quickly as she could. She looked like a beatnik from some earlier era, Reo was thinking, as Zeke answered his own question.

"Move to a more expensive place," he said. "Trust me, it works every time."

"Oh, yeah? Just like that?"

"Just like that. No, not just like that. Because you have to work for it, and since rent is just a part of what you make, you end up making more overall. You start making the right decisions because you have to."

"You guys want anything else?" the waitress spoke up, not entirely ignoring the conversation.

"Another quaalude for my friend," Zeke said, "and two for me."

"Coming right up," she mock curtsied, and went away.

Reo gave the phone number to Zeke, and to Tony O, stopping by in the late afternoon just after the club opened. There he met Renaldo, the slim, quiet Apache with the long, wavy black hair, following him to Tim Marcek's large third-floor loft over a falafel restaurant on MacDougal

Street for a session around the wooden picnic table in his living room. There were a dozen songwriters hanging out, including Sara somebody, a petite and ravaged country girl with dirty blond hair and a voice soaked in whiskey for half her thirty years. Reo loved her singing, went to see her at Folk Life, where Tony O had hired her, and at the end of the week she invited him onstage to play harmonica with her. He wailed along behind an old Patsy Cline tune, secretly pleased he got through without any really bad notes.

He was walking up Sixth Avenue with Ted, Jonas and Jason, who got Reo laughing with his imitation of Proust Wild, launching into a soliloquy of non-sequiters, all punctuated by emphasizing the last syllable of a phrase:

> Four score and seven years aGOOO

Jason would sneer, mimicking the distinctive nasal whine. His impression prompted Jonas to stop dead in his tracks.

"Yeah, it's funny," he said in his raspy whisper. "But in this scene you have to sing your own work."

"What about traditional songs?" Ted replied. "Those are bona fide, you might say."

"The good ones have all been done to death," Jonas remarked, and as Reo looked past him he spied Duke la Monte through the window, drinking at the bar in Mavis', a local dive with a pool table.

He went right inside and, instead of saying hello, dove right in.

"Got a question for you, Duke. What role do you think traditional songs should have in the current scene?"

La Monte exploded into laughter, filling the room with his wheezy, gruff guffaws. He was clearly loaded, and drinking alone, as he waved at the empty stools and sat back down.

"You got a lot of nerve," he sputtered. "And why am I not surprised."

"Hey Duke," the others said, standing around. Reo didn't know if Duke remembered him from Chicago, but it didn't take long to find out.

"I oughta never speak to you again," Duke said, looking at him.

"Why's that?" Reo asked.

"You got me so drunk that I almost missed my gig the next night in Milwaukee, that's why."

"Well, Duke, who the hell wants to go to Milwaukee anyway?"

Duke nearly fell off his stool laughing at that one, as the other three men stood around, wondering what was so funny. Reo didn't say a word, until Duke recovered and nodded.

"Okay. What was it you asked."

Now Ted stepped forward, wanting in on the conversation.

"Traditional songs. Are they still important?"

Duke la Monte took a long slug from his beer bottle, looking down the bar toward the bartender, who immediately came over and refilled the shot glass beside it. Then, his voice emerging from his chest as a loud grumble that broke like a wave into full gruffness, he let loose.

"I know you guys. You think you're the new guys, the ones that're gonna change things. And maybe you will." He shrugged his shoulders, picked the tiny shotglass up in his thick fingers and tossed its contents against the back of his throat.

"But the trouble is you have no respect for them what's come befoah. You have to place yourself in context or else you're nowhere." Duke said "nowhere" with emphasis, as if it were "no wheaaahh," and with his gravelly voice behind it, it made them all laugh, Duke the loudest of all. Reo loved that about Duke, that he could laugh at himself with total abandon.

"But I'm serious," he said when the laughter subsided, spreading his palms wide. "It's what ya gotta do. Or else it ain't folk music."

"It's been done to death," Jonas declared from behind a beer glass.

"Ignore it at your own peril," Duke shook his head, stood up and walked over to the rack of cue sticks on a near wall.

"Who wants to bet?" he said to them. "One game. I win, you learn a traditional song. And perform it in public. I lose, I learn one of yours."

"I'll take that bet," Reo said, standing up immediately. "You're on." To have Duke sing one of his songs, he'd risk anything for that, he thought.

They racked up a game of eight ball, and Duke broke the rack, sinking two low balls on the break. He ran three more before missing, leaving Reo no clear shot at anything. He barely managed to hit one of the high numbers and avoid scratching, before Duke sunk two more of his. He had only the eight ball to make.

"Hey Duke, I didn't know you were so good at this," Ted called from his side of the table. Reo wondered if he was trying to throw him off, the way a coach will call time out before an opponent's important kick or shot.

"I'm not," la Monte growled. "But I have the gods on my side this time." He slammed home the eight ball into the corner pocket, then broke into his loud, boisterous laugh.

Reo spent the next afternoon combing through some old songbooks and recordings in a used record store. Most of what he found were either well known or made no sense, having been handed down through generations of singers who had taken verses from one song and added it to another, until the story was lost. In one verse the words said

> I love my gal, she's the finest gal in town,
> I don't want no other girl, I'm staying right at home

followed in the next by

> I'm going' down to Abilene, find me a girl to love

clearly just pieces of music from different songs, thrown together. Reo knew several singers who did this kind of song well, but it didn't interest him. He was looking for something more.

The store owner, a tall nervous man with greasy blond hair and glasses, watched him looking through the stacks of old songbooks, carefully replacing each one without buying it.

"Looking for anything in particular?" he asked.

Reo continued thumbing through the stacks, determined to look at as many as he could before the man ran him out.

"Traditional folk songs," he said. "I'm looking for something singable no one else has done."

"Ah," the man replied, stroking his chin, as if that one word said it all. "Finding any?"

"Not really."

"Why don't you try the Harry Smith *Anthology*?. It's by the old Victrola, in the corner. That's the Bible all the old guys studied. Far as folk songs are concerned, that is."

Reo turned and studied the display in the corner. It was an inch-thick box, leaning diagonally against a display case so the letters could plainly be seen: *Anthology of Folk Music.*

"Go ahead. Take a look."

It was a three disc collection, with a book of notes written in the 1940s by the collector of the original 1920s recordings. For each song there were lyrics and an explanation of its origins, and there were dozens of songs, most of their titles new to Reo. It cost a lot, all his lunch money for the week, but he bought it and took it back to Bryce's, playing it all afternoon until Bryce begged him to stop.

"Please," he said, "I can't take anymore."

He shut it off.

"It's oral history," Reo said. "It's what was on people's mind at that time. That's what a traditional song is, a record, not just a recording, but a document, of its time."

"I don't care," Bryce said. "Well, okay, I get your point, you're looking for a classic song, an undiscovered gem. Hear anything yet?"

"I like the one where the rejected lover throws him down the well."

"Great."

"He sings to this bird, to help him get back up. The bird says no, if I help you she'll kill me too."

"Nice."

"And it's all very sweet and calmly sung."

Bryce, walking around the apartment, stopped and put his hands in his pockets. Slightly taller than Reo, just short of six feet, he had the look of someone trying to figure out a puzzle, thinking over a strategy.

"You know, I think the secret to that type of song is to understate it. To sing it calmly, as if relating a story but not getting involved inside it. It's different than declarations of love and that sort of thing. For those you want to get wound up."

Reo sat and thought that over, swirling his cup, studying the surface of the dark brew as if it held some answer. In the silence Bryce poured another coffee for himself and set it down, just as the loud ring of the telephone interrupted.

"Hold that thought," said Bryce.

31–Now We're Getting Somewhere

Ted Imbonante was onstage with his band, singing one of his songs about leaving New York for the quiet life of a mountain cabin out west, the words written by a poet friend who had done just that, moved west. Ted did not write lyrics, only music, and was dependent upon the poems of his distant friend, a guy he had gone to high school and college with. And then he unfolded a piece of paper and stuck it on the mike stand with a piece of tape, pointing sideways at Reo, seated in the L-shaped corner booth just inside the archway.

"The guy who wrote this is right there," he told the crowd, and counted a quick, one-two-three-four and started strumming. Reo heard the familiar chords of his song, followed by Ted's big, round voice.

> Late last night a stranger came crawlin'
> Crawlin' down my fire escape

The band responded with a fierce rendition of Reo's chord changes, a chord progression he had made to fit the words, a chord progression he had not seen anywhere else. A guitar solo rose above the band, ending punctually with a drum fill, and Veronica's soaring violin running behind the words framed the ending of the song. True to his word, Ted sang

> You better getta your shotgun ready
> 'cause hard times
> Is out on the edge of town

The crowd, many of them the band's friends from Queens, broke into applause, as Reo looked up and saw a tall blond man handing him a beer.

"You wrote that," he said, a statement rather than a question, and slid down into the booth.

"Yes. I did."

The man had a high, nasal voice and the downbeat assurance of someone who had seen it all.

"Ya know, I see a lot. It's a jungle out theah. But until now, I didn't hear it. In here, I mean."

Reo took a sip of the beer, raised the glass.

"Thanks," he said, not knowing what else to say.

"Exactly," the tall man nodded. "You're welcome."

After the show Ted slapped Reo on the back, took him to the bar and bought him another beer.

"Royalties. Call it an advance payment."

"For what?"

"I'm gonna make an album."

"That's great," Reo smiled. "Soon?"

"Soon," Ted grinned, took a long slug of beer, and walked away.

Nine days before his job as Alice's opening act, he went to the open mike on a Monday night. The place was packed, one of those nights when ninety people signed up to play. Reo MacGregor knew almost none of them, so he sat in the back and waited until his number came up. The biggest surprise was Lila, the bartender, who answered number 8C; she had a small blond guitar, big soft brown eyes, and a tight pair of jeans that wiggled in time with the music. Seemingly unaware of the hungry eyes staring at her torso, her cool, kittenish voice sailed through the songs effortlessly, totally in tune, as if the possibility of hitting a wrong note never existed. Reo watched her set, captivated, moved to sadness when she hit a warm, lower register.

What do you say when
It's over?

and as she finished, someone exhaled loudly near the stage, then burst into applause. A slow wave of handclaps traveled around the room as she gathered her case and headed toward the bar, then stopped. She stood there, broke into a big smile, and seemed about to say something, when she heard, from the other end of the bar, Tony O, calling her back to work.

Reo worked the next day at the print shop, slicing strips of printed stories into readable lines and paragraphs. The afternoon turned into a long evening, everything running late and tempers running over.

"Uh, oh," he said to himself.

"What?" overheard Burt, the newspaper's editor, a tall, wavy brown-haired man with a blue and white striped shirt and a nervous way of pacing back and forth in front of the pages they were assembling.

"You have 'the president says giving a break to wealthier people will be to everyone's benefit' over here," Reo told him.

"Yeah. So?"

"President is always spelled with a capital P. At least The President."

Burt exhaled a long breath as if letting steam escape. He had about had it with this paste-up guy who was correcting his copy after it had been edited, typed, printed on expensive paper, and pasted on the large master sheets waiting to be photographed for the actual print edition. In other words, it was way too late in the process to be changing things. Burt also knew that to be taken seriously, especially as a journalism critique, you can't have careless mistakes in your stories.

"Can you fix it?"

Reo scratched his chin. He hadn't shaven in three days, was hungry and was wondering if they'd ever finish the job. But he scanned the adjoining page and found a story about a Lester Padonov, an upstate police chief sentenced that afternoon for taking bribes from an erotic dance club offering girls for outcalls.

"This story ran long, didn't it?" he asked Burt.

"Yes."

"Where are the extra galleys, the columns that were cut?"

"Over there." Burt waved. Reo searched the pile of typed columns and found three instances of Padonov with a capital P; cutting a small square around one with a razor tip, he dropped the letter on the story and steered it into place, sealing it with transparent tape.

"There you go," he said.

"You are a wizard," Burt shook his head. "A real pain in the ass. But a wizard. Thank you."

One afternoon he went to Alice's, playing guitar with her and Joshua for hours, learning her chords and songs in her one-room apartment. Her tree-lined West Village neighborhood of brick townhouses and diagonal streets smelled fresh and crisp in the last days of Indian summer, the dry scent of leaves turning from green to dust. It was a favorite time of year, for it reminded Reo of his childhood front yard, and always filled him with longing. Longing for what? he asked himself every year, and knew this year he would not know the answer, any more than in previous years.

Diners in sidewalk cafes had their jackets on now, and couples walked more closely entwined, young lovers and casual friends wrapped in animated conversation. He passed a café window displaying a man-made powdered dessert, stopped before an art gallery with a large painting taller than himself, entirely of fire red, and three thin, yellow, vertical stripes. It stared back at him like a huge square eye with an immense hangover.

"Well, look who it is," said a familiar voice.

It was Bryce, and a woman taller than Reo, standing erect beneath an impressive structure of curled silver hair, dyed or painted to look way beyond the years of her round face.

"This is Reo," Bryce said to her. "He's the singer I was telling you about. Reo, Glenna."

She offered a small, pale hand and he took it, getting a firm shake.

"Why don't we go in this café and have coffee," Bryce said, and they walked past the powdered desserts to a circular table no bigger than a basketball, perched on one cheek on the metal chair, and ordered a cappuccino, a latte with decaf espresso, and, for Reo, a black coffee.

"So, Reo" Bryce said. "Take a look at Glenna and tell me what you think she does for a living."

He looked her over. She was not beautiful, but had an animal quality to her that made her interesting, watchable, and he said the first thing that came to mind.

"I think she's an actress, in theaters, maybe, underground stuff."

Glenna snorted. Bryce stirred his coffee and kept on with it.

"Underground stuff."

"Something like that."

"Very good," Bryce nodded. "She is indeed in the underground, and furthermore is an actress, in movies. Porn movies, in fact. And in case you're wondering, it is a real job, with real pay and long hours."

"I'll bet," said Reo. "It must be real hard work, too."

"Ah, yes, I'll bet it is," Bryce smiled. "And Reo, my dear, is a singer.

And songwriter. And a paste-up artist, too, I understand. My goal is to make him stop doing newspaper work."

Reo laughed and looked her over a second time. She met his eyes with a bemused expression, and was, on some level, genuinely unattractive, at least to him.

"How you gonna do that?" she asked, smiling, peeling off a jacket and settling onto the thin bench. She was wearing no makeup and had her feet across Bryce's legs. Reo wondered if the hair was a wig. It certainly looked real except for the color.

"It's real," she said as if she knew what he was thinking. "I'm in a show."

"Was I that obvious?"

"Everybody stares at her hair," Bryce broke in. "Anyway, to answer your question, I'm going to take Reo up to meet Jeffrey Harriman."

In the front window a tall, blond man was twirling a long, pliant strand of dough into a foot-long cruller, dipping it in syrup, setting it on a tray to be baked. A tall, thin girl with long blond hair wound in a circle on top of her head, like a crown stitched right into her locks, picked the tray up and backed through two swinging doors into a kitchen in the back.

"Are you listening?"

Reo turned toward Bryce but saw Glenna first. She was smiling at him, as if she knew Bryce was on to something. And he was.

"I called his office. He remembers your tape, said it was okay," he began, stretching out the last word. "That's the phrase he used, anyway. 'Okay.' He wants to meet you. Friday afternoon."

Reo was silent, waiting for some sign it was a joke, that Bryce was pulling his leg. What's the punch line?

"This is serious. It's happening. You are going to see Jeffrey Harriman. The real question is, what are you going to do then?"

32–To See The Great Man

On a creaky, waist-high stool of blond wood, Reo MacGregor sat with his guitar across his legs, flatpick in hand, when it occurred to him that many very famous singers had probably sat on this stool at some point in time. For a moment he glimpsed spotlights and footlights—colored phantasmas, the singer as canvas—and he tuned the guitar, listening to the notes ring out in the room. It was the moment when he always thought about what the previous performer had done, imagined himself in someone's footsteps, wondering where to start, how to channel that information into a real performance of his own. Now, he sat back and watched as his host looked in one drawer after another, until he found the piece of paper he was searching for and placed it on his desk, a large and cluttered slab of gray where he nonetheless maintained a bare spot right in front of him. Reo let his eyes wander around the small cubicle; it was high above the city streets, its window a view of formless sky, its insides crammed with open boxes of old tapes and recordings, spilling framed gold records as if they meant nothing to their owner, stacked on top of each other. Photographs apparently were more his thing, covering every inch of wall space with snapshots of famous musicians and singers, each one with his arm around Jeffrey Harriman, who stood grinning and beaming with pride at the success of his star. Each photo was signed with "To Jeffrey" and some uniquely flattering phrase: "To Jeffrey, the man who knows my soul." "To Jeffrey, with everlasting gratitude." "To Jeffrey, love always." "To Jeffrey, the main man." And each signer had probably been in this office, and stood before the tall, energetic man in the gray tweed sport jacket, white shirt open at the collar, crew cut and great big smile.

"So what have you written lately?" he asked.

Reo sang him “Hard Times,” finding it hard to look at the man while he sang, just staring straight ahead.

“Well that’s something,” Harriman said with a big grin. “How about something with some humor.” He pronounced humor as “humah,” neither dwelling on it nor dragging it out.

Reo had been working on something lately, thought he might as well give it a try.

You want to take me out for dinner
I think your idea’s a winner
Always glad to meet a patron of the arts
Have some caviar and crackers
Open up your little smackers
Tell the waitress how she’s looking very smart

You’re a patron of the arts
You’re a patron of the arts
You deserve a certificate at least
Though I know my stuff is trying
And I’m really glad you’re buying
Please excuse me for a minute while I eat

Reo sang in waltz time, strumming the simple chords, trying not to think but to sing the melody.

“All right,” said Harriman, rubbing his hands together. “We’re not buying just yet, but we’re making progress.”

“Do you mind waltzes?” Reo asked.

“Not a bit, love ‘em.”

A tale in the papers
of prison escapers
hiding in the woods nearby
who were serving six years
for stealing some beers
from a grocer with connections up high
Was read by the prelate
who finds out but too late

They've taken three of his school's boys
And they're demanding an airplane
and freedom in exchange
For letting the three of them go

And he says tear down the woods
Cut down the trees
Bring down the outside world to its knees
Take all the children and bring us the best
Making it safe for an academy desk
Safe for an academy desk

It was a long, slow song, and ended badly when the cops showed up and started a bloodbath.

"Oh, I like that," Harriman beamed. "Safe for an academy desk. Were you an academy student yourself?"

Reo looked at Bryce, then back at his host.

"I was," he said.

"There's someone here who knows you," Harriman said. "Roy Edelstein, says he went to Columbia with you. Did you go to Columbia Law School?"

The question hung in the air like a helium balloon against the ceiling. Reo believed when people say musicians need something to "fall back on," they aren't taking your work seriously. He wanted Jeffrey Harriman to take him seriously. And he didn't want to lie.

"I'm impressed,' Reo said, "Ten minutes and you know my bio."

"Oh, it's quite accidental, I assure you," Harriman waved. "Roy saw your name on my calendar and mentioned it. So it's true."

"Yes."

"Do you intend to practice?"

"No."

Harriman studied him with a frank but open expression, then broke into his broad smile.

"Well, good for you," he said. "I think you've made a wise choice."

Bryce Warterburn leaned forward and tapped Reo on the knee.

"How about 'Hollywood Movie'?"

"What's that?" Harriman asked.

"A song about the Kennedy assassination."

Jeffrey Harriman nodded and squinted at Bryce.

"I know he must have a lot of songs. He's a very bright young man, I can see that."

Bryce leaned back.

"But," he said simply.

"I have been informed that I can't sign anyone without their say-so. I think you have some promise though, so let's record a handful of songs next week. I can do that without asking anyone."

"Really?" Reo sat up.

"You sound surprised," said Jeffrey Harriman, leaning back in his chair, stretching his hands behind his head.

Reo laughed quietly.

"No, nothing really surprises me, I guess. Or everything. It's truly an honor, Mr. Harriman, that's all."

The great man looked at him and broke into a reluctant laugh. He was well aware of his own reputation in the music world.

"I guess you can look at it that way, if you want to," he answered in his smooth, melodic tone. "I want to mention something to you, though. When you sing, and play, and especially when you make a recording, you have to remember that the person listening may be doing nothing more than pushing a broom around the house, or dancing by the sink. They may not be listening to the words at all."

"You mean watch my time," Reo smiled, relaxing, holding his guitar across his legs.

"I mean all music is essentially dance music," shrugged Jeffrey Harriman exaggeratedly, palms up. "Even protest music. Or a solo piece. That's all I mean. It's a fact."

Reo took the subway to the Village, dragging his guitar to a couple of his favorite cafes without seeing anyone he knew. It was a chilly, dry evening, and he felt good to have the time alone, holding onto the secret that Jeffrey Harriman had invited him to record some songs. He did not want to jinx himself, and did not want anyone to know before it happened; by mid-evening Reo was, as he had been for three evenings in a row, locked in his nearly empty apartment, what Bryce referred to as "his tower."

"You're like the madwoman up there, no furniture, no food, just you and your guitar," he said.

"That's how I like it," Reo answered. "Good acoustics."

He hung out in the back room, where there was a mattress with his sleeping bag. Two bed sheets from a church second-hand store curtained the windows, one overlooking the empty real estate that had burned to a distant traffic light, where cars slid over the glistening asphalt under a thin mist, punctuated by horns, yelling, buses, ambulances and the occasional fire truck. Inevitably, his single metal folding chair ended up at this window, where he watched the intersection, strumming the guitar. He watched the light change, again and again, from red to green to yellow, red and green and yellow; he closed his eyes. When he opened them again it was yellow, then red; he blinked slowly again and it was green.

And he wrote:

There's no music
There's no sound
There's no window
Through the clouds
All I get's a restless moaning
Kind of wind
There's no flame
There's no light
There's no love in sight tonight
All I know's these
Sleepless nights
Got to end

He had a second verse and a bridge when he ran out of words, stood up, grabbed his guitar and began strumming a chord, listening for the melody. It was a floating, high melody, and he had to sing it in a full voice to hit the notes. He sang it again and was trying to decide if it was enough, or if it needed one more verse, when he looked out the window at the moment when night stops and day has not yet begun. He had seen it other nights: no traffic, the streets empty, still. One night he counted three green lights before morning crawled in: a bus, a taxi horn, a steadily increasing flow of traffic and noise, and the day arrived.

Usually he went to bed. He set down the guitar, put on his thin denim jacket and went out into the mist. He walked quickly through the gray, pre-dawn stillness to the East River bank, watching a furious ball of red sun fight its way through a hazy gap across the water.

A chilly breeze picked up; he wrapped his arms around his chest and started home. A truck pulled up at the curb ahead. A man jumped out and opened a newspaper vending machine with one hand, a bundle of newspapers in the other. He yanked a single page from the machine, thoughtlessly sent it fluttering into the stiff breeze, then dropped the fresh days' news into place and slammed the door. The truck was gone before the now-homeless front page, separated from its bigger self, floated back to the sidewalk, where its large, block letters stared straight at Reo:

JoZ: 'It's A Secret'

It was a story about JoZ, an actress so famous, so desired, so well promoted, that the mere fact she would not answer a question was front-page news, so important that her three-letter name was enough to identify her to millions. He, on the other hand, was to play his first real set at the Folk Life tonight, and thus remembering it was Wednesday, saw it had been Tuesday's paper. Must have been a pretty slow day for news, even old news, he thought, wondering what had really happened that day, what was really going on, what didn't the suits want people to know, that they had filled the air with JoZ.

He picked up the page of day-old print and rolled it into a tube, threading it into his jacket. Walking down the sidewalk, hands in his side pockets, he began the last verse.

Newspaper blowing across the road
Just like me another day old
And all I know's these
Sleepless nights
Got to end

33–The Gig

He started his first set promptly on time. The stage was bare except for the mikes and Joshua's guitar on a stand. Jake, a short, heavy man with a long gray pigtail and beard sat behind the mixing board, through which Reo's voice rattled around the empty audience.

Wednesday's news indeed had different headlines; a dozen local men had gone into Washington Square Park and beaten up the loose federation of drug salesmen and their friends with baseball bats. The newspapers had all carried the story on the front page; at Folk Life, one of the regulars had walked in, breathlessly taken off his overcoat, and announced "the streets are officially deserted!" The respectable people from other parts of the city, from Uptown, the West or East Side, and Brooklyn or Queens, or Jersey, were nowhere to be seen. The only customers were the locals, the guys who sat at the bar to drink, without regard to who was singing on the stage.

"They're afraid of getting beaten up," someone said.

"Why would they be afraid of that? They don't go in the park."

"It's all the press. I even saw it on TV."

Alice was pretty upset and only partly mollified when a few of her fans drifted in during Reo's last song, timing it perfectly. She put on a great show, sassy and funny, and several left saying "I'm coming back this weekend." But no one stayed for his second show, until Bryce and Glenna walked in during his third song. Bryce looked around and raised his eyebrows, standing there, slowly taking off his coat in the archway.

"Where shall we sit?" he inquired politely, scanning the sea of empty chairs. The evening's waitress climbed off a bar stool, wearing a short leather skirt and blue leggings, three-inch gold hoops dangling from her ears, and led Glenna to a table along the back wall. Her name was Madeline, Reo recalled.

"Hey," Reo said. "Glad you made it."

"Glad somebody made it," Bryce replied. Reo stepped back, eyed the room and went straight into "In The Morning," remembering Bryce had once asked him about it. Jake, the sound man, caught Reo's eye and held up a single finger: one more song. He finished with "Hard Times," had planned it that way, expecting more of a crowd, and played it aggressively, singing with all the energy he could put into it, and earned a respectful round of applause from the bar customers, off in the dark beyond the arch.

"They liked that one," Bryce said, as Reo sat down. Another small crowd trickled in for Alice's set. Reo watched her singing to a dozen fans as if to a packed house, never losing her smile.

On the second night, he sat at the bar during her second set, amid the men who drank there every night, for whom Folk Life was their neighborhood bar.

"*The New York Times* should be here," declared Tommy Castro, a fast-talking man with a well-trimmed, prematurely gray beard. "You get that review and they come to you. Except Waverly, he's the only one I ever knew, got a review in the *Times* and didn't get a record deal."

"You mean Jonas?" Reo asked.

"First week he played here," replied Castro. "We had him uptown; first thing he does, marches right in and starts telling everybody what to do. I swear, didn't wait five minutes."

"Uptown? You work there yourself? Where?" Reo asked.

"I work in the art department, drawing and illustrating promos, cd covers, ads, whatever. So I hear about it, you know?" He turned back to a shot of some golden-colored liquid in a short glass, watching his hand swirl it around over the ice.

"You just don't do that," he finished.

There were six of them, fellow drinkers holding down the fort on a slow night. Reo sat next to Carl, a tall man with straight blond hair cut right across his shoulders, giving his head the appearance of having wings. Reo sat and listened to his high-pitched New York accent, recalling it was Carl who had bought him a beer at Ted's gig.

"I can tell you're not a drinking man," he said, leaning back and looking at Reo sideways. "That's not a bad thing, ya unnerstan. It's just that I can always tell a drinking man. You're a good songwrita; oh I hear it from here, don't think I don't. That 'Hard Times' is real strong, you should record that one now while it mattahs."

After one of Alice's racier songs, Carl spoke loud enough for the others at the bar to hear.

"Watching this chick reminds me, I gotta get laid soon," he said.

"Need a helping hand?" crooned Jamie, who stood next to Carl in a muted blue plaid suit and wiggled his hips.

"Get away from me, you pervert," Carl replied in a fake snarl, and everyone at the bar laughed loudly. Reo looked up and saw Alice, in the distance, frowning at them from the stage.

The streets remained empty until Friday, when the city made some arrests. Reo played for his first crowd that evening and it felt good, a different level of energy than a coffeehouse, everyone drinking and dressed up for a good time. He was surprised to feel them responding to his serious songs, more than when he tried to be entertaining, and by Saturday he had a short, tight set together.

"I think you're ready for him," Bryce told him, when he came back on Sunday, this time alone. "I've been hearing you practice upstairs. And check this out."

He flashed the cover of *Minstrel,* one of the entertainment industry's main magazines, folded it open to a middle page and read it out loud, softly, just for Reo, as Alice and Joshua tuned up and got ready to go on.

"Reo MacGregor's debut at the Folk Life Café showed a young man with a lot on his mind. A fluent singer with a rough tenor and straightforward delivery, MacGregor worked his way through folk, jazz, light rock and blues before landing on 'Hard Times,' his own standout tune. MacGregor's songs are rich in detail and observation, and with the help of his mentor Jeffrey Harriman, he is a young man who offers a lot of promise."

Reo blinked twice.

"When was he here?"

"Beats me," said Bryce. "Just shows you never know who's out there. You have to always be on."

A few open mikers showed up too, including Ted, Jonas, Jason, and Tim Marcek, and after Alice's last set they all went to a late-night restaurant a few blocks away, ordering omelets and pancakes.

"So," growled Jonas across the table. "What did yeew do to get a review in *Minstrel*?"

"Yeah," echoed Ted. "What's this about Jeffrey Harriman?"

Reo took a bite of his Denver omelet, ham and cheese with some tomatoes thrown in for an extra 75 cents.

"I met him," he answered simply.

"And?"

"I played a few songs for him."

"He calls him your mentor," Ted observed.

"I am hoping to work with him," Reo shrugged.

"Methinks," Jonas rasped in a stage whisper, silence spreading around the table, "he knows more than he pretends."

Tim Marcek stirred his coffee.

"Good for you," he said in his big, round voice, silencing the table. They watched as he took a four-inch tan cylinder from his shirt pocket, produced a cigarette from his other pocket, planted it in one end, and, without lighting it, waved it slowly before them. It reminded Reo of a video he had once seen of Franklin Roosevelt, as Tim continued in his casual, elegant tone.

"Don't tell him a thing." Marcek waved his cigarette at Jonas and nodded, smiling at Reo. "Not a thing."

Reo chewed deliberately through a piece of rye toast before replying.

"Tell you what, Jonas," he said. "When there's something to tell you, I'll let you know." They watched as he slid his fork under a big, flat chunk of fried potatoes and stuffed it into his mouth, smiling, enjoying his first real meal in days.

34–Lightning Strikes

He sat all afternoon with a notepad on his lap, trying to be a writer; occasionally, he would get up and walk around, then get an idea, sit down, write it down quickly, and sit back. Slowly a shape emerged in the background, words became lines, lines became rhymes and then pairs of rhymes. Each verse became a mini-story within itself, a piece of a life, perhaps his own, perhaps only a life he imagined. This last realization, that it did not need to be about himself, but instead be a fully-realized character speaking, left him leaning back against his metal folding chair, feet up on the windowsill, thinking of his own memories.

> I took down an old volume
> of your letters to me
> and laid them out to read
> just yesterday
> and though I tried to regain
> the feelings you named
> I couldn't bring 'em back
> In any easy way

A second verse on the beach—dancing hand in hand with a lovely young lady in the moonlight, only to wake alone, face down on the sand—yielded to a third spent on the highway, unable to stay away from the "city's silver lights." Two more followed, and he was looking at the last one, thinking it seemed to be the right one for a chorus, when he heard Bryce's voice coming through the hole in his kitchen floor.

"Hey, you have a phone call."

"Just a minute, I'll come down," he said. He set the guitar on the bed and went out, locking the door behind him. He went downstairs and took the phone from an impatient Bryce.

"Hello?"

"Reo? Hi. It's Lila. I hope you don't mind me calling, I got the number at the bar."

"Lila? Oh. Hi. It's okay. Hi."

"I was in the neighborhood and, well, I have most of the night off, Tony O told me he didn't need me tonight, so I don't have to be back to the bar til one."

"Where are you now?" Reo asked her.

"The Del Rico, the coffee place on Eighth. Do you know it?"

He did, and said he would come meet her.

"Can you come right away? There's some guy bothering me."

He left at once, found her five minutes later in the cafe, alone and slightly scared. He scanned the small crowd of customers and saw no one staring at her.

"Is your apartment nearby?" she asked him, and he took her back to his building, to Bryce's cleaner, furnished place. Bryce had his jacket on.

"I have to meet Glenna," he said. "Keep it locked." They heard his key turn in the lock as he left.

He led her to the small table; she unbuttoned her denim jacket, unraveled the scarf around her neck, and remained standing.

"You can feel the winter, just around the corner," she said in her soft, cool voice.

"Do you want some coffee?" he asked. She began walking around the apartment, looking casually through open doorways.

"Where do you sleep?" she asked him.

"Actually, I live in the apartment just above this one," he said. "I brought you here because mine is, well, kind of empty."

She went into the small bedroom, its mattress on the floor made up with a pillow, sheet. and blanket. "For guests," Bryce called it.

"Is this your friend's room?"

"No," he said. "It's the guest room."

She smiled and came back out. She walked over and took him by the hand, led him back through the doorway and to the mattress. He sat next to her, their backs against the wall, as she shook off her shoes.

"Thanks for coming for me," she said. "I haven't seen you since you stayed at my place."

"Yeah," he said. "I didn't know what to say to you. I was pretty drunk."

She smiled and took his hand.

"You don't have to say anything," she said, and looked right in his eyes. They drifted easily into a kiss and slid down from the wall, stretching side by side on the mattress, removing jackets, sweaters, tee-shirts, unbuttoning buttons, unzipping zippers, sliding things off, until they were naked on the bed. Straddling him on his back, she tossed her thick black hair backwards and rested her hands on his chest.

"You're not drunk now," she smiled, stretching her shoulders back. He lay back and looked at her; none of her beauty was from makeup, styling or fake, and he enjoyed looking at her.

"I mean, I know you're in love with Callisto and all that," she went on. "Everybody knows that."

He gave her a look of genuine surprise.

"I'm in love with Callisto?"

"Well, you wrote that song. And I see how you look at her."

He ran his fingernail along her side; she shivered with pleasure.

"Aren't you in love with her?" she asked.

He took his hand away, stretched his arms behind his head and lay back on the pillow.

"Just now, it was the farthest thing from my mind," he said.

"She told me she slept with you."

He didn't reply to that, and was trying to think of a different conversation, when she continued.

"It's okay. I mean, I have a boyfriend. You know him. I probably shouldn't be doing this, but I am, I guess."

He wasn't sure he knew him, or why she was doing this; she slid forward on his legs.

"Well, I don't have all night," she exhaled. "And it always takes me such a long time to come. So, what do ya say?."

It did feel good, so good that when it was over they lay still; and after some time, they began again in a dreamier state of mind. Later, as she was quietly resting in his embrace, the sound of breaking glass in the distance broke their mood. She laughed softly.

"Hey, Did you hear what happened last night?" she asked him. "This suit came in and said 'the guys uptown are about to sign someone to a deal. Someone from around here.'"

She paused.

"I'm not kidding, that's what he said," she added.

"Someone you know?"

"I've seen him before. One of the regulars says the guy does work for a label."

He watched her brush curly, black strands of hair from her eyes.

"So who do you think it is?" she asked him, widening her eyes and cocking her head to one side. "Got a theory? Everyone else does."

"You mean who do I think the suits will sign?"

"Yes."

He had no idea, had heard nothing first-hand.

"I don't know. Is it you?"

"Me? That would be nice. But if it's me no one has said anything about it."

He didn't reply to that.

"I was wondering if it's you."

"Me?" he looked at her, surprised.

"Well, you were mentioned in that magazine. With that producer."

"Yeah," he said, "that's true. Well, no one has said anything yet to me either."

They heard the door open, the tumbling of a cylinder, the creak of hinges, the rubber edging on its base sliding across the linoleum floor. They heard Bryce walk to another part of the apartment, footsteps crisp on the refinished wood.

"I should go," she whispered. "Can you walk me to a cab?"

Quickly, they got up and dressed, and she let him find a taxi on the nearby avenue, kissing him on the cheek as she slipped into the back seat.

"This is crazy," she said. She didn't want him to accompany her back to Folk Life, so he said good night and watched her cab drive away. There was a sudden flash of lightning, followed by a loud crack of thunder blocks away. He bought a sandwich at a nearby market and headed back to his building, climbing six flights of stairs with no overhead bulbs, dark landings with windowless doors, the walls exploding into shadows as the white flashes drew closer outside. He opened his door and a blast of air hit him in the face, suddenly cold, and as he crossed the room a massive bolt of lightning streaked somewhere over the skyline, followed immediately by thunder. Inside, the rain was coming in, soaking his room.

The window was empty except for a few jagged, remaining triangles of glass wedged into the frame; the rest of it lay on the floor, beneath the crumpled curtain, and crunched beneath his feet as he turned around.

His bed, usually covered by a sleeping bag, was a bare mattress, and that meant only one thing.

His guitar was gone.

35–The Search

He and Bryce crisscrossed the entire roof in the post-thunderstorm mist, the lightning now gone out to sea; no one was out, and there was nothing to be done until morning. He rose early in Bryce's guest room, dressed quickly and had some coffee, his host awake and ready to go.

They spent the morning in pawn shops on Third Avenue, asking vaguely "if we could see some guitars." Offered cheap knock-offs, Reo mentioned he was interested in a Gibson, and they said he could see "what's in the back" if he came back with five hundred dollars. When he mentioned he was looking for a Gibson Country & Western model, with trapezoidal inlay on the fret board and a pickguard with scalloped edges, they were told to leave. After five attempts, they stopped for lunch.

"That's how it works, isn't it," Reo said disconsolately. "The guys who steal work for these guys, who keep everything locked away."

They talked with a policeman in the small café, who said there was "nothing I can do unless you have a warrant," which, he said, would be impossible to get without knowing the guitar was really in one of the shops.

"By now, whoever has yours probably has gotten it out of town anyway," Bryce ventured after the cop had left.

"Is that supposed to make me feel better?" Reo scoffed. "I bet it's back there, in one of those stores, right now. You could tell from the way they act, any of them would buy it, and keep us from seeing it."

Bryce was about to tell Reo he was being irrational, blaming everyone for his loss; but he knew better.

In the early afternoon they grabbed a few random tools—a flashlight, a stubby, firm-handled kitchen knife—and went up on the roof. They found a rope hidden behind an old, empty box. It was less than an inch thick; whoever used it was not very heavy.

"That's how he got in," Reo said. "He came down from the roof."

"Pretty desperate people," Bryce mused, standing there, his hands in his pockets. Reo climbed onto the higher rooftop next door, walked a large circle and stopped at the back edge, where a fire escape trailed down.

Bryce came puffing up behind him.

"Are there people living in all these buildings like this? Coming in from the windows instead of the doors?" Reo asked him.

Bryce bent over and caught his breath.

"I suppose so. I don't know."

Reo took the flashlight, hopped onto the edge of the roof and studied the flimsy metal structure snaking down to the topmost window. Its white paint long peeled away to rust, it only went that far; markings on the wall showed it once extended down to the ground, but now only the top section remained. It looked as if it might disengage from the wall at any moment, crashing to the street seven flights below.

"What are you thinking?" Bryce asked.

"Tie this down," was his answer, as he tied the rope around his waist and handed the other end to Bryce. He worked his way carefully down the rickety steps, past the turn, toward the open window a flight below. It was dark inside, and he listened for a sound. There was none, so he leaned in and shone the light on the walls and floor. Empty. He was about to leave when something caught his eye on the floor, something strangely familiar.

He sat backwards on the threshold and looked up. Bryce was staring at him from the roof.

"Stay there and wait" he whispered as loudly as he could. Quickly, he slid inside, shining the light on the floor.

It was a small orange flatpick, slightly worn on the edges. He turned it over and read .60, the thickness he himself preferred. There was nothing else in the room; alert, he stepped soundlessly into the adjoining room, where his sleeping bag was stashed against the wall. Excited, he shone the flashlight into every corner, but found nothing else.

Leaving the bag as he had found it, he tied the rope back on and climbed back up, trying to make no sound. Bryce called the police, and at about ten pm, two uniformed officers showed up at the door.

“I'm Officer Schaefer. You said there are some stolen goods,” declared a stocky, pockmarked-faced blond man with thick, meaty hands. The second cop, a wiry, olive-skinned man with dark glasses, stared as Reo explained what he had found and where. And that he wanted to catch the person in that apartment, and find out where his guitar was.

““We can't go in there,” Schaefer said.

“It's an empty apartment. No one lives there legally,” Bryce said.

“How do you know that? We can't just break in because you say you saw something. What the hell's a flat pick?”

They were about to leave when Reo had an idea.

“What if someone let you in?”

“How are you going to do that?” Schaefer asked.

“I guess that's not your problem,” Reo replied.

The two cops looked expressionlessly at each other.

“You can go to the top of the stairs in the building right next door to this one. Be there in ten minutes,” Reo said.

“Ten minutes,” Schaefer said. “That's all.” And abruptly they turned and started walking downstairs.

Reo grabbed the flashlight and put on his jacket.

“You're even crazier than I thought,” Bryce protested.

“You go with them,” Reo said. “If you hear a noise, yell, ‘everything ok in there?’ The guy will open the door himself.”

“That's the dumbest idea ever,” Bryce said.

“Just do it, okay? I'm going down that fire escape.”

“Jesus H Christ,” Bryce shook his head. “At least take this.” And he handed Reo the small, stubby knife.

He was over the other roof quickly, quietly tiptoeing down the flimsy metal steps. Looking out, distracted by the lights flickering in distant windows, disoriented, motionless, he listened for any warning sound and thought of those creatures who live every day of their lives in some abandoned building, stealing from wherever they could. Well, he told himself, all I want is my guitar back.

He was the intruder now, vulnerable to someone shoving him off the fire escape or shooting him; he was the one sneaking around. At the window he inched forward, leaned forward without moving his feet, and at last could see into the room, first a corner, then the far wall.

As his eyes adjusted, he spied a lumpy form on the floor, near the back wall. Quickly, he shone the light inside and pulled it back; when nothing happened he shone the light inside again. Nothing.

Heart pounding, he stepped across the windowsill and landed with a soft thump. The shape never stirred, and he moved swiftly through the layout he had memorized; he turned the knob softly and opened the door on Bryce and the two policemen, shifting their weight from leg to leg.

"He's in there," Reo said, waving toward the bedroom on his right, behind him. "Lying on my sleeping bag."

Without a word Schaefer and his partner stepped past him, unholstered and drew their guns, cautious, about to walk blindly into a dark apartment. They went into the room behind their police flashlights; Reo watched the unidentified policemen grab a skinny young man and yank him to his feet. Schaefer turned around and walked toward Reo, backing him out of the room; there was the crunch of the young man thrown against the wall, and, for the first time, the voice of the other cop.

"You little motherfucker, you piece of shit, what the fuck do you think is going on here?" the cop ranted in a wheedling, piercing tone, followed by the body being tossed a second and third time, until the boy cried out in a thin, high-pitched wail and sank to the floor.

"You hurt me," he sobbed.

Schaefer, standing in the doorway, blocking Reo and Bryce from seeing anything, turned and holstered the gun he had silently had ready.

"We'll take it from here," he said. With no trace of a smile, he pointed at the stairs with a thick finger. "Go back to your apartment. We'll come talk to you after this is settled."

But Reo stood there, unwilling to leave.

"Get the fuck out of here," the cop said. "Now."

An hour later Schaefer was at their door, alone. His partner was downstairs, "waiting in the car, so I don't have long, but I climbed up here to give you this." And he handed Reo his sleeping bag.

"He's fifteen, lives up the street with his father," he continued. "We took him home. Precinct knows him, says they won't press charges."

Reo stood there and waited. The cop turned to go.

"Is that it? What about my guitar?"

"He didn't say anything about that."

"Did you ask?"

The husky, blond cop stepped forward right into Reo's chest.

"You know, you're lucky we don't make you for B & E," he said quietly. "If I were you I wouldn't take this any further." And without waiting for an answer, he turned and left.

36–Recording Session #2

"I can't believe that, it's too crazy," said Lila Mazursky, drawing her robe closed around her waist. He had shown up out of nowhere in the middle of the night, looking like he hadn't slept in days, wired up and wild-eyed, exhausted from walking around all day, unable to sit still or go home.

"That's really what he said? That instead of getting back your guitar he was going to arrest you?"

"Those were his words," Reo exhaled, slowly sinking into the chair, stirring the coffee she had made for him. "You think the cops are working for you, but in reality they're working for the pawn shops. If they were to ask that kid where he took that guitar, all hell might break loose."

She watched him, clearly agitated and unable to pull himself together.

"You know, you think it's about the money, or about the guitar, but it's really about being violated, having something that's a part of you ripped away and then being prevented from looking for it."

She sighed heavily and sipped a coffee. She could see how deeply hurt he was, and felt sad for him; but it was not how she had planned to spend her evening off, playing therapist to someone coming unglued.

"Hey, do you have a guitar around?" he asked suddenly.

"Um, yeah," she said, somewhat slowly.

"Can I play it for a minute? Don't worry, I'm not asking to borrow it or anything, I was working on a song and I want to sing it before I forget it."

"All right," she said, and got up to get her guitar. By the time she returned, he had a piece of paper on the table and was looking it over. She handed him her guitar, a small-bodied Martin with the shine of being recently polished; he ran his fingers over the strings, as if dazed, while she settled down on her chair, becoming quiet and warily attentive. He picked a few notes and nodded.

"Nice. Okay, here goes." He started with his fingers, but, hesitating, thumbed a single note, a solitary low tone on the A string. He fell into a very slow fingerpicking, leaving the second string open, letting the B drone on top. It had a quiet, meditative sound, an incomplete quality that implied it might resolve into a chord, and as he finished the verse, his eyes jumped ahead to the last verse, and it became a chorus.

> I built me a castle on the sand
> I made those towers with my own hand
> Just when you believe you made them strong enough
> They go washing out to sea
> When the waves get rough

It was a long, slow song, quieter and quieter until it reached a last verse, with a higher note that was hard to sing in a whisper.

> I come to you with roses
> I come to you again
> I know we are just castles on some shore
> Though the night be filled with darkness
> I shall not close my eyes
> Til these petals fall down
> Forgotten to the floor

he sang, and the last, hypnotic notes, an A chord with the B droning on top, were unresolved, as Reo stared at the floor and could not look in her face.

"That's the last song I wrote on that guitar," he said quietly. He began to shiver, letting out the pent-up emotion he had contained through the two days since he had seen her, tears smearing his face, unable to see.

Lila lifted the guitar from his hands and set it on the table; she stood above him a moment, then sat on his lap and wrapped her arms around him, holding him as he sobbed, her lips on his eyes, kissing him softly.

"That's why I love you," she whispered, then got serious. "But you have to go."

Bryce woke him in the late afternoon.

"You know," Bryce said, "You've got that session with Jeffrey Harriman tomorrow. Do you want me to see if I can postpone it?"

Reo sat on the bed and looked around. He had one bag of clothes, a pair of shoes, and no guitar.

"No," he said.

"Well, you need a guitar, then." Bryce said. "I made a couple calls, talked to someone at Folk Life. They already knew about it."

Reo tried to stand up and fell back on the mattress.

"Come on, get up," Bryce said. "Pull yourself together. We have to move on."

They were sitting around the table, Bryce talking about a movie he'd seen once, filling the space with what to Reo was meaningless chatter. He had hardly said a word when the phone rang. Bryce answered and looked out the window.

"He's right here," he said, and handed Reo the phone.

"Reo," croaked the strangely familiar voice of Jonas Waverly. "I hear you need a guitar for some reason."

"Yes," Reo heard himself say.

"I have one you can borrow," Jonas said. "You'll have to come here and get it, and return it later. Do you have somewhere safe to keep it?"

Hours later, he arrived at Jonas' apartment to find him "gone for a few days," leaving the guitar with Jason, a large man with shoulder-length blond hair, who bounced lightly back two steps to let Reo enter.

"Come on in. Sit down," Jason said.

Reo found a small, wooden chair beside the kitchen table, where the numerous handwritten names of those who had sat there before him were written in pen, magic marker, fingernail polish, and even carved in, slanting every which way on the wooden slab.

"A lot of people have sat here," Reo said.

"Yeah. Feel free to add yours if you like."

"That's okay. Some other time."

Jason stood with his back to the sink and crossed his arms.

"When's the last time you ate anything?" he asked.

Reo blinked and looked up.

"I don't know. Yesterday?"

Jason handed him a large mug of coffee and told him to take off his jacket. He dug into the fridge and emerged with an armful of bags and small, covered dishes. Ten minutes later he set down two plates, each with a large half of omelet, two slices of wheat toast, a chunk of watermelon, and a sprig of parsley. He sat across the table and laughed, a deep, hearty laugh that made Reo relax and pick up the fork in front of him.

"I don't even like parsley," said Jason, shaking his head. "What's the big deal about it anyway?"

After they ate, Jason handed him a guitar, a light-brown Martin D-18 that had been around, judging from the wear on its lower front and its rich sound; it was much more valuable than the one Reo had lost.

"Play something," Jason told him, sweeping the neck of a large wooden standup bass into view. Reo started strumming some chords, an old familiar song he couldn't remember, then slid into a blues in G, giving them some chords to play together.

"Play something of yours," Jason said when the blues had run its course. They played for two hours, as Reo went through his songs, one at a time, losing himself in the music, trying to forget what he had lost.

But Reo didn't take the guitar with him; he'd decided to leave it safely there. The next afternoon, when he went back to get it for his recording session, Jason grabbed his bass and drove them uptown in a small red sedan with the bass neck extending through the open back window.

"I've gotta get a bigger car or a smaller bass," Jason said.

He'd asked Bryce about bringing Jason; Bryce was all for it, had heard him and said it would make the music better. And it did; they swung through a version of "Hard Times" that Reo sang as well as he had ever sung it. The only problem was, Jeffrey Harriman didn't like the song.

"Okay," he said, somewhat impatiently. "I get what you're getting at. Let's play something else. Got anything funny?"

He tapped on the guitar a minute, then bent down to his case and found a piece of paper. He played the blues in G, the same chords as yesterday, when he and Jason first played together; now they had words.

This is the ballad of Harry Reems
A fellow who's now a star
An actor of some esteem
Not getting very far
One day the director said

'Harry lie down on your back
And let our starlet work you over'
And this girl could really act

With Jason walking the bass behind him, they took off on a lengthy jam after the second verse, and were cruising through the chords, the deep rhythm of Jason's bass keeping Reo right on time.

They couldn't prove what Harry did was
Anything bad for your health
They couldn't prove what Harry did was
Something you couldn't do yourself
They couldn't prove what Harry did was
Something that wasn't done all the time
So they convicted him of conspiring to
Do it across state lines

Two verses later the song ended, and Harriman spoke over his control-room mike as the last notes faded away.

"Oh, I like that. Do you remember the solo you did after the second verse?"

"Yeah," Reo said.

"Can you sing it again, straight through, without that?"

He looked over at Jason, who was grinning at him.

"Sure," he said.

Later, they played "In The Morning," Jason's favorite a day earlier, its verse and chorus easy to follow. There was a loud click, and Harriman was speaking into his earphones.

"Okay. Let's try something. You remember how you played four bars of strumming after each chorus, before going into the next verse?"

"Yes," Reo replied into his mike.

"Can you do it again without them? Oh, and in the middle part, where you strummed four extra measures, can you leave those out, too?"

They played the song again, Reo carefully executing what Harriman had suggested, and once again heard his distinctive, resonant voice.

"That was good. Can you do it once more? This time I want you to sing the chorus once at the end, not twice. Can you do that?"

"Sure," Reo said.

"Good. And the things you left out the last time, leave those out this time too."

They played it again. And waited.

"That's good. We got that one down from four minutes and fifteen seconds down to three minutes and ten seconds. Good job."

At the end of the session Harriman asked if he had any new songs he would like to sing.

"We have time for one more," he said through the mike. They had been playing, without a break, for nearly three hours. Out of ideas, Reo searched his case and discovered the handwritten page of "Sand Castles." Lines were crossed out and scrawled over, wound around corners and crammed together as arrows pointed from one section to another, sometimes leading the eye to a single word.

He played it just as he had played it for Lila, slow and careful, letting the low notes of the guitar ring out, keeping it quiet and meditative. He played a short piece in the middle, watching his fingers execute the simple pattern perfectly, as if they had always known them, ending in a dramatic downward flourish that stopped, trailed off, and started again at its slow pace. Jason floated through the chord changes as if he knew the song, though Reo was sure he had not played it for him, and they each let the last low note ring out until they blended into one sound, a deep moan slowly drifting toward silence. They stood perfectly still until it had faded entirely away, without a squeak or a noise interrupting.

Harriman, Bryce, and Harold, the engineer running the machines, stared through the glass in silence. They had ended the song clean, after seven minutes, and it was over. After several seconds of silence they heard the click of a microphone being turned on.

"That was mahvelous," Jeffrey Harriman said. "Truly beautiful. Why don't you come on in here now."

37–A Place To Call Home

The next day, Bryce told Reo that Jeffrey Harriman was officially retiring; he had said at the session it was "somewhat against my wishes."

Bryce shrugged.

"He didn't tell you because he wanted you to respond to the situation just as you normally would. So I followed his wishes. It's a shame, really, you played some great stuff."

Months later, Harriman's office mailed a tape to Reo, but it was blank.

Reo, meanwhile, saved some money from two singing jobs and the print shop and went guitar shopping on 48th Street, playing guitars at three different stores before finding, for what seemed a low price, a big round-sounding Martin D-28. He found it hanging on a wall in a large, single-room store on 48th Street in New York. He liked that it was hanging right out in public, and after playing it for fifteen minutes, bought it with his cash.

He went to visit Jason, finding Ted and Jonas there too, along with a slim young woman in a grey skirt. He thanked Jonas for the guitar with a smile, wanting to show he appreciated the favor.

"You'd do the same for me," Jonas said, shrugging his shoulders and waving toward the corner. "Have you met my wife, Mary?"

She was reading in the corner under a solitary wooden lamp, a patterned brown shade forming a circle of light around her and the book. Her light hair tied back around a narrow face, dressed in a button-down sweater over a white blouse, she looked up, smiled, and went back to her book without speaking. Ted, on his third coffee, interrupted the quiet mood with "a rumor circulating since Saturday, when some suit walked in and told everyone at the bar the guys uptown are about to sign someone to a deal."

"Someone from around here, you mean," Jason said from the table.

"That's the general idea."

"No idea who?" Jonas spoke from the back. "Who told you about it?"

"Lila, the bartender. She was there."

"And what did she say?" Jonas went on, walking back into the kitchen with a notebook in his hand.

"Just what I told you," Ted said. He was perched on a couch, and apparently was sleeping there as well; a rolled-up mattress was pushed into the corner, an item Jason had referred to as "my crib" once or twice. Jonas and Mary had the bedroom.

It was crowded and hot, and Reo was restless. No one wanted to join him at the moment; maybe they'd see him later, they said. He thanked Jonas again for the guitar, and went out, down the stairs, into the darkening evening air. It was crisp and cold, the edge of winter making its first visit. He buttoned his denim jacket and headed along Houston Street. A cab screeched to a stop, the driver rolling down a window.

"Where ya going'?" the driver said.

"No, thanks," Reo said, stuffing his hands in his jacket pocket.

The night sky, lit in blue and white stripes by the Empire State Building to the north, glittered beyond the low neighborhoods of the Village. He entered an open gate to a long concrete walkway and a large plaza, where a statue several stories tall twisted into the arc of the spotlights anchored on the grass below. He walked slowly around it, the great marble bust of a woman, a youth on one side, hair streaming around a fair face; then, on the other, it became an old woman, her hair drawn back in a tight bun, lines of wisdom etched at the edges of her eyes.

Reo stood silent, as if she were speaking to him. Maybe it's over, he told himself; the guitar's gone, the audition's done, there's nowhere to call home, and I don't owe anyone my time. I can head West, find some new places to sing, meet some new people. Get an idea what's out there. Find out what's next for me. Hitchhike? Bus? Train? To where? He knew he was welcome at Martin Lehman's in Chicago, at least for a while. But he doubted he'd want to stay there permanently, either.

"Hey buddy," a voice said, and when he turned, a security guard was waving a flashlight at him.

"You can't walk on the grass," he said, and watched Reo leave. He bought a falafel sandwich at MacDougal and Bleecker streets, watching a limousine pull up a few houses away. A woman emerged from the basement doorway of a large gray townhouse, her head wrapped in a white scarf, four children following her into the long black car. The limo's brake lights came on once, twice, three times, as people walked in front.

He was wandering up MacDougal Street when he encountered Madeline, from Folk Life. She was wearing a suede miniskirt and a black leather jacket, her brown hair cut into curls across the top of her forehead.

"Do you know anyone who needs an apartment?" she asked him. "We're moving to Austin."

He gave it less than a moment's thought.

"I do," he said.

"Do you want to see it?"

"Sure, but I'll take it anyway."

She walked him to the middle of the block, to the same building where he had visited Sonoma Sal, to the first floor apartment right next door. She left him there and went upstairs for the super, who shook his hand and said "call me Phil." Phil had some other words as well.

"I don't want no problems. No deadbeats, no weird stuff, no loud parties, no garbage lying around."

"I can do that," Reo said; Phil seemed unimpressed.

"Another musician," he said, shaking his head. He went into the hall and rapped on Sal's door. Sonoma Sal appeared.

"Hey, Phil? Que pasa?"

Phil went inside and closed the door behind him. After a brief conversation Phil reappeared, telling Reo he needed the last month's rent in advance, plus this month's. He had been living rent-free for months; now, as he pulled together the last of his money and gave it to Phil, he was broke, but no longer without a place to live.

"You mean I can't be kicked out," he told Sal two days later, as he bought him a beer to thank him. He had moved in that day.

"That's right. Long as you pay."

He called Jonas and Jason's number and got who he wanted, Ted.

"Hey, Ted," he said. "How would you like a room of your own?"

A raw wood bed made of two-by-fours and a sheet of plywood extended from wall to wall in the back, taking up half the room. Reo found a slanted wooden ladder, understanding what the previous tenant had been planning: a loft bed. He lifted up the bed, got under it, raised it over his head and turned himself around. He walked it to the door. It fit snugly into the other end of the room, over the doorway, and Ted nailed it to the door frame and ladder, leaving almost four feet of overhead space. Now, he had the floor back.

Ted, now established in the living room with a mattress and chair, said he was thirsty and went out. Reo surveyed the small kitchen: a flat, polished slab of wood cut in a large oval sat on the bathtub. A refrigerator and stove stood across the room, separated by a single window to an airshaft and a brick wall six feet away. By the door a beat-up basin was attached to the wall and propped on a single 2 x 4 wedged under it. The dingy white sink, which looked as if it had been there since the building was built, had two chrome knobs and one spigot, and there was a mirror plastered directly into the wall above it.

Reo washed his hands, looked into the mirror, and smiled. He opened the nearby refrigerator and found a beer in the back corner. He faced himself in the mirror, popped the can and spoke out loud.

"Home," he grinned, and took a big slug.

He climbed into his loft with two books, a notebook, a folder of scribblings, his guitar, and a large candle in a glass container. He lit the candle, carefully worked it into the corner, and picked up the notebook. The sounds of New York City drifted in occasionally, bits of music from a nearby bar, the low dull thud of a bass on a jukebox somewhere; he imagined the hustle of the city night, everything and everyone in motion, while somehow sitting in the center of it all, quiet. Three hours later he had finished a long lyric sheet, arrows running every which way, lines upon lines upon lines. He copied it onto another sheet of paper so he could read it, and was working on a guitar piece to go with it when the door opened. Ted was talking to someone. Reo climbed down the slanted stairway and met them in the kitchen, still holding the piece of paper he was working on.

"What's that?" Lila said, instantly reaching for it, holding it to the light, reading it out aloud.

> New York City rain
> I don't know if it's making me dirtier or clean
> went for the subway but there was no train
> and the tunnel was crumbling for repairs again

> and the sign said welcome to American
> Jerusalem

She read it exactly as the lines broke, as if it were a poem.

"Here," said Ted, handing her a can of beer, turning to Reo.

"Want one?"

Reo took the beer and popped the tab. They went into the living room, Ted's room, and found seats; Lila sat on the wooden chair, Ted on his bed. Reo sat on a tree stump that was, beside the bed in the back, the only thing already in the apartment.

"So you heard the news," Lila said. "It was Callisto."

He hadn't heard anything, he said, he was in his loft.

"She signed with S & L on Wednesday, after they did a showcase Tuesday night. Place was sold out, all industry people. I guess she has some heavy manager now, his brother's some big producer and they brought her in and got her a deal."

"Callisto," he said, just repeating the name.

"One guy at the bar said 'I don't see what anybody sees in her,' she's scrawny and doesn't even sing, she just talks,'" Lila said in a perfect parody of Carl's voice from the bar. It made them all laugh.

"Well, what do you think?" Ted directed the question at Reo. "Aren't you surprised?" he added with an upraised eyebrow.

"I always liked her music," Reo said. "So no, I'm not."

They spent an hour in the living room, Ted's room, trading songs and drinking the beers Ted had brought. Reo sang from his new lyric:

> I been around
> You could spend forever looking for a friend in this town
> and all you get to do is lay your dollar down
> til you're stumbling drunk up the stairs again
> and the sign says Welcome to American
> Jerusalem

he sang, as Ted nodded and tapped his fingers on the beer can.

"Good song!" Ted said enthusiastically, and immediately grabbed his own Martin D-35 and launched into a strum.

I want to be on the
Open road
The open road
That's where I want to be
I want to be where
Skies are blue
And the city can't
Get to me

he sang, and they all sang with him. Lila sang two songs, both written by "my boyfriend, Brian," and Reo picked quietly along. Ted sang harmony to the chorus, a tale of "meeting the perfect lover."

You're always searching
For that moment to come
When that moment is always right here
You're always waiting for the world to stop
When it's moving on everywhere

Lila's other song was a tale of heartbreak; Reo wondered which one the boyfriend had written about Lila, as Ted expounded on the virtue of a strong melody.

"Gotta have a good tune," he said twice.

Lila had to go; she was meeting Brian at the Folk Life. Ted stared into the empty refrigerator and volunteered to walk her back to the bar.

""We're out of beer anyway," he told Reo. "Coming? It's only two. The night is still young."

38–Here

"So that's it," Zeke said, dipping a piece of tortilla shell into the small metal bowl of salsa. "Jonas got married in upstate New York last week. Who expected that? I hear she's nice, though."

Reo was working his way through his guacamole as Zeke continued.

"And it was Callisto who got a record deal. Oh, I heard all the rumors floating around. That sure was a shock to a hell of a lot of people. But she'll still be around, take it from me. And I bet she's not the last one, there will be others now too, once the ice is broken like that. This could be a good time to be around here. I've been here for six years and never seen a better time. Maybe you should stick around awhile."

"Well, I have a lease," Reo reminded him, "a place to live in my own name. I might do that."

The waitress, a slim red-haired girl with baggy shorts and long legs, came to their table. She set down a handful of napkins and refilled their water glasses, giving Zeke a big, goofy smile as she left.

"She likes you," Reo said.

"They all do that," Zeke said. "It's because they know I want nothing to do with them."

As winter approached, he worked extra days for the newspaper and had a two-night booking at an upstate coffeehouse, a log cabin with a fireplace and forty people on chairs. They were good listeners, despite the absence of microphones; he enjoyed both concerts, and, except for the organizer, was the only one at both of them, the only one to compare them. He thought he played very well on Friday, had gotten a lot of sound from the new guitar. Saturday's concert had been quieter but intense, the crowd taking the words more seriously; and when they applauded and stood, he felt a great satisfaction that he'd sung what was important, current, and meaningful to him, and they had gotten it. After the second night's show, he found himself watching the fire, drinking a tea, when an elderly woman with a cane approached him.

"Can I offer a suggestion?" she asked politely.

"Okay," he said.

"Look at your audience, at least once in awhile. Oh, and smile," she said. "That's all." And she turned and went back out to the café.

The host, a heavy, nervous man who drove him to and from the coffeehouse in a van with three little kids bouncing around, told him the children were "disappointed."

"I'm sorry," he said, taken aback. "What did I do?"

"Nothing," his host replied with a laugh. "They were expecting Rudy McGaggle."

Reo laughed, too. Rudy McGaggle was a rooster, in reality an actor who played a rooster on TV, advertising the hamburgers for a national chain of drive-thru restaurants. He had shocking pink hair and a big blue nose.

One Monday he was back at Folk Life, watching several acts by himself. Eventually it was his turn, and he stood at the mike and spoke to the restless crowd, milling around with guitar cases banging into chairs, everyone waiting to play.

"I lost a bet recently and had to learn a traditional song," he finally said. "This is what I learned."

> Get down, get down, little Henry Lee
> and stay all night with me
> The very best lodging I can afford
> will be far better'n thee
> I can't get down, and I won't get down
> and stay all night with thee
> For the girl I have in that merry green land
> I love far better'n thee

The room listened; he held their attention through the entire old ballad, as the deed was done.

Some take him by his lily-white hand
some take him by his feet.
We'll throw him in this deep, deep well
more than one hundred feet

Reo let his voice drift off melody a few times, searching for some adjacent note that would be more interesting, willfully exploring the song. He got lost momentarily in the middle of the fourth verse, then pulled it together quickly and sailed to the end.

I can't fly down, or I won't fly down
and alight on your right knee
A girl who would murder her own true love
would kill a little bird like me

The crowd response was respectfully formal, and Reo stepped back, thinking he should play something fast, fun, energetic, get back in a good mood. He heard a voice from the bar, Lila's voice, calling above the crowd.

"Aren't you going to play 'American Jerusalem?'"

He looked toward the bar, not seeing her at first; she had already retreated to the far end, and was resting against the back cabinet, staring at him, her arms across her chest.

"Okay, sure," he said.

It was not the fast, energetic song he sought, but something he had written for himself; still, he snapped the capo on the guitar and checked his tuning. He admired the smooth flat neck and new strings of his Martin, the 1969 rosewood dreadnought he had miraculously been able to afford, a much better instrument than the one he had lost. He touched the D string lightly with his pick and was about to start the song, when he heard it: the ebb and flow of the note, from the beautiful guitar, drifting out over the room, the simple note weaving a silence throughout the crowd, the silence of expectation, of desire, of a need to be entranced, to be moved, to be captivated, the quiet of an audience risking its attention, giving him a chance to cut through the normal half-attention, half indifference that was the norm. Though he was unaware of it, they were raptly waiting, giving him a moment to earn, or lose, their regard for him forever; and he swung into the song without a pause, letting the introduction emerge from the same notes he had played while tuning.

With a moving melodic line under the chords, it was, for Reo, a specific guitar piece, and he stared at his fingers to the second bridge. He looked up, stood up straight, and, concentrating on getting the words right, met people's eyes in the quiet crowd. He felt his voice change to a quieter, more personal sound, as the words rolled along on their own.

In the alleys of American Jerusalem
The homeless lie down at the dawn
The pretty people wonder what they're on
And how they afford it
In the ashes of American Jerusalem
The prophets live their deaths out on the corner
The pretty people say there should've been a warning
But nobody heard it

Carried along by the music, Reo drifted away, letting the words hang in the air, waiting for the next phrase to come to him. It was right there, the possibility that he might be lost, forget the words, forget the song itself; sliding into the next guitar line, he found the words without thinking about it, as if they were waiting for him.

Then shadows lick the sun
The streets are paved with footsteps on the run
Somebody must've got double, 'cause I got none
I forgot to collect my share again
So go west to breathe the cleansing air again
go Niagara for your honeymoon again
go on the road if you're going to sing your tune again
go to sea to learn to be a man again
til you come on home to American
Jerusalem

It was a long song, and here he was stretching it out, slowing down with every line, the guitar ending on the last word, his voice ebbing slowly over it. Reo heard someone exhale loudly nearby, then burst into applause. A slow wave of handclaps built in its wake, filling the room until long after he had gathered his case and headed toward the bar. He stopped midway along the railing, catching Lila's eye as she poured someone a beer.

"Thanks for the request," he grinned at her. She looked up, smiled, gave a slight nod and held the glass under the tap.

"I love that song," she said, watching the foam rise.

"Hey, I don't know if I ever told you this, you're really good," Reo went on. "You have a beautiful voice."

She stood there and broke into a big smile. She seemed about to say something, then heard "Lila" at the other end of the bar. It was Tony O; she stepped back shyly and went away.

"So you got a song fa me?"

He turned and saw Jack, the New Yawk folksinger, as he had called himself onstage, standing there with his guitar.

"Hey, I remember you. Haven't seen you in awhile," Reo noted.

"I was away. I'm back."

"Great."

"So youse still wanta sing my song?"

"What do you have?" Reo asked.

"Nothin. I mean, yeah, I got songs. But I was thinkin' you don need to sing any."

Reo looked at him and, remembering their other brief conversation, wondered if the guy was thinking of throwing a punch.

"Okay," Reo shrugged. "Sure. Whatever."

"An I don't sing one a yoahs."

"Seems fair enough," Reo smiled. He held a hand out and Jack shook it almost automatically, giving Reo the chance to end it right there.

"Okay, then, see you around," he said, and, picking up his case, walked straight toward the door, out into the street. He took a quick glance back to see he was alone, walked down the block and bought a slice of pizza at the corner. A steady stream of people passed, some in a hurry, some just walking aimlessly. He sauntered down MacDougal Street, past a cafe of tiny, ironwork chairs filled with groups of students, books and coffee cups scattered around the small, circular marble tabletops. It was a fine evening, the crisp winter air clear up to the clouds high above the buildings, with the promise of a cold night ahead.

"Well, well. MacGregor."

In the middle of the block, the greasy-haired, nearly toothless man who had played the guitar onstage with him at his first open mike was leaning against an ironwork railing.

"Mick," Reo said.

The man grinned as if pleased he'd remembered his name.

"Got a cigarette?"

"No. I don't smoke."

"Too bad."

Reo watched him fidget around; unshaven, standing with one foot on the sidewalk and another on the stoop, he looked like he was posing, sweeping his blue woolen overcoat backward with his hand.

"How do you know my name?" Reo asked him.

"Well now, that's a question," Mick nodded, as if that answered everything. "I know more than you can ever tell."

"But no more than you can tell."

"Ah, yes. Very good. Listen, do you have a guitar handy? I have this song I need to play." He had a nervous way of talking, like he was in a hurry for an answer.

"I don't, sorry," Reo said, setting down his case, sitting on the steps. "Can you sing it?"

Mick shook his head.

"No, no." He shook his head, looking up and down the street, speaking to Reo without looking at him.

"I suppose you know by now you're not getting out for some time," he said, brushing something off the knee of his pants.

"What do you mean?"

"Some of the others, they come and go, and that's what they're supposed to do. You're here from now on."

Reo followed Mick's gaze, up and down the block, as the words settled in. He often imagined himself somewhere else, surrounded by green trees and a wide-open sky.

"You mean, like, right here? Around here? Or just plain here."

Mick laughed, running his hand through his greasy black hair.

"Not around here. Here," he said, moving his hand in a circle, palm up, soundlessly describing the crowded sidewalk, the street clogged with backed-up traffic, the chaos of competing car radios blasting their music like missionaries intent on converting the heathen to hip hop, ska, reggae or ringing, vibrato-drenched guitar notes, the smell of ground lamb burning in a nearby restaurant window, the subtle chill of what would soon be deep winter in the night air.

Abruptly, still without looking at him, Mick reached across and tapped Reo's shoulder with a dirty fingernail.

"Tag, you're it," he said, and, straightening up, walked quickly toward a well-dressed man and woman in fine overcoats passing by on the sidewalk. As they slowed down, not sure if they should stop and respond to, or get away as fast as possible from the greasy-haired stranger, Mick grinned and fell in step, his voice drifting away as he trailed them down the street.

"Excuse me. Got a cigarette?"

Afterword

Greenwich Village as Prevailing Hero

The Open Mike evolved from a series of short stories that Rod MacDonald composed during the early 1980s, and which comprise much of the material found in the novel's opening section, *The Book of Reo.* Rod had kept the stories—as well as two quite different but fascinating unpublished novels—in some old cardboard boxes that he described as his archives: writings he had composed not as song lyrics but as serious fiction. In April of 2007, when I first interviewed Rod, he told me that his fiction meant a lot to him, but he did not think he would ever find the time or energy to prepare any of it for publication. Having published a volume of literary work by former Weavers' member Lee Hays—a book that Rod admired and had included in his own courses in Music Americana at Florida Atlantic University—I now saw the potential for another such book that would introduce the prose and literary achievements of a respected singer/songwriter. As I rummaged through Rod's "papers," I was delighted to discover a substantive body of work worth pursuing, as I had with Lee Hays' papers housed at the Smithsonian Institute.

Better still, though, was the opportunity to work not only with an artist whose work I had admired for years, but with one who was still alive, active—and my friend.

By 2007, Rod had completed two novels, engaging reads in their contrasting approaches: 1). *American Guerillas*, a complex magical realist text with rich treatment of the Hopi Indian Reservation in Arizona where Rod had spent a spiritually-redemptive period of his life in 1981; and, 2). *Our Little Secret*, a political potboiler which features the controversial nomination of an anti-abortion African-American Supreme Court justice nominee—while the Attorney General charged with confirming the pre-Clearance Thomas era figure was urging his own daughter to terminate her pregnancy.

Striking me as less burdensome to a novice reader being first introduced to Rod MacDonald as a fiction writer, the short stories emerged as the most publishable material.

The Book of Reo, thus, derived from an old manila folder's contents of three-decades-old typewritten pages on a dog-eared, withering yellow notepad. Composed while Rod was living in New York's Greenwich Village, these fictions evoked a rich texture of Place and Time, a kind *of* Bildungsroman, a novel of one's coming to adulthood.

The collection originally titled *The Book of Rico* consisted of narratives based on people Rod had known and who, though peers of his, had stories and issues of their own. These were people he had observed closely enough to depict in the style of Hemingway that he so admired: showing how objective descriptions of gestures, mannerisms, body language—and awkward silences—suggest deep and complex layers of subjective consciousness.

Finding himself once again working with these early manuscripts, Rod expanded them into a more coherent series of chapters, a novel in its own right. Meanwhile, Rod had continued writing new stories and, building on them, he conceived the second and longer section, itself called *The Open Mike*. This he finished 30 years after he had composed the original stories that had been titled *The Book of Rico*. By that time, Rod had relocated to South Florida and started a family of his own with his Swiss wife Nicole: both of these major life changes seem evident in the lighter and crisper tone of both his songs and his fiction.

Writing *The Open Mike* as a unified volume to be published as literature provided Rod with poetic and mythic insights that had not occurred to him earlier. The first thing to go was the protagonist's name *Rico*. Drawing instead from his own Scotch ancestry and historical bent, Rod now preferred the name Reo MacGregor, instead. Readers familiar with Sir Walter Scott's 1817 novel *Rob Roy* will recognize the surname as the ambiguous, rough-edged, mysterious figure who emerges as a most unlikely hero.

But, the history of Reo's surname is what intrigued Rod the most. As Scott's novel itself documents, the family name MacGregor had belonged to a highland Scotch clan (also known as Clan Gregor) that had been disenfranchised—the very name itself officially banned—in Scotland between 1603 and 1774, after a series of unsuccessful battles against the Clan Campbell. Thus, *The Book of Reo* first introduces, as a newcomer to America's best-known bohemia, a famous and once-prosperous family name that now has no value except historically.

Rather than the familiar Italian name *Rico*, (which would make it more recognizable in the historically Italian West Village) the Spanish-sounding though oddly-spelled *Reo* struck MacDonald as more befitting his protagonist whom people could not quite "figure out" or "place": an individual who had graduated from Columbia law school, but who now had recreated himself as an anonymous young-man-with-a-guitar writing of his "hard times" in New York.

Though the newer, second section of *The Open Mike* could have stood on its own, Rod preferred to keep many of the earlier vignettes for their more youthful—thus, volatile and alienated—personae. To my mind, *The Open Mike*—written in Delray Beach, Florida— seems more tightly woven, but a touch removed from the aura of Greenwich Village where the entire novel is set, but where only the initial portions were actually composed. I find a similar, darker sensibility in his earlier albums (such as *No Commercial Traffic* and *Highway to Nowhere)*, the ones Rod had recorded while living in New York, contrasted with the brighter mood of those he has recorded since his move to South Florida in 1995 (such as *Into the Blue* and *Songs of Freedom*). Rod will be the first to note, however, that all of his studio albums have been recorded in New York, regardless of where he was living at the time.

The novel as a whole is set in New York, amongst the backdrop of W. 4th Street, the area now known as the West (Greenwich) Village. His earliest years there, as just another guitar player aspiring to connect with people as a songwriter, provide the context for this late-Twentieth Century American Reo MacGregor.

The similarities between Rod MacDonald and his fictional creation Reo MacGregor are notable, but not entirely representative. Having declined more prestigious traditional—and lucrative—careers as an historian, naval officer, and attorney, Rod himself had arrived in New York's famed Greenwich Village with a guitar, a handful or original songs, and a fiercely optimistic determination to succeed as a professional musician.

Raised in Connecticut, the son of a Canadian immigrant, Rod MacDonald first moved to New York in 1970 to attend Columbia Law School. After his graduation in 1973, Rod moved to the Village—Rod might say that he "squatted" more than settled—and began playing open mikes. The neighborhood he found there had passed its 1960s prime, but he would play a major role in reviving it with a new generation of singer/songwriters. Indeed, the year Rod played his first Village open mikes, 1973, turned out to be a touchstone year for the West Village: That year, Bob Dylan moved away from his MacDougal Street residence for the final time, and John and Yoko Lennon also left the Village for the Dakota apartment on Manhattan's Upper West Side where Lennon would be gunned down seven years later. The coincidental departure of Dylan suggests the passing of a metaphysical torch to MacDonald's generation, just as the relocation of Lennon to the site of his untimely death underscores the fact that Lennon's move did not bring him to a place more conducive for him to call home. Curiously, the Greenwich Village that Rod encountered in 1973, like the Greenwich Village I first adopted as a summer residence in 2007, was a lively place, to be sure, but not the "scene" of bohemian spirit that it had been a decade earlier. The Village of cheap rents was gone; but, the Village of young creative musical talent remained, as it does to this day.

However, nostalgia for a lost community of personal and artistic freedom has been endemic to virtually every generation of Village "regulars" ever since Washington Square Park emerged out of the potter's field and Minetta Swamp that is the historical palimpsest of the neighborhood between Houston and 14th Streets. Indeed, this is the very nature of any so-named Bohemia—be it the Left Bank or the West Village—as aptly described by Ross Wetzsteon in his 2002 book *Republic of Dreams: Greenwich Village: The American Bohemia, 1910-1960*:

> [Despite]…the rhapsodizing about "happy days and happy nights," from its very birth, bohemia seemed to exist in the past. "Bohemia is dying," even its most ardent residents lamented; "the great days of bohemia are over." This sense of lost grandeur has been felt in every generation—just as Floyd Dell said *in the teens* [emphasis mine] that "the Village isn't what it used to be,"

> [Henri] Murger's followers were saying in the 1850s that "Paris isn't what it used to be." "Whatever else bohemia may be," a Village magazine editorialized in 1917, "it is almost always yesterday." (9)

Fortunately, MacDonald offers a more aesthetic and spiritual dimension of the West Village. Readers of *The Open Mike* will encounter a refreshing relief from Wetsteon's largely sexually-obsessed study. More recently, John Strausbaugh's 2013 volume *The Village: 400 years of Beats and Bohemians, Radicals and Rogues: A Village History* covers much of the Village's creative, activist community history. However, when it comes to detailing the 1970s and 1980s—the years when Rod, Jack Hardy, David Massengill, Shawn Colvin, John Gorka, Suzanne Vega, and *Fast Folk* magazine spurred a new folksinger/songwriter revival in the West Village—Strausbaugh's impressive new volume follows Wetzsteon's methodology: painstakingly characterizing the historical significance of the 1980s Village as homosexual activity on the dilapidated piers along the lower Hudson while making not a single reference to the existence of *Fast Folk* and the musical scene along MacDougal Street that reignited the famed folk clubs of a previous generation, including Gerde's Folk City.[1] The other major folk clubs where Rod became most active and influential were the Musician's Cooperative at the Speakeasy on MacDougal Street (now the Grisly Pear) and Kenny's Castaways on Bleecker Street between Thompson and Sullivan Streets. Max's Kansas City, where he first opened for Peter Yarrow, closed in 1974 but reopened briefly in 1980 where Bruce Springsteen, among others, recorded live performances.

The historical amnesia concerning Greenwich Village's more recent acoustic music activity is something this volume hopes to remedy, at least as a start.

Throughout *The Open Mike*, Rod MacDonald portrays the Village's renewal of creative—and, yes, sexual—energy during his early years there.

---

1. In a friendly exchange of e-mails with the author in July 2013, Strausbaugh acknowledged his omissions of numerous Village phenomena worthy of note. By the time he got to the 1980s, Strausbaugh explained, the book was already becoming unwieldy and he felt obligated to examine the spread of A.I.D.S. and the demographic changes that charged the Village's atmosphere after the Stonewall Riots of 1969.

Although Reo MacGregor and his peers never perceive their local open mike-hopping as anything worthy of historical note, Ted Imbonanti—Reo's first and best friend in the music scene—does remind Reo on a few occasions of the milieu's musical history, including their own traversing of the geographical paths travelled by the early Bob Dylan. As far as the present-day Village is concerned, I am pleased to invite anyone to the Monday night open mike at Caffe Vivaldi, at 32 Jones Street, just off Bleecker Street—Jones Street being the location where the famous photo of Dylan and Suze Rotolo was taken, the cover of *The Freewheelin' Bob Dylan.* Experience the high quality, young generation of songwriters and acoustic performers who now roam the Village streets with guitars and who now constitute the evening bills at such newer acoustic venues as the Vivaldi, the songwriter showcase at the Bitter End on Bleecker—and such East Village venues as Rockwood Music Hall and the Sidewalk Café—and you will need no further proof that the demise of Greenwich Village "as we knew it" has been greatly exaggerated by those who have long since left. But, that is for another book.

The historical setting of *The Open Mike* is, however, a period when the vacuum of "hard rock" had sucked up the folk revival first introduced to the national popular music charts in 1950 when big band leader Gordon Jenkins struggled, fought, and eventually prevailed with his Decca Records producers to include the Weavers as lead singers for his own orchestra and chorus on his chart-topping recordings. The first "popular" musician to record Village "folk" singers for a major record label, Jenkins had become the Weavers' biggest fan and advocate after he became a "regular" at Max Gordon's Village Vanguard on 7th Avenue during the Weavers' six-month residence at the club, better-known to contemporary clientele for its jazz bookings.

For the next decade and a half, folk music flourished in Greenwich Village.

On the other hand, Reo MacGregor's Greenwich Village almost seems a-historic. He does not experience a bohemia whose time had passed. Like the group of musicians Rod MacDonald met there, Reo's contemporaries focus on original writing and are reluctant to use the term "folk music" to describe their genre. Unlike Reo MacGregor, however, Rod MacDonald did first perceive a West Village haunted by the ghosts of the so-called "Folk Scare" of the 1960s whose participants included the likes of Rev. Gary Davis, Bob Dylan, Phil Ochs, Mississippi

John Hurt, Judy Collins, Dave Van Ronk, Noel (Paul) Stookey, and Fred Neil. Though not centered in the Village itself, iconic figures such as Pete Seeger and Joan Baez appeared at the Village's best-known clubs Gerde's Folk City and the Gaslight. Indeed, Seeger's 1962 Columbia Records release *The Bitter and the Sweet* was one of the first albums recorded at the Bitter End on Bleecker Street between Thompson and LaGuardia Streets. The Bitter End, then a new venue for live music, remains as one of the leading clubs featuring both blues and aspiring songwriters. The 60s generation of the so-called "folk scare" were indeed the beneficiaries of the dues paid during the 1950s genuine "red scare" by the Weavers.

By 1980, the 1960s crowd had largely vanished. Only Dave Van Ronk remained as a Village resident, and thus Dave became the connecting link between the 1960s and 1980s Greenwich Village folk scenes, just as Pete Seeger had been the connecting link between the 1950s and 1960s folk scene. The feisty and gravel-voiced Van Ronk offered Rod, just as he had done two decades earlier with Rev. Gary Davis and countless others, a singularly influential friendship and wise counsel, as one who had been on the scene for a generation. Indeed, Van Ronk's memoir *The Mayor of MacDougal Street*—posthumously finished by Elijah Wald—includes extensive material from recorded conversations between Rod MacDonald and Van Ronk.

But even that is getting ahead of the game. Accepting the hospitality of Robin Hirsch and his Cornelia Street Café, Rod joined a group of young songwriters in the late 1970s who formed the Songwriter's Exchange, an informal organization whose early compilation of recordings Hirsch backed and that also constituted the genesis of *Fast Folk* Magazine. Hirsch's support included producing the 1980 album *Cornelia Street: The Songwriter's Exchange*, released by Stash Records. Although not one of its main editors, (that work was piloted by Jack Hardy and Richard Meyer—both of whom had died before I had a chance to interview either one of them for this project), Rod did contribute to *Fast Folk* 21 songs, several articles, and an interview with Pete Seeger.

The new generation of musicians whose articles were published and—more importantly—whose songs were recorded for distribution accompanying *Fast Folk* distinguished itself from those of the 1950s and 60s. Though they respected both traditional and more popular material of their predecessors, particularly Bob Dylan and Phil Ochs, the acoustic performers of the 1980s ushered in the genre that is now known as the singer/songwriter. Until his death nearly three decades later, Jack Hardy facilitated a weekly meeting of songwriters whose task was to bring new original material each week for one another's scrutiny—and support.

Two female singer/songwriters—Shawn Colvin and Suzanne Vega—emerged as the most commercially successful of the group surrounding Jack Hardy's magazine and song circles. As booking chairman of the Musicians' Co-operative at the Speakeasy on MacDougal Street, Rod MacDonald promoted Colvin, Vega, Lucy Kaplansky, Christine Lavin, John Gorka, and many others who continue to compose, record, and perform nationally and internationally to this day. Rod welcomed anyone who was seriously interested in performing, and he first booked Shawn Colvin as his own opening artist. Interestingly, Colvin began to perform Rod's plaintive, imagistic balled "American Jerusalem"—featured as Reo MacGregor's newest song in the closing sections of *The Open Mike*—as a regular part of her own sets when she emerged as a headliner in her own right. A live version of the song was included in Colvin's first demo recording, although she never released a recording of the song until her 2012 Nonesuch album *All Fall Down*, with harmonies provided by Emmy Lou Harris.

MacDonald had the charismatic appeal, boundless energy, and local influence that attracted musicians, friends, and fans alike. Like the poet Allen Ginsberg who at that time was still living in the East Village, he became a central figure in the development and dissemination of a new generation of talented and dedicated writers: songwriters. But Rod also recruited better-known musicians from the 1960s revival, including Van Ronk, Richie Havens, Peter Yarrow and Odetta to join with his own generation of performers for the Greenwich Village Folk Festival, first held in October 1987.

Greenwich Village is a community of acoustic musicians and songwriters in *The Open Mike*, as well. Though his career is only in its infancy, Reo MacGregor also seeks a kind of fellowship with his fellow songwriters as he shares his writing, recording, and performing opportunities as best he can. The invitation from Micky and Molly Fresh, for example, plants this seed of cooperation among musicians that Reo will join as a growing, organic element.

* *

Perhaps what most distinguishes Rod MacDonald's generation, as has been alluded to above, is its dedication to song*writing*, to the notion that songs share personal stories and observations, and yet aimed to strike a chord (pardon the pun) with listeners. Although they do not harmonize with one another often, or host "sing-alongs," these songwriters do share mutual respect and communal support, although there is a lot of good-natured competition in *The Open Mike*. Folk music (for lack of a better term) meant personal expression that melds literary and musical language. This is a crucial departure (though never an intentional rupture) from the traditional—and often academic—understanding of folk music as an historical process: the continuation of an a-literary tradition of symbolic stories and motifs handed down through generations via oral transmission. A progression of scholarly folklorists—from Francis James Child, through Albert Friedman to Jan Harold Brunvand and their adherents—may insist that music be termed *folk* only if is at least 300 years old, is of unknown authorship, and has been learned solely through one generation's physically singing the song in the immediate presence of a younger generation. However, MacDonald (and Colvin, for that matter) were raised in a musical culture whose main mode of transmission was AM rock radio. In this sense, more recent writers and recorded performers of note see modern technological innovations, unavailable in the past, as crucial to the maintenance and expansion of the folk tradition.

Since the time when Gordon Jenkins introduced the Weavers and folk music to a mass popular audience, however, the "folk process" itself has been re-evaluated. Readers may now consult Gene Bluestein's 1994 book *Poplore: Folk and Pop in American Culture* and former Weavers' member Lee Hays' 1959 essay "The Folk Song Bridge." Significant performers themselves, Bluestein and Hays would have no difficulty attributing their own valuable contributions to the dissemination of folk music as the result of a combination of traditional means of performance with contemporary means of production (recording). In this respect, Dad's portable radio may serve the same function as Grandma's rocking chair on a Sunday afternoon: both are vehicles for the transmission and inheritance of music shared by a previous generation. Rod MacDonald himself has defined Chuck Berry's 1950s rock standard, "Johnny B. Goode" as one of America's greatest folk songs due to its widespread recognition by multiple generations of Americans who now sing it in pubs, concert halls, parties—even at campfires late in the evenings of major folk festivals. Radio, recordings, and Internet file-sharing have not replaced but have advanced the cause of the "people's music."

Rod MacDonald's public consciousness and wide readings of history and literature are central to his songwriting and performance. His primary objective as a writer is to be honest. His main goal as a performer is not to entertain, but to "move" his audiences. Perhaps one reason he is yet to "make it big" from a commercial standpoint is his insistence on sincerity—not to mention his refusal to fixate on self-promotion. He feels he has succeeded with audiences when they know that he believes in what he presents. By contrast, he has devoted relatively little energy to manufacturing a striking or particularly memorable stage presence. Similarly, Reo MacGregor and his contemporaries are devoted to effective writing and technical mastery of their musical instrument. What stage presence they may have grows out of their songs, never the other way around.

Amongst Rod MacDonald's "fans," he may well be marked as "tall, dark, handsome, and cool." If he looks like a remnant of the 1960s garage band-type lead singer (a la Mick Jagger or Van Morrison), it is a blessing of coincidence. Wanting most to *move* his audience, Rod's charisma ultimately lies in his integrity as an artist and as a man. In this respect, he resembles Pete Seeger and Joan Baez far more than he does Arlo Guthrie or Phil Ochs, as examples—the latter two being as well-known for their humor as storytellers as for their musicianship in performances. Certainly, Rod can hold audiences with his warmth as a chronicler and troubadour.

Thus, it is Rod's role as public intellectual that most distinguishes him from his first fictional protagonist.

* *

The Greenwich Village scene, as Rod experienced it in his early days, is poignant in the novel's opening vignette. We first encounter Reo MacGregor as a competent but virtually invisible nightclub performer in "The Last Audient," which opens *The Book of Reo*. His only listener is an attractive German graduate student. The club owner reluctantly pays Reo his meager night's pay, although the text implies that Reo is somewhat of a "regular" performer there. His musical career is in its infancy, as is his relationship with women and with Greenwich Village. He fails to hold his audience's attention just as he fails to find a soul mate in this woman who enjoys his company and conversation as they walk to a nearby diner for coffee. As they walk, she places her hand in his coat pocket, as if curious to know the "real" man behind the "act." She links her arm in his and does not mention her live-in boyfriend until Reo tries to kiss her. In love, as in music, Reo has the power to "get to first base," as it were, but (continuing the baseball analogy) does not get home—I hesitate to say "score." Significantly, however, Reo hopes to prove her intellectual equal before he tries to become her romantic partner. She, in turn, encourages his music, but rejects his romance.

In the end, he seeks solace from one of nature's tiniest but most musical creatures. Unable to find an invitation himself, Reo finishes the episode by addressing a park sparrow: "I'm all out of songs, myself. Sing one for me." Where does Reo commune only with singing sparrows, on this chilling winter morning? Though unnamed, the geography described as Reo dazedly walks "home" leads him to Washington Square Park. Once famed for its Sunday afternoon folk "jams," the only musicians there now are the birds. Reo is their lone "audient."

As his editor, I urged Rod to open the curtain with "The Last Audient," just as I had encouraged him to consider Hemingway's claim regarding *The Sun Also Rises* by making the earth—in Rod's case, the Village—the final "hero" of the piece. Thus, the reader is brought full circle from Reo's finding companionship only with the birds in the park to Reo's finding his own apartment in the Village and being acknowledged as one of the few musicians "on the scene" who will remain. Like Odysseus, he survives temptations and momentary glimpses of stardom, only to discover not only his "place," (e.g. his own apartment on MacDougal Street), but also a true *sensibility* of Place: where geographical location interconnects with metaphysical wholeness.

Robert S. Koppelman
Senior Professor of English
Broward College
Ft. Lauderdale, FL
May 2014

Selected Bibliography

Bluestein, Gene. *Poplore: Folk and Pop in American Culture.* Boston: U Massachusetts P, 1994.

Cohen, Ronald D. *Rainbow Quest: The Folk Music Revival and American Society.* Amherst: U Massachusetts P, 2002.

Herman, Arthur. *How the Scots Invented the Modern World.* New York: Crown Publishers, 2001.

Koppelman, Robert S. *"Sing out, Warning! Sing out, Love!": The Writings of Lee Hays.* Boston: U Massachusetts P, 2003.

Strausbaugh, John. *The Village: 400 Years of Beats and Bohemians, Radicals and Rogues.* New York: HarperCollins, 2013.

Wetzsteon, Ross. *Republic of Dreams: Greenwich Village: The American Bohemia, 1910-1960.* New York: Simon & Schuster, 2002.

Selected Recordings

Cornelia Street: The Songwriter's Exchange. Stash Records 1980. Reissued 2006.

The entire Fast Folk catalogue is available from Smithsonian Folkways at http://www.folkways.si.edu/explore folkways/fast folk folk.aspx. A live version of "American Jerusalem" is the opening cut on the first Fast Folk compilation produced by Smithsonian/Folkways.

For a list of Rod MacDonald's recordings and videos, see http://www.rodmacdonald.net/recordings.htm.

Acknowledgements

I wish to thank the following individuals for their assistance, insights, and personal remembrances:

Jamal Alnasr, Alan Anapu, David Bernz, David Bromberg, Ellen Bukstel, Ron Cohen, Bob Fass and Bill Propp of WBAI radio in New York, Mark Dann, James Durst, Karen Garthe, Robin Hirsch, Mike Lieber, Adriane Pontecorvo of Archway Publishing, Sherwood Ross, Pete Seeger, Mark Stenzler, Michael Stock of WLRN radio in Miami, John Strausbaugh, and Elijah Wald.

Special thanks to Ellen Bukstel of Design Workshop Group, Inc. and to Todd Segal of OnPoint Productions for designing the book cover. Also, thanks are due to Pascal Aebli for permission to use his photograph of Rod MacDonald.

Most of all, I am grateful to Rod MacDonald for graciously sharing his time and personal materials with me. His frequent hospitality has been matched only by that given so generously by his family: his wife Nicole, and their two daughters Ella and Alena.